21世纪英语专业系列教材

总主编 胡壮麟

英语泛读教程

第2册

主 编：潘守文 胡文征

编 者：孙明丽 沈红梅 侯冰洁 唐颖 周晓凤

北京大学出版社
PEKING UNIVERSITY PRESS

图书在版编目(CIP)数据

英语泛读教程.第2册/潘守文,胡文征主编.—北京:北京大学出版社,2008.9
(21世纪英语专业系列教材)
ISBN 978-7-301-14085-7

Ⅰ.英… Ⅱ.①潘…②胡… Ⅲ.英语—阅读教学—高等学校—教材 Ⅳ.319.4

中国版本图书馆CIP数据核字(2008)第111118号

书　　名:英语泛读教程　第2册
著作责任者:潘守文　胡文征　主编
责 任 编 辑:刘　强
标 准 书 号:ISBN 978-7-301-14085-7/H·2036
出 版 发 行:北京大学出版社
地　　址:北京市海淀区成府路205号　100871
网　　址:http://www.pup.cn
电　　话:邮购部 62752015　发行部 62750672　编辑部 62765014　出版部 62754962
电 子 邮 箱:zbing@pup.pku.edu.cn
印 刷 者:北京大学印刷厂
经 销 者:新华书店
787毫米×1092毫米　16开本　10印张　258千字
2008年9月第1版　2008年9月第1次印刷
定　　价:22.00元

总 序

北京大学出版社自2005年以来已出版《语言与应用语言学知识系列读本》多种，为了配合第十一个五年计划，现又策划陆续出版《21世纪英语专业系列教材》。这个重大举措势必受到英语专业广大教师和学生的欢迎。

作为英语教师，最让人揪心的莫过于听人说英语不是一个专业，只是一个工具。说这些话的领导和教师的用心是好的，为英语专业的毕业生将来找工作着想，因此要为英语专业的学生多多开设诸如新闻、法律、国际商务、经济、旅游等其他专业的课程。但事与愿违，英语专业的教师们很快发现，学生投入英语学习的时间少了，掌握英语专业课程知识甚微，即使对四个技能的掌握也并不比大学英语学生高明多少，而那个所谓的第二专业在有关专家的眼中只是学到些皮毛而已。

英语专业的路在何方？有没有其他路可走？这是需要我们英语专业教师思索的问题。中央领导关于创新是一个民族的灵魂和要培养创新人才等的指示精神，让我们在层层迷雾中找到了航向。显然，培养学生具有自主学习能力和能进行创造性思维是我们更为重要的战略目标，使英语专业的人才更能适应21世纪的需要，迎接21世纪的挑战。

如今，北京大学出版社外语部的领导和编辑同志们，也从教材出版的视角探索英语专业的教材问题，从而为贯彻英语专业教学大纲做些有益的工作，为教师们开设大纲中所规定的必修、选修课程提供各种教材。《21世纪英语专业系列教材》是普通高等教育"十一五"国家级规划教材和国家"十一五"重点出版规划项目《面向新世纪的立体化网络化英语学科建设丛书》的重要组成部分。这套系列教材要体现新世纪英语教学的自主化、协作化、模块化和超文本化，结合外语教材的具体情况，既要解决语言、教学内容、教学方法和教育技术的时代化，也要坚持弘扬以爱国主义为核心的民族精神。因此，今天北京大学出版社在大力提倡专业英语教学改革的基础上，编辑出版各种英语专业技能、英语专业知识和相关专业知识课程的教材，以培养具有创新性思维的和具有实际工作能力的学生，充分体现了时代精神。

北京大学出版社的远见卓识，也反映了英语专业广大师生盼望已久的心愿。由北京大学等全国几十所院校具体组织力量，积极编写相关教材。这就是说，这套教材是由一些高等院校有水平有经验的第一线教师们制定编写大纲，反复讨论，特别是考虑到在不同层次、不同背景学校之间取得平衡，避免了先前的教材或偏难或偏易的弊病。与此同时，一批知名专家教授参与策划和教材审定工作，保证了教材质量。

当然，这套系列教材出版只是初步实现了出版社和编者们的预期目标。为了获得更大效果，希望使用本系列教材的教师和同学不吝指教，及时将意见反馈给我们，使教材更加完善。

航道已经开通，我们有决心乘风破浪，奋勇前进！

胡壮麟

北京大学蓝旗营

前言

英语专业的本分是什么？英语语言能力的重要性毋庸置疑，却不是英语专业的本分。与高校许多文科专业相类似，英语专业的本分是人文素质的培养，是洞察人文现象的能力的培养，是思考力、鉴别力、判断力的培养，依此洞悉、鉴别、吸收英语国家的文化成就，并与中华文化精华融会贯通，促进人的全面发展和社会进步。

然而实际情况却不能尽如人意。很多人误以为英语专业的本分就是英语语言能力的提高，客观上将英语语言能力培养与人文素质培养割裂开来，使之相互脱节，导致英语教学效率低下，加上应试教育推波助澜，英语专业学生对英语国家文化只停留在现象的表面，而无意追问现象背后的文化内涵和精髓，不去深入思考，不追求理论高度，不能构建系统的专业知识，不能洞察、鉴别、吸收英语国家优秀文化，更谈不上与中华文化融会贯通，不能履行英语专业的本分，因此在高校处境尴尬。常有人说英语专业不是一个专业，这让英语专业师生痛心疾首。不是一个专业意味着不是一门学问，不是一门学问意味着没学问、没知识、没头脑、没思想，只能当匠人，不能成大器，不能成为民族的栋梁。

成为民族的栋梁，是英语专业师生的梦想。时代在发展，旧的人才标准已经不能适应时代发展的要求，只具有英语语言技能的人才已经算不上真正的人才。时代的发展要求英语专业必须充分利用所属高校的人文资源，逐步打通文、史、哲的界限，构建以学术研究为核心的英语人才培养体系，以学术研究促进英语实践能力、独立思考能力和人文素质的提高，培养英语基本功扎实、独立思考能力强、通晓英语国家文化和中华文化、人文素质优秀的新型英语人才。实践证明，将学生当学者，将课文当文献，英语语言能力、独立思考能力、自主学习能力、人文素质同时培养，不仅符合《高等学校英语专业英语教学大纲》的要求，而且切实可行，理应成为英语教材编写的指导原则。本册书在上述英语教学理念指导下完成，与以往以应试为目的的英语泛读教材有所不同，现就本书特点说明如下：

1. 本书供高校英语专业一年级第二学期使用，起点高，要求学生具有较好的英语基础和人文修养，旨在帮助学生从语言技能与人文修养两个方面提高自己。

本书所选的24篇课文不仅语言规范而且具有相当的思想内涵，大部分作者为英语国家的文化精英。课文不仅涉及英语国家的文化现象，更包含英语学者对这些文化现象的深入思考，不是单纯的语言技能训练资料，而是英语专业学生洞察英语国家文化不可或缺的参考文献。

2. 课文开门见山，直接进入课文题目和内容，引导学生迅速进入阅读状态，集中精力捕捉关键信息。

3. 生词释义简洁明了，完全采用英文释义，完全回避汉译，旨在引导学生完全进入英语状态并运用英语进行判断思维。本书为一些生词提供了多个释义，旨在培养学生鉴别语言细微差别的能力。

4. 文化注释言简意赅，意在为学生提供便捷的文化参考，具有百科全书的功能。

5. 本书意在为学生的独立思考提供广阔的空间，无意将本书编者对课文的理解强加于学生，因此取消了以往常见的多项选择题，淡化唯一答案和绝对答案，努力将以学生为中心的英语教学理念落到实处，设计了具有探讨性、启发性、辐射性的练习题，引导学生穿越语言现象和文化现象的表面进入英语国家文化的深层，独立探索，独立判断。

6. 练习I、II围绕课文内容进行提问，旨在锻炼学生的判断力、逻辑推理能力、文献综述能力和快速组织语言进行表达辩论的能力。练习III、IV仍然围绕课文内容展开训练，旨在训练学生灵活使用英语的能力和英译汉的能力。练习V、VI为扩展练习，既为了督促学生有目的地扩大阅读范围，也为了引导学生举一反三，将刚学到的内容与以往学到的内容融会贯通，形成完整而良好的知识结构。

本册教材由吉林大学外国语学院英语系负责编写，由潘守文、胡文征担任主编，负责整体设计与审稿，并与孙明丽、沈红梅、侯冰洁、唐颖、周晓凤老师一起承担选材及编写工作，其间得到了本套教材其他分册主编的帮助，北京大学出版社张冰主任、刘强编辑也为本册书编写付出了心血，编者在此一并表示感谢。本册教材疏漏之处，诚请广大读者批评指正，提出宝贵意见和建议。

编　者

2008年8月

Contents

Unit One

Text A

Reading

*Benjamin Franklin**

From a child I was fond of reading, and all the little money that came into my hands was ever laid out in books. Pleased with the *Pilgrim's Progress**, my first collection was of John Bunyan's works in separate little volumes. I afterward sold them to enable me to buy R. Burton*'s *Historical Collections*; they were small chapmen's books, and cheap, 40 or 50 in all. My father's little library consisted chiefly of books in polemic divinity, most of which I read, and have since often regretted that, at a time when I had such a thirst for knowledge, more proper books had not fallen in my way, since it was now resolved I should not be a clergyman. Plutarch*'s *Lives* there was in which I read abundantly, and I still think that time spent to great advantage. There was also a book of De Foe*'s, called *An Essay on Projects*, and another of Dr Mather*'s, called *Essays to Do Good,* which perhaps gave me a turn of thinking that had an influence on some of the principal future events of my life.

This bookish inclination at length determined my father to make me a printer, though he had already one son (James) of that profession. In 1717 my brother James returned from England with a press and letters to set up his business in Boston. I liked it much better than that of my father, but still had a hankering for the sea. To prevent the apprehended effect of such an inclination, my father was impatient to have me bound to my brother. I stood out some time, but at last was persuaded, and signed the

lay out a. to extend at length b. to spread out in order c. to arrange d. *(Informal)* to spend

chapman /ˈtʃæpmən/ *n.* (plural chapmen) an itinerant dealer. Here it means cheap.

polemic /pəˈlemɪk/ *adj.* of or involving dispute or controversy; controversial; also, polemical

divinity /dɪˈvɪnɪti/ *n.* a. the quality of being divine b. deity c. theology

resolved /rɪˈzɒlvd/ *adj.* determined

letter /ˈletə/ *n.* (Printing) a piece of type that prints a single character

hankering /ˈhæŋkərɪŋ/ *n.* a longing; craving

apprehended /ˌæprɪˈhendid/ *adj.* a. fully understood or grasped b. worried

stand out to persist in opposition or resistance

indentures when I was yet but twelve years old. I was to serve as an apprentice till I was twenty-one years of age, only I was to be allowed journeyman's wages during the last year. In a little time I made great proficiency in the business, and became a useful hand to my brother. I now had access to better books. An acquaintance with the apprentices of booksellers enabled me sometimes to borrow a small one, which I was careful to return soon and clean. Often I sat up in my room reading the greatest part of the night, when the book was borrowed in the evening and to be returned early in the morning, lest it should be missed or wanted.

And after some time an ingenious tradesman, Mr. Matthew Adams, who had a pretty collection of books, and who frequented our printing-house, took notice of me, invited me to his library, and very kindly lent me such books as I chose to read. I now took a fancy to poetry, and made some little pieces; my brother, thinking it might turn to account, encouraged me, and put me on composing occasional ballads. One was called *The Lighthouse Tragedy*, and contained an account of the drowning of Captain Worthilake, with his two daughters; the other was a sailor's song, on the taking of Teach (or Blackbeard) the pirate. They were wretched stuff, in the Grub-street -ballad style; and when they were printed he sent me about the town to sell them. The first sold wonderfully, the event being recent, having made a great noise. This flattered my vanity; but my father discouraged me by ridiculing my performances, and telling me verse-makers were generally beggars. So I escaped being a poet, most probably a very bad one; but as prose writing has been of great use to me in the course of my life, and was a principal means of my advancement, I shall tell you how, in such situation, I acquired what little ability I have in that way.

There was another bookish lad in the town, John Collins by name, with whom I was intimately acquainted. We sometimes disputed, and very fond we were of argument, and very desirous of confuting one another, which disputatious turn, by the way, is apt to become a very bad habit, making people often extremely disagreeable in

indenture /in'dentʃə/ *n.* a contract by which a person, as an apprentice, is bound to service

journeyman /'dʒɜːnɪmən/ *n.* a. one who has fully served an apprenticeship in a trade or craft and is a qualified worker in another's employ b. a competent but undistinguished worker

acquaintance /ə'kweɪntəns/ *n.* a person whom one knows, esp. through work or business but who may not be a friend

ingenious /ɪn'dʒiːniəs/ *adj.* having or showing cleverness at making or inventing things

frequent /'friːkwənt/ *v.* to be often in a place

fancy /'fænsi/ *n.* a like formed without the help of reason

turn to account to derive profit

put on a. to cause to be performed b. (Informal) to tease (a person)

taking /'teɪkɪŋ/ *n.* arrest

wretched /'retʃɪd/ *adj.* a. of inferior quality b. in a deplorable state of distress or misfortune

Grub-street a street in London, England, formerly inhabited by many impoverished minor writers and literary hacks; now called Milton Street. Here it implies bad quality.

make a noise to be the object of general notice and comment

turn /tɜːn/ *n.* a. a movement of partial or total rotation b. disposition

company by the contradiction that is necessary to bring it into practice; and thence, besides souring and spoiling the conversation, is productive of disgusts and, perhaps enmities where you may have occasion for friendship. I had caught it by reading my father's books of dispute about religion. Persons of good sense, I have since observed, seldom fall into it, except lawyers, university men, and men of all sorts that have been bred at Edinborough.

A question was once, somehow or other, started between Collins and me, of the propriety of educating the female sex in learning, and their abilities for study. He was of opinion that it was improper, and that they were naturally unequal to it. I took the contrary side, perhaps a little for dispute's sake. He was naturally more eloquent, had a ready plenty of words; and sometimes, as I thought, bore me down more by his fluency than by the strength of his reasons. As we parted without settling the point, and were not to see one another again for some time, I sat down to put my arguments in writing, which I copied fair and sent to him. He answered, and I replied. Three or four letters of a side had passed, when my father happened to find my papers and read them. Without entering into the discussion, he took occasion to talk to me about the manner of my writing; observed that, though I had the advantage of my antagonist in correct spelling and pointing (which I ow'd to the printing-house), I fell far short in elegance of expression, in method and in perspicuity, of which he convinced me by several instances. I saw the justice of his remarks, and thence grew more attentive to the manner in writing, and determined to endeavor at improvement.

About this time I met with an odd volume of the *Spectator* * . It was the third. I had never before seen any of them. I bought it, read it over and over, and was much delighted with it. I thought the writing excellent, and wished, if possible, to imitate it. With this view I took some of the papers, and, making short hints of the sentiment in each sentence, laid them by a few days, and then, without looking at the book, try'd to complete the papers again, by expressing each hinted sentiment at length, and as fully as it had been expressed before, in any suitable words that should come to hand. Then I compared my *Spectator* with the original, discovered some of my faults, and corrected them. But I found which I thought I should

thence /ðens/ *adv.* a. from there; b. therefore, for that reason
sour /ˈsaʊə/ *v.* to cause to become unpleasant
enmity /ˈenmɪti/ *n.* a feeling or condition of hostility; hatred; ill will; animosity; antagonism
propriety /prəˈpraɪəti/ *n.* rightness of social or moral behavior
eloquent /ˈeləkwənt/ *adj.* able to express ideas or opinions well, so that the hearers are influenced
bear down to press or weigh down
observe /əbˈzɜːv/ *v.* to make a remark; say
pointing /ˈpɔɪntɪŋ/ *n.* punctuation
elegant /ˈelɪgənt/ *adj.* having the qualities of grace and beauty —elegance *n.*
perspicuity /ˌpəːspiˈkju(ː)iti/ *n.* lucidity
endeavor /ɪnˈdevə/ to work hard
sentiment /ˈsentɪmənt/ *n.* a. tender or fine feeling of pity, love b. thought or judgment

have acquired before that time if I had gone on making verses; since the continual occasion for words of the same import, but of different length, to suit the measure, or of different sound for the rhyme, would have laid me under a constant necessity of searching for variety, and also have tended to fix that variety in my mind, and make me master of it. Therefore I took some of the tales and turned them into verse; and, after a time, when I had pretty well forgotten the prose, turned them back again. I also sometimes jumbled my collections of hints into confusion, and after some weeks endeavored to reduce them into the best order, before I began to form the full sentences and complete the paper. This was to teach me method in the arrangement of thoughts. By comparing my work afterwards with the original, I discovered many faults and amended them; but I sometimes had the pleasure of fancying that, in certain particulars of small import, I had been lucky enough to improve the method or the language, and this encouraged me to think I might possibly in time come to be a tolerable English writer, of which I was extremely ambitious. My time for these exercises and for reading was at night, after work or before it began in the morning, or on Sundays, when I contrived to be in the printing-house alone, evading as much as I could the common attendance on public worship which my father used to exact on me when I was under his care, and which indeed I still thought a duty, though I could not, as it seemed to me, afford time to practise it.

import /ɪm'pɔːt/ *n.* meaning; importance; significance
measure /'meʒə/ *n.* meter
jumble /'dʒʌmbəl/ *v.* to mix in a confused mass; put or throw together without order; to confuse mentally; muddle
particular /pə'tɪkjʊlə/ *n.* an individual item, fact, or detail; an item or detail of information or news
evade /ɪ'veɪd/ *v.* to escape from by trickery or cleverness; to avoid doing or fulfilling
exact /ɪg'zækt/ *v.* to demand or obtain by force

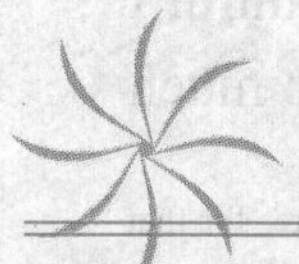

Cultural Notes

1. **Benjamin Franklin** (1706—1790) was an American public official, writer, scientist, and printer. After the success of his *Poor Richard's Almanac* (1732—1757), he entered politics and played a major part in the American Revolution. Franklin negotiated French support for the colonists, signed the *Treaty of Paris* (1783), and helped draft the *Constitution* (1787—1789). His numerous scientific and practical innovations include the lightning rod, bifocal spectacles, and a stove. "Reading" is an excerpt from his *Autobiography*.
2. ***Pilgrim's Progress*** (1678), written by John Bunyan (1628—1688), an English preacher and author, is an allegorical tale of Christian's journey from the City of Destruction to the Celestial City.

3. Nathaniel Crouch (*c.* 1640—1725?) wrote popular histories under the name of **Richard Burton.**
4. **Plutarch** (*c.* 45—125 A.D.) was a Greek historian, biographer, and essayist. His *Lives* was biographies of famous Greeks and Romans.
5. **Daniel Defoe** (1659?—1731) was an English novelist, pamphleteer, and journalist, author of *Robinson Crusoe* (1719), a story of a man shipwrecked alone on an island. Along with Samuel Richardson, Defoe is considered the founder of the English novel. Before his time stories were usually written as long poems or dramas. He produced some 200 works of nonfiction prose in addition to close 2 000 short essays in periodical publications.
6. **Dr. Cotton Mather** (1663—1728) was an American clergyman and author, and the most celebrated of all New England Puritans.
7. ***Spectator*** was an English daily periodical published jointly by Joseph Addison (1672—1719) and Richard Steele (1672—1729) with occasional contributions from other writers.

Comprehension Exercises

I. Please answer the following questions according to the text you have just read.

1. What's the function of the first paragraph in the whole text?
2. How did prose writing influence Benjamin Franklin's life?
3. How did Franklin think about the disputatious temperament of a person?
4. What is the relationship between reading and writing?
5. What's your reflection on Franklin's way of learning to write?

II. Are the following judgments correct according to the text? Write "T" if the judgment is correct, or "F" if the judgment is wrong.

1. Franklin was not interested in religion.
2. Franklin afterward sold John Bunyan's works because he didn't like them any more.
3. By reading his father's books of dispute about religion, Franklin caught the disputatious temperament.
4. His father thought Franklin was stronger in elegance of expression than his antagonist.
5. Franklin's view on educating the female sex in learning and their abilities for study was negative because he looked down upon women.
6. Franklin thought public worship was rather a duty than a belief.

III. Please paraphrase the following sentences:

1. Plutarch's *Lives* there was in which I read abundantly, and I still think that time spent to great advantage.
2. To prevent the apprehended effect of such an inclination, my father was impatient to have me bound to my brother.
3. An acquaintance with the apprentices of booksellers enabled me sometimes to borrow a small one, which I was careful to return soon and clean.
4. They were wretched stuff, in the Grub-street-ballad style; and when they were printed he sent me about the town to sell them.
5. He was naturally more eloquent, had a ready plenty of words; and sometimes, as I thought, bore me down more by his fluency than by the strength of his reasons.

IV. Please translate the following sentences into Chinese:

1. My father's little library consisted chiefly of books in polemic divinity, most of which I read, and have since often regretted that, at a time when I had such a thirst for knowledge, more proper books had not fallen in my way, since it was now resolved I should not be a clergyman.
2. So I escaped being a poet, most probably a very bad one; but as prose writing has been of great use to me in the course of my life, and was a principal means of my advancement, I shall tell you how, in such situation, I acquired what little ability I have in that way.
3. We sometimes disputed, and very fond we were of argument, and very desirous of confuting one another, which disputatious turn, by the way, is apt to become a very bad habit, making people often extremely disagreeable in company by the contradiction that is necessary to bring it into practice; and thence, besides souring and spoiling the conversation, is productive of disgusts and, perhaps enmities where you may have occasion for friendship.
4. With this view I took some of the papers, and, making short hints of the sentiment in each sentence, laid them by a few days, and then, without looking at the book, try'd to complete the papers again, by expressing each hinted sentiment at length, and as fully as it had been expressed before, in any suitable words that should come to hand.
5. The continual occasion for words of the same import, but of different length, to suit the measure, or of different sound for the rhyme, would have laid me under a constant necessity of searching for variety, and also have tended to fix that variety in my mind, and make me master of it.

V. How would you respond to each of the following statements?

1. Persons of good sense seldom fall into the disputatious temper.
2. Disputatious temper will produce disgusts and enmities where you may have occasion for friendship.
3. A man is never too old to learn.
4. Common sense is not common.

VI. Please provide a text, which might support your view on one of the statements in *Exercise V.*

Text B

A Love Affair with Books

*Bernadete Piassa**

When I was young, I thought that reading was like a drug which I was allowed to take only a teaspoon at a time, but which, nevertheless, had the effect of carrying me away to an enchanted world where I experienced strange and forbidden emotions. As time went by and I took that drug again and again, I became addicted to it. I could no longer live without reading. Books became an intrinsic part of my life. They became my friends, my guides, my lovers—my most faithful lovers.

I didn't know I would fall in love with books when I was young and started to read. I don't even recall when I started to read and how. I just remember that my mother didn't like me to read. In spite of this, every time I had an opportunity I would sneak somewhere with a book and read one page, two pages, three, if I was lucky enough, always feeling my heart beating fast, always hoping that my mother wouldn't find me, wouldn't shout as always: "Bernadete, don't you have anything to do?" For her, books were nothing. For me, they were everything.

enchanted /ɪn'tʃɑːntɪd/ *adj.* bewitched, captivated, delighted

addicted /ə'dɪktɪd/ *adj.* compulsively or physiologically dependent on sth. habit-forming

intrinsic /ɪn'trɪnsɪk/ *adj.* inherent; belonging to a thing by its very nature

sneak /sniːk/ *v.* to go stealthily or furtively

In my childhood I didn't have a big choice of books. I lived in a small town in Brazil, surrounded by swamp and farms. It was impossible to get out of town by car; there weren't roads. By train it took eight hours to reach the next village. There were airplanes, small airplanes, only twice a week. Books couldn't get to my town very easily. There wasn't a library there, either. However, I was lucky: my uncle was a pilot.

My uncle, who owned a big farm and also worked flying people from place to place in his small airplane, had learned to fly, in addition, with his imagination. At home, he loved to sit in his hammock on his patio and travel away in his fantasy with all kinds of books. If he happened to read a best-seller or a romance, when he was done he would give it to my mother, who also liked to read although she didn't like me to. But I would get to read the precious book anyway, even if I needed to do this in a hiding place, little by little.

I remember very well one series of small books. Each had a green cover with a drawing of a couple kissing on it. I think the series had been given to my mother when she was a teenager because all the pages were already yellow and almost worn out. But although the books were old, for me they seemed alive, and for a long time I devoured them, one by one, pretending that I was the heroine and my lover would soon come to rescue me. He didn't come, of course. And I was the one who left my town to study and live in Rio de Janeiro*, taking only my clothes with me. But inside myself I was taking my passion for books that would never abandon me.

I had been sent to study in a boarding school, and I was soon appalled to discover that the expensive all-girls school had even fewer books than my house. In my class there was a bookshelf with maybe fifty books, and almost all of them were about the lives of saints and the miracles of Christ. I had almost given up the hope of finding something to read when I spotted, tucked away at the very end of the shelf, a small book already covered by dust. It didn't seem to be about religion because it had a more intriguing title, *The Old Man and the Sea*. It was written by an author that I had never heard of before: Ernest Hemingway*. Curious, I started to read the book and a few minutes later was already fascinated by Santiago, the fisherman.

hammock /'hæmək/ *n.* a hanging bed of canvas or rope netting (usu. suspended between two trees)
patio /'pæːtiəu/ *n.* paved outdoor area adjoining a residence
fantasy /'fæntəsi/ *n.* **a.** imagination unrestricted by reality **b.** fiction with a large amount of fantasy in it
devour /dɪ'vaʊə/ *v.* **a.** to enjoy avidly, as of a book **b.** to eat greedily
appalled /ə'pɔːld/ *adj.* struck with fear or dread
tuck /tʌk/ *v.* **a.** to fold under **b.** to press into a narrower compass
intriguing /ɪn'triːgɪŋ/ *adj.* capable of arousing interest or curiosity

I loved that book so much that when I went to my aunt's house to spend the weekend, I asked her if she had any books by the man who had written it. She lent me *For Whom the Bell Tolls,* and I read it every Sunday I could get out of school, only a little bit at a time, only one teaspoon at a time. I started to wait anxiously for those Sundays. At the age of thirteen I was deeply in love with Ernest Hemingway.

When I finished all of his books that I could find, I discovered Herman Hesse*, Graham Greene*, Aldous Huxley*, Edgar Allan Poe*. I could read them only on Sundays, so during the week I would dream or think about the world I had discovered in their books.

At that time I thought that my relationship with books was kind of odd, something that set me apart from the world. Only when I read the short story "Illicit Happiness" by Clarice Lispector*, a Brazilian author, did I discover that other people could enjoy books as much as I did. The story is about an ugly, fat girl who still manages to torture one of the beautiful girls in her town only because the unattractive girl's father is the owner of a bookstore, and she can have all the books she wants. With sadistic refinement, day after day she promises to give to the beautiful girl the book the girl dearly wants, but never fulfills her promise. When her mother finds out what is going on, she gives the book to the beautiful girl, who then runs through the streets hugging it and, at home, pretends to have lost it only to find it again, showing an ardor for books that made me exult. For the first time I wasn't alone. I knew that someone else also loved books as much as I did.

My passion for books continued through my life, but I had to surmount another big challenge when, at the age of thirty-one, I moved to New York. Because I had almost no money, I was forced to leave all my books in Brazil. Besides, I didn't know enough English to read in this language. For some years I was condemned again to the darkness; condemned to live without books, my friends, my guides, my lovers.

But my love for books was so strong that I overcame even this obstacle. I learned to read in English and was finally able to enjoy my favorite authors again.

Although books have always been part of my life, they still hold a mystery for me, and every time I open a new one, I ask myself

sadistic /sə'dɪstɪk/ *adj.* deriving pleasure from inflicting pain on another
refinement /rɪ'faɪnmənt/ *n.* the quality of excellence in thought and manners and taste
dearly /'dɪəli/ *adv.* **a.** at a high price or terrible cost **b.** very much
ardor /'ɑːdə/ *n.* intense feeling of love
exult /ɪg'zʌlt/ *v.* **a.** to express great joy **b.** to feel extreme happiness
surmount /səː'maʊnt/ *v.* to deal with successfully
condemn /kən'dem/ *v.* **a.** to express strong disapproval of **b.** to force someone into an unhappy state of affairs

unveil /ʌn'veɪl/ *v.* to reveal by removing a veil from (a person or sth. new)
seduce /sɪ'djuːs/ *v.* to lure or entice away from duty, principles, or proper conduct
dazzled /'dæzəl/ *adj.* stupefied or dizzied by sth. overpowering
fraction /'frækʃən/ *n.* a small part or item forming a piece of a whole
abyss /ə'bɪs/ *n.* a bottomless gulf, or pit; hell
infatuate /in'fætjueit/ *v.* to arouse unreasoning love or passion in and cause to behave in an irrational way
point /pɔɪnt/ *n.* idea contained in sth. said or done
tiresome /'taiəsəm/ *adj.* a. annoying b. tiring or uninteresting
subversive /səb'vɜːsɪv/ *adj.* in opposition to a civil authority or government
lackluster /'læk,lʌstə/ *adj.* lacking brilliance or vitality

which pleasures I am about to discover, which routes I am about to travel, which emotions I am about to sink in. Will this new book touch me as a woman, as a foreigner, as a romantic soul, as a curious person? Which horizon is it about to unfold to me, which string of my soul is it bound to touch, which secret is it about to unveil for me?

Sometimes, the book seduces me not only for the story it tells, but also because of the words the author uses in it. Reading Gabriel Garcia Marquez*'s short story "The Handsomest Drowned Man in the World," I feel dazzled when he writes that it took "the fraction of centuries for the body to fall into the abyss." The fraction of centuries! I read those words again and again, infatuated by them, by their precision, by their hidden meaning. I try to keep them in my mind, even knowing that they are already part of my soul.

After reading so many books that touch me deeply, each one in its special way, I understand now that my mother had a point when she tried to keep me away from books in my childhood. She wanted me to stay in my little town, to marry a rich and tiresome man, to keep up with the traditions. But the books carried me away; they gave me wings to fly, to discover new places. They made me dare to live another kind of life. They made me wish for more, and when I couldn't have all I wished for, they were still there to comfort me, to show me new options.

Yes, my mother was right. Books are dangerous; books are subversive. Because of them I left a predictable future for an unforeseeable one. However, if I had to choose again, I would always choose the books instead of the lackluster life I could have had. After all, what joy would I find in my heart without my books, my most faithful lovers?

Cultural Notes

1. **Bernadete Piassa**, a senior project director of the marketing research team of

Mattson Jack Group, Inc. based in Philadelphia, grew up in rural Brazil. In this prize-winning essay from a national writing contest, she describes how she was eager to read but was discouraged from reading the few that she could find.

2. **Rio de Janeiro** is the former capital and 2nd largest city of Brazil, famous as a tourist attraction.
3. **Ernest Hemingway** (1899—1961) was a famous American novelist and short-story writer and is regarded as one of the great American writers of the 20th century. During World War I he served as an ambulance driver in the Italian infantry and was wounded. Later, while working in Paris as a correspondent for *the Toronto Star*, he became involved with the expatriate literary and artistic circle surrounding Gertrude Stein. During the Spanish Civil War, Hemingway served as a correspondent on the loyalist side. From this experience came his novel, *For Whom the Bell Tolls* (1940). He fought in World War II and then settled in Cuba in 1945. His novel *The Old Man and the Sea* (1952) celebrates the indomitable courage of an aged Cuban fisherman—Santiago. In 1954, Hemingway was awarded the Nobel Prize for Literature. Increasingly plagued by ill health and mental problems, he committed suicide by shooting himself in 1961.
4. **Herman Hesse** (1877—1962), a German-Swiss writer, received the Goethe Prize of Frankfurt in 1946 and the Peace Prize of the German Booksellers in 1955.
5. **Graham Greene** (1904—1991) was an English playwright, novelist, short story writer, travel writer and critic whose works explore the ambivalent moral and political issues of the modern world. Greene combined serious literary acclaim with wide popularity. Although Greene objected strongly to being described as a "Catholic novelist" rather than as a "novelist who happened to be Catholic", Catholic religious themes are at the root of many of his novels. Works such as *The Quiet American* also show an avid interest in international politics.
6. **Aldous Huxley** (1894—1963) was an English writer and one of the most prominent members of the famous Huxley family, best known for his dystopian novel *Brave New World* (1931). Besides novels, he published travel books, histories, poems, plays, and essays on philosophy, arts, sociology, religion and morals.
7. **Edgar Allan Poe** (1809—1849) was an American poet, short story writer, editor, critic and one of the leaders of the American Romantic Movement. Best known for his tales of the macabre, Poe was one of the early American practitioners of the short story and a progenitor of detective fiction and crime fiction. He is also credited with contributing to the emergent science fiction genre.

8. **Clarice Lispector** (1920—1977) was a Brazilian writer universally recognized as the most original and influential Brazilian woman writer of her time. In feminist circles, she is revered as an intensely feminine writer who articulates the needs and concerns of every woman in pursuit of self awareness.
9. **Gabriel García Márquez** (1928—) is a Colombian-born author and journalist, winner of the 1982 Nobel Prize for Literature and a pioneer of the Latin American "Boom." His masterpiece, *One Hundred Years of Solitude*, tells the story of the rise and fall, birth and death of a mythical town of Macondo through the history of the Buendi'a family.

Comprehension Exercises

I. Please answer the following questions according to the text you have just read.

1. What's the main idea of the text?
2. In what ways were books "like a drug" to Piassa?
3. Why did Piassa's mother discourage her from reading?
4. How did books affect her life?
5. What might you get to know about the Brazilian culture?

II. Are the following judgments correct according to the text? Write "T" if the judgment is correct, or "F" if the judgment is wrong.

1. Piassa's mother did not enjoy reading.
2. As a child, Piassa had to struggle to find access to books.
3. The books Piassa read were largely romance.
4. Piassa was not interested in books with religious contents.
5. Piassa implies that girls interested in reading books are usually beautiful.
6. Piassa finally understands her mother's reasons for keeping books from her.

III. Please paraphrase the following sentences:

1. With sadistic refinement, day after day she promises to give to the beautiful girl the book the girl dearly wants, but never fulfills her promise.
2. For some years I was condemned again to the darkness; condemned to live without books, my friends, my guides, my lovers.
3. Which horizon is it about to unfold to me, which string of my soul is it bound to touch, which secret is it about to unveil for me?
4. Sometimes, the book seduces me not only for the story it tells, but also because of the words the author uses in it.

5. I read those words again and again, infatuated by them, by their precision, by their hidden meaning.

IV. Please translate the following sentences into Chinese:

1. When I was young, I thought that reading was like a drug which I was allowed to take only a teaspoon at a time, but which, nevertheless, had the effect of carrying me away to an enchanted world where I experienced strange and forbidden emotions.
2. At home, he loved to sit in his hammock on his patio and travel away in his fantasy with all kinds of books.
3. I had almost given up the hope of finding something to read when I spotted, tucked away at the very end of the shelf, a small book already covered by dust.
4. At that time I thought that my relationship with books was kind of odd, something that set me apart from the world.
5. When her mother finds out what is going on, she gives the book to the beautiful girl, who then runs through the streets hugging it and, at home, pretends to have lost it only to find it again, showing an ardor for books that made me exult.
6. Reading Gabriel Garcia Marquez's short story "The Handsomest Drowned Man in the World," I feel dazzled when he writes that it took "the fraction of centuries for the body to fall into the abyss."
7. What joy would I find in my heart without my books, my most faithful lovers?

V. How would you respond to each of the following statements?

1. Forbidden fruit is often the sweetest.
2. Books are dangerous.
3. Books give people wings to fly.
4. A book tightly shut is but a block of paper.
5. It often requires more courage to read some books than it does to fight a battle.

VI. Please provide a text, which might support your view on one of the statements in *Exercise V.*

Unit Two

Text A

The Triumph of the Yell

*Deborah Tannen**

I put the question to a journalist who had written a vitriolic attack on a leading feminist researcher: "Why do you need to make others wrong for you to be right?" Her response: "It's an argument!"

That's the problem. More and more these days, journalists, politicians and academics treat public discourse as an argument—not in the sense of *making* an argument, but in the sense of *having* one, of having a fight.

When people have arguments in private life, they're not trying to understand what the other person is saying. They're listening for weaknesses in logic to leap on, points they can distort to make the other look bad. We all do this when we're angry, but is it the best model for public intellectual interchange? This breakdown of the boundary between public and private is contributing to what I have come to think of as a culture of critique.

Fights have winners and losers. If you're fighting to win, the temptation is great to deny facts that support your opponent's views and present only those facts that support your own.

At worst, there's a temptation to lie. We accept this style of arguing because we believe we can tell when someone is lying. But we can't. Paul Ekman*, a psychologist at the University of California at San Francisco, has found that even when people are very sure they can tell whether or not someone is dissembling, their judgments are as likely as not to be wrong.

vitriolic /ˌvɪtrɪˈɒlɪk/ *adj.* very cruel and angry towards someone

dissemble /dɪˈsembəl/ *v.* to hide one's true feelings, thoughts etc.

If public discourse is a fight, every issue must have two sides—no more, no less. And it's crucial to show "the other side," even if one has to scour the margins of science or the fringes of lunacy to find it.

scour /ˈskaʊə/ v. to search very carefully and thoroughly through an area, a document etc.
lunacy /ˈluːnəsi/ n. a situation or behavior that is completely crazy; mental illness
fanatic /fəˈnætɪk/ n. a person who shows very unreasoning keenness for some religious or political belief
rationalize /ˈræʃənəlaɪz/ v. to invent an explanation for one's behavior so that it does not seem as bad
dissemination /dɪˌsemɪˈneɪʃən/ n. the spread of information or ideas to as many people as possible
confront /kənˈfrʌnt/ v. to face boldly or threateningly
couch /kaʊtʃ/ v. to express in a certain way
eloquence /ˈeləkwəns/ n. the power of expressing one's ideas and opinions well, esp in a way that influences people
sputter /ˈspʌtə/ v. to talk quickly in short confused phrases, esp. because you are angry or shocked
scrutinize /ˈskruːtɪnaɪz/ v. to examine someone or sth. very carefully
free-wheeling adj. not worried about rules or what will happen in the future

The culture of critique is based on the belief that opposition leads to truth: when both sides argue, the truth will emerge. And because people are presumed to enjoy watching a fight, the most extreme views are presented, since they make the best show. But it is a myth that opposition leads to truth when truth does not reside on one side or the other but is rather a crystal of many sides. Truth is more likely to be found in the complex middle than in the simplified extremes, but the spectacles that result when extremes clash are thought to get higher ratings or larger readership.

Because the culture of critique encourages people to attack and often misrepresent others, those others must waste their creativity and time correcting the misrepresentations and defending themselves. Serious scholars have had to spend years of their lives writing books proving that the Holocaust* happened, because a few fanatics who claim it didn't have been given a public forum. Those who provide the platform know that what these people say is, simply put, not true, but rationalize the dissemination of lies as showing "the other side." The determination to find another side can spread disinformation rather than lead to truth.

The culture of critique has given rise to the journalistic practice of confronting prominent people with criticism couched as others' views. Meanwhile, the interviewer has planted an accusation in readers' or viewers' minds. The theory seems to be that when provoked, people are spurred to eloquence and self-revelation. Perhaps some are. But others are unable to say what they know because they are hurt, and begin to sputter when their sense of fairness is outraged. In those cases, opposition is not the path to truth.

When people in power know that what they say will be scrutinized for weaknesses and probably distorted, they become more guarded. As an acquaintance recently explained about himself, public figures who once gave long, free-wheeling press conferences now limit themselves to reading brief statements. When less information gets communicated, opposition does not lead to truth.

Opposition also limits information when only those who are adept at verbal sparring take part in public discourse, and those who cannot handle it, or do not like it, decline to participate. This winnowing process is evident in graduate schools, where many talented students drop out because what they expected to be a community of intellectual inquiry turned out to be a ritual game of attack and counterattack.

One such casualty graduated from a small liberal arts college, where she "luxuriated in the endless discussions." At the urging of her professors, she decided to make academia her profession. But she changed her mind after a year in an art history program at a major university. She felt she had fallen into a "den of wolves." "I wasn't cut out for academia," she concluded. But does academia have to be so combative that it cuts people like her out?

In many university classrooms, "critical thinking" means reading someone's life work, then ripping it to shreds. Though critique is surely one form of critical thinking, so are integrating ideas from disparate fields and examining the context out of which they grew. Opposition does not lead to truth when we ask only "What's wrong with this argument?" and never "What can we use from this in building a new theory, and a new understanding?"

Several years ago I was on a television talk show with a representative of the men's movement. I didn't foresee any problem, since there is nothing in my work that is anti-male. But in the room where guests gather before the show I found a man wearing a shirt and tie and a floor-length skirt, with waist-length red hair. He politely introduced himself and told me he liked my book. Then he added: "When I get out there, I'm going to attack you. But don't take it personally. That's why they invite me on, so that's what I'm going to do."

When the show began, I spoke only a sentence or two before this man nearly jumped out of his chair, threw his arms before him in gestures of anger and began shrieking—first attacking me, but soon moving on to rail against women. The most disturbing thing about his hysterical ranting was what it

sparring /ˈspɑːrɪŋ/ *n.* boxing; dispute or argument

winnow /ˈwɪnəu/ *v.* to get rid of the things or people that you do not need or want from a group

casualty /ˈkæʒjuəlti/ *n.* someone or something that suffers as a result of a particular event or situation

luxuriate /lʌgˈzjʊərieɪt/ *v.* to relax and enjoy sth.

academia /ˌækəˈdiːmiə/ *n.* the activities and work connected with education in universities and colleges

combative /ˈkɒmbətɪv/ *adj.* ready, willing, or eager to fight

disparate /ˈdɪspərɪt/ *adj.* consisting of things or people that are very different and not related to each other

rail /reɪl/ *v.* to curse or complain noisily

rant /rænt/ *v.* to talk or complain in a loud excited and rather confused way because you feel strongly about sth.

sparked in the studio audience: they too became vicious, attacking not me (I hadn't had a chance to say anything) and not him (who wants to tangle with someone who will scream at you?) but the other guests: unsuspecting women who had agreed to come on the show to talk about their problems communicating with their spouses.

spark /spɑːk/ *v.* to lead into action; incite
tangle /ˈtæŋgəl/ *v.* to argue or fight with someone
animosity /ˌænɪˈmɔsɪti/ *n.* strong dislike or hatred
demonize /ˈdiːmənaiz/ *v.* to represent someone or sth. as an evil spirit or force
overwhelming /ˌəuvəˈwelmɪŋ/ *adj.* large or great
exalt /ɪgˈzɔːlt/ *v.* to put someone or sth. into a high rank or position; to praise someone, esp God
preclude /prɪˈkluːd/ *v.* to prevent sth. or make sth. impossible
stifle /ˈstaɪfəl/ *v.* to stop someone from breathing comfortably

This is the most dangerous aspect of modeling intellectual interchange as a fight: it contributes to an atmosphere of animosity that spreads like a fever. In a society where people express their anger by shooting, the result of demonizing those with whom we disagree can be truly demonic.

I am not suggesting that journalists stop asking tough questions necessary to get at the facts, even if those questions may appear challenging. And of course it is the responsibility of the media to represent serious opposition when it exists, and of intellectuals everywhere to explore potential weaknesses in others' arguments. But when opposition becomes the overwhelming avenue of inquiry, when the lust for opposition exalts extreme views and obscures complexity, when our eagerness to find weaknesses blinds us to strengths, when the atmosphere of animosity precludes respect and poisons our relations with one another, then the culture of critique is stifling us. If we could move beyond it, we would move closer to the truth.

Cultural Notes

1. **Deborah Tannen** (1945—) is an American professor of linguistics at Georgetown University. Tannen is best known as the author of *You Just Don't Understand: Women and Men in Conversation* (1990), which was on the *New York Times Best Seller* list for nearly four years, including eight months as No. 1, and has been translated into 24 languages. Tannen's insight brought gender differences in communication style to the forefront of public awareness, and her work has been featured in most major newspapers and magazines. The text was first published in the *New York Times*, January 14, 1994.
2. **Paul Ekman** (1934—) is a professor of psychology at the Department of Psychiatry at the University of California in San Francisco. In addition to his basic research on emotion and its expression, he has, for the last thirty years,

also been studying interpersonal deception. In 2001, he was named by the American Psychological Association as one of the most influential psychologists of the 20th century based on publications, citations and awards.

3. **Holocaust** is a word of Greek origin meaning "sacrifice by fire". The Nazis, who came to power in Germany in January 1933, believed that Germans were "racially superior" and that the Jews, deemed "inferior," were an alien threat to the so-called German racial community. The Holocaust was the systematic, bureaucratic, state-sponsored persecution and murder of approximately six million Jews by the Nazi regime and its collaborators.

Comprehension Exercises

I. Please answer the following questions according to the text you have just read.

1. What is the difference between *making* an argument and *having* an argument?
2. What effects may occur when argument is reduced to fighting?
3. What does the author mean by "the culture of critique"?
4. What is the ideal form of "critical thinking"?
5. What is the responsibility of media?

II. Are the following judgments correct according to the text? Write "T" if the judgment is correct, or "F" if the judgment is wrong.

1. People can easily tell whether or not someone is lying.
2. The culture of critique is based on the belief that opposition leads to truth.
3. Opposition may lead to truth if truth is a crystal of many sides.
4. Information is lost, not gained, when opposition is given solely for the sake of having an argument.
5. On the television talk show, a guest attacked the author because he didn't like her book.
6. The hostility that comes with having an argument would lead to a dangerous atmosphere of animosity.
7. Politicians, journalists, and academics should be held accountable for perpetuating the culture of critique.

III. Please paraphrase the following sentences:

1. Paul Ekman, a psychologist at the University of California at San Francisco, has found that even when people are very sure they can tell whether or not someone is dissembling, their judgments are as likely as not to be wrong.

2. It's crucial to show "the other side," even if one has to scour the margins of science or the fringes of lunacy to find it.
3. The culture of critique has given rise to the journalistic practice of confronting prominent people with criticism couched as others' views.
4. One such casualty graduated from a small liberal arts college, where she "luxuriated in the endless discussions."
5. Truth is more likely to be found in the complex middle than in the simplified extremes, but the spectacles that result when extremes clash are thought to get higher ratings or larger readership.

IV. Please translate the following sentences into Chinese:

1. The theory seems to be that when provoked, people are spurred to eloquence and self-revelation.
2. Some people are unable to say what they know because they are hurt, and begin to sputter when their sense of fairness is outraged.
3. This winnowing process is evident in graduate schools, where many talented students drop out because what they expected to be a community of intellectual inquiry turned out to be a ritual game of attack and counterattack.
4. Opposition does not lead to truth when we ask only "What's wrong with this argument?" and never "What can we use from this in building a new theory, and a new understanding?"
5. This is the most dangerous aspect of modeling intellectual interchange as a fight: it contributes to an atmosphere of animosity that spreads like a fever.
6. In a society where people express their anger by shooting, the result of demonizing those with whom we disagree can be truly demonic.
7. When opposition becomes the overwhelming avenue of inquiry, when the lust for opposition exalts extreme views and obscures complexity, when our eagerness to find weaknesses blinds us to strengths, when the atmosphere of animosity precludes respect and poisons our relations with one another, then the culture of critique is stifling us.

V. How would you respond to each of the following statements?

1. Truth is more likely to be found in the complex middle than in the simplified extremes.
2. The determination to find another side can spread disinformation rather than lead to truth.
3. The aim of intellectual inquiry is to build a new theory and a new understanding.
4. Successful intellectual interchange is based on mutual respect.

VI. Please provide a text, which might support your view on one of the statements in *Exercise V*.

Text B

The Eloquent Sounds of Silence

*Pico Iyer**

Every one of us knows the sensation of going up, on retreat, to a high place and feeling ourselves so lifted up that we can hardly imagine the circumstances of our usual lives, or all the things that make us fret. In such a place, in such a state, we start to recite the standard litany: that silence is sunshine where company is clouds; that silence is rapture, where company is doubt; that silence is golden, where company is brass.

But silence is not so easily won. And before we race off to go prospecting in those hills, we might usefully recall that fool's gold is much more common and that gold has to be panned for, dug out from other substances. "All profound things and emotions of things are preceded and attended by Silence," wrote Herman Melville*, one of the loftiest and most eloquent of souls. Working himself up to an ever more thunderous cry of affirmation, he went on, "Silence is the general consecration of the universe. Silence is the invisible laying on of the Divine Pontiff's hands upon the world. Silence is the only Voice of our God." For Melville, though, silence finally meant darkness and hopelessness and self-annihilation. Devastated by the silence that greeted his heartfelt novels, he retired into a public silence from which he did not emerge for more than 30 years. Then, just before his death, he came forth with his final utterance—the luminous tale of *Billy Budd**—and showed that silence is only as worthy as what we can bring back from it.

retreat /rɪ'triːt/ *n.* a quiet, secluded place that one goes to in order to rest
fret /fret/ *v.* **a.** to be agitated or irritated **b.** to make resentful or angry
litany /'lɪtəni/ *n.* a prayer consisting of a series of invocations by the priest with responses from the congregation
company /'kʌmpəni/ *n.* **a.** companionship; fellowship **b.** a group of people together for some purpose
rapture /'ræptʃə/ *n.* **a.** a state of being carried away by overwhelming emotion **b.** a state of elated bliss
prospect /'prɒspekt/ *v.* to explore for useful or valuable things or substances, such as minerals
fool's gold a common mineral that has a pale yellow color, sometimes mistaken for gold
pan /pæn/ *v.* to wash dirt in a pan to separate out the precious minerals
lofty /'lɒfti/ *adj.* of unusually high quality of thinking, feeling, desires, etc.
consecration /ˌkɒnsɪ'kreɪʃən/ *n.* a solemn commitment of your life or your time to some cherished purpose
laying on the act of contacting sth. with your hand
pontiff /'pɒntɪf/ *n.* (usu. cap.) the Pope
annihilation /əˌnaiə'leiʃən/ *n.* total destruction
devastate /'devəsteɪt/ *v.* to destroy completely
come forth **a.** to come out of **b.** to happen or occur as a result of something
luminous /'luːmɪnəs/ *adj.* softly bright or radiant

We have to earn silence, then, to work for it: to make it not an absence but a presence; not emptiness but repletion. Silence is something more than just a pause; it is that enchanted place where space is cleared and time is stayed and the horizon itself expands. In silence, we often say, we can hear ourselves think; but what is truer to say is that in silence we can hear ourselves not think, and so sink below ourselves into a place far deeper than mere thought allows. In silence, we might better say, we can hear someone else think.

Or simply breathe. For silence is responsiveness, and in silence we can listen to something behind the clamor of the world. "A man who loves God, necessarily loves silence," wrote Thomas Merton*, who was, as a Trappist, a connoisseur, a caretaker of silences. It is no coincidence that places of worship are places of silence: if idleness is the devil's playground, silence may be the angels'. It is no surprise that silence is an anagram of license. And it is only right that Quakers* all but worship silence, for it is the place where everyone finds his God, however he may express it. Silence is an ecumenical state, beyond the doctrines and divisions created by the mind. If everyone has a spiritual story to tell of his life, everyone has a spiritual silence to preserve.

So it is that we might almost say silence is the tribute we pay to holiness; we slip off words when we enter a sacred space, just as we slip off shoes. A "moment of silence" is the highest honor we can pay someone; it is the point at which the mind stops and something else takes over (words run out when feelings rush in). A "vow of silence" is for holy men the highest devotional act. We hold our breath, we hold our words; we suspend our chattering selves and let ourselves "fall silent" and fall into the highest place of all.

It often seems that the world is getting noisier these days: in Japan, which may be a model of our future, cars and buses have voices, doors and elevators speak. The answering machine talks to us, and for us, somewhere above the din of the TV; the Walkman preserves

repletion /ri'pliːʃən/ *n.* the state of being replete; superabundant fullness
clamor /'klæmə/ *n.* a loud continuous usu. confused noise or shouting
Trappist /'træpɪst/ *n.* member of an order of monks noted for austerity and a vow of silence
connoisseur /ˌkɒnə'sɜː/ *n.* an expert able to appreciate a field; esp. in the fine arts
anagram /'ænəgræm/ *n.* a word or phrase spelled by rearranging the letters of another word or phrase
license /'laɪsəns/ *n.* **a.** excessive freedom; lack of due restraint **b.** a legal document giving official permission
ecumenical /ˌiːkju'menɪkəl/ *adj.* universal, general
tribute /'tribjuːt/ *n.* sth. given or done as an expression of esteem
slip off words to be silence
devotional /dɪ'vəʊʃənəl/ *adj.* relating to worship
din /dɪn/ *n.* **a.** a loud harsh noise **b.** the act of making a noisy disturbance

a public silence but ensures that we need never—in the bathtub, on a mountaintop, even at our desks—be without the clangor of the world. White noise becomes the aural equivalent of the clash of images, the nonstop blast of fragments that increasingly agitates our minds. As Ben Okri*, the young Nigerian novelist, puts it, "When chaos is the god of an era, clamorous music is the deity's chief instrument."

There is, of course, a place for noise, as there is for daily lives. There is a place for roaring, for the shouting exultation of a baseball game, for hymns and spoken prayers, for orchestras and cries of pleasure. Silence, like all the best things, is best appreciated in its absence: if noise is the signature tune of the world, silence is the music of the other world, the closest thing we know to the harmony of the spheres. But the greatest charm of noise is when it ceases. In silence, suddenly, it seems as if all the windows of the world are thrown open and everything is as clear as on a morning after rain. Silence, ideally, hums. It charges the air. In Tibet, where the silence has a tragic cause, it is still quickened by the fluttering of prayer flags, the tolling of temple bells, the roar of wind across the plains, the memory of chant.

Silence, then, could be said to be the ultimate province of trust: it is the place where we trust ourselves to be alone; where we trust others to understand the things we do not say; where we trust a higher harmony to assert itself. We all know how treacherous are words, and how often we use them to paper over embarrassment, or emptiness, or fear of the larger spaces that silence brings, "Words, words, words" commit us to positions we do not really hold, the imperatives of chatter, words are what we use for lies, false promises and gossip. We babble with strangers; with intimates we can be silent. We "make conversation" when we are at a loss; we unmake it when we are alone, or with those so close to us that we can afford to be alone with them.

In love, we are speechless; in awe, we say, words fail us.

clangor /'klæŋgə/ *n.* a sharp, harsh, ringing sound

blast /blɑːst/ *n.* a. a sudden very loud noise. b. an explosion (as of dynamite) c. a strong current of air

agitate /'ædʒɪteɪt/ *v.* to cause to be excited

deity /'deɪɪti/ *n.* a god or goddess; a heathen god

exultation /ˌegzʌl'teiʃən/ *n.* the utterance of sounds expressing great joy

signature tune a melody used to identify a performer or a dance band or radio/TV program

charge /tʃɑːdʒ/ *v.* to fill

province /'prɒvɪns/ *n.* the proper sphere or extent of your activities

assert /ə'sɜːt/ *v.* a. to insist on having one's opinions and rights recognized b. to affirm solemnly and formally as true

treacherous /'tretʃərəs/ *adj.* a. tending to betray b. dangerously unstable and unpredictable

paper over to cover up; to conceal

imperative /ɪm'perətɪv/ *n.* some duty that is essential and urgent

babble /'bæbəl/ *v.* a. to talk foolishly b. to utter meaningless sounds like a baby, or utter in an incoherent way

unmake /'ʌn'meik/ *v.* to deprive of certain characteristics

awe /ɔː/ *n.* a. an overwhelming feeling of wonder or admiration b. a profound fear inspired by a deity

Cultural Notes

1. **Pico Iyer** (1957—) is one of the most revered and respected travel writers alive today. He was born in England, raised in California, and educated at Eton, Oxford, and Harvard. His essays, reviews, and other writings have appeared in *Time, Conde Nast Traveler, Harper's, the New Yorker, Sports Illustrated,* and *Salon.com.* His books include *Video Night in Kathmandu, The Lady and the Monk, Cuba and the Night, Falling off the Map, Tropical Classical,* and *The Global Soul.* They have been translated into several languages and published in Europe, Asia, South America, and North America.
2. **Herman Melville** (1819—1891) was an American author, best-known for his masterpiece *Moby Dick* (1851), a whaling adventure recognized as a masterpiece 30 years after Melville's death. The fictionalized travel narrative of *Typee* (1846) is Melville's most popular book during his lifetime. ***Billy Budd*** is the novel he wrote in the last five years of his life and published posthumously in 1924.
3. **Thomas Merton** (1915—1968) was arguably the most influential American Catholic author of the twentieth century. His autobiography, *The Seven Storey Mountain,* has sold over one million copies and has been translated into over fifteen languages. He wrote over sixty other books and hundreds of poems and articles on topics ranging from monastic spirituality to civil rights, nonviolence, and the nuclear arms race.
4. **Quakers** are members of the Religious Society of Friends, a faith that emerged as a new Christian denomination in England during a period of religious turmoil in the mid-1600's, and is practiced today, in a variety of forms, around the world. To members of this religion, the words "Quaker" and "Friend" mean the same thing.

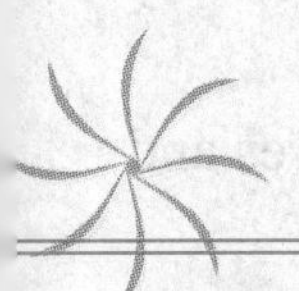

Comprehension Exercises

I. Please answer the following questions according to the text you have just read.

1. What might be the most essential statement that the author tries to convey?
2. Why is silence not so easily won?
3. Why do Quakers almost worship silence?
4. When is silence best appreciated?

5. Why does the author think silence could be said to be the ultimate province of trust?

II. Are the following judgments correct according to the text? Write "T" if the judgment is correct, or "F" if the judgment is wrong.

1. Everybody loves the sensation of going up to a high place.
2. Herman Melville was finally destroyed by silence.
3. Silence is just a pause, an absence and emptiness.
4. The author does not like sports and music at all.
5. The greatest charm of noise is when it is absent.

III. Please paraphrase the following sentences:

1. White noise becomes the aural equivalent of the clash of images, the nonstop blast of fragments that increasingly agitates our minds.
2. In love, we are speechless; in awe, we say, words fail us.
3. Silence, then, could be said to be the ultimate province of trust.
4. Silence is responsiveness, and in silence we can listen to something behind the clamor of the world.
5. If idleness is the devil's playground, silence may be the angels'.

IV. Please translate the following sentences into Chinese:

1. Silence is sunshine where company is clouds; silence is rapture where company is doubts; silence is golden where company is brass.
2. Before we race off to go prospecting in those hills, we might usefully recall that fool's gold is much more common and that gold has to be panned for, dug out from other substances.
3. Devastated by the silence that greeted his heartfelt novels, he retired into a public silence from which he did not emerge for more than 30 years.
4. Silence is an ecumenical state, beyond the doctrines and divisions created by the mind.
5. We hold our breath, we hold our words; we suspend our chattering selves and let ourselves "fall silent" and fall into the highest place of all.

V. How would you respond to each of the following statements?

1. An inability to stay quiet is one of the most conspicuous failings of mankind.
2. Words can make a deeper scar than silence can heal.
3. There are times when silence has the loudest voice.

4. Speech is silver, silence is golden.
5. It is better to do well than say well.
6. A word spoken cannot be recalled.

VI. Please provide a text, which might support your view on one of the statements in *Exercise V*.

Unit Three

Text A

Your Speech Is Changing

*Bergen Evans**

If a contemporary Rip van Winkle* had slept for forty years and awakened today, he would have to go back to school before he could understand a daily newspaper or a magazine. He would never have heard of atomic bombs, babysitters, coffee breaks, flying saucers, or contact lenses — nor of eggheads, mambo, microfilm, nylons, neptunium, parking meters, or smog.

Many new words have been added to the English language in the past forty years; and since Shakespeare*'s time the number of words in the language has increased more than five times, from 140,000 to somewhere between 700,000 and 8000,000. Most of these new words have not come from borrowing, but from the natural growth of language—adaptation of elements already in the language.

The language has always changed, but the rate of change has been uneven; minor changes have slowly accumulated in every generation, but there have been periods of rapid change as well. The most important of these periods occurred during the two hundred and fifty years after 1066, the year the Normans conquered England*. Before the conquest, the inhabitants of England spoke Anglo-Saxon*, a complex Germanic language. The Normans were Norsemen who, after generations of raiding, had settled in northern France in the

babysitter /ˈbeibiˈsitə/ *n.* a. a person to take charge of a child while the parents are temporarily away b. warship used for convoy, guard and anti-submarine purposes
coffee break a brief rest, as from work
flying saucer UFO
egghead /ˈeghed/ *n.* a person who is very highly educated but not very good at practical things
mambo /ˈmæmbəu/ *n.* a fast ballroom dance of Carib-bean origin, rhythmically similar to the rumba and cha-cha but having a more complex pattern of steps
microfilm /ˈmaɪkrəʊfɪlm/ *n.* a film for photographing a printed page reduced to a very small size
neptunium /nepˈtjuːniəm/ *n.* a radioactive metallic element that is chemically similar to uranium and is obtained in nuclear reactors esp as a by-product in the production of plutonium
somewhere /ˈsʌmweə/ *adv.* used when you are giving a number that is not exact
accumulate /əˈkjuːmjʊleɪt/ *v.* to make or become greater in quantity or size

tenth century and by 1066 were speaking a f orm of French. After their conquest of England they instituted Norman French as the dominant language—the language of the upper classes, of law, of government, and of such commerce as there was.

institute /'ɪnstɪtjuːt/ *v.* to introduce or start sth.
dominant /'dɒmɪnənt/ *adj.* most important, prevailing
commerce /'kɒmɜːs/ a. an interchange of goods on a large scale between different countries or different parts of the same country; trade; business b. social communication
anybody /'eniˌbɔdi/ *pron.* a person of some importance
churl /tʃəːl/ *n.* ill-bred person
dress /dres/ *v.* to prepare meat or fish for cooking or eating by removing the parts that are not usually eaten
alteration /ˌɔːltə'reɪʃən/ *n.* a change in sth.
comic /'kɒmɪk/ funny or humorous
villain /'vɪlən/ *n.* the main bad character in an old play, film, or story
draw apart to move slowly away from each other
riot /'raɪət/ *v.* a. to behave violently in a public place b. to indulge without restraint
defiant /dɪ'faɪənt/ *adj.* showing lack of respect or a refusal to obey someone
exuberance /ɪg'zjuːbərəns/ *n.* luxuriance, state of being full of life and vigor
overlord /'əʊvəlɔːd/ *n.* ruler

For more than two centuries nobody who was anybody spoke Anglo-Saxon. It is doubtful that Richard the Lion-hearted*, for example, spoke one word of English in his entire life—*Angle-ish* was strictly for the churls. As Wamba the Jester pointed out to Curth the Swineherd in Scott's *Ivanhoe**, while animals were living and had to be cared for, they were Saxon—*cow, calf, sheep,* and *pig*—but when they were dressed for the table, when the rewards of labor were to be enjoyed, they were Norman French—*beef, veal, mutton,* and *pork.*

Nevertheless, the masses went right on speaking Anglo-Saxon. It was used every day for generations, by millions of common people who merely said things as effectively as they could and then got on with the business of living; never did a language become more "corrupted" by alterations, foreign words, and errors. By about three hundred years after the Norman conquest, Anglo-Saxon had re-established itself as the language of the upper classes, as *English,* and had become a flexible, exact, splendid, and moving instrument of expression. Norman French, meanwhile, had become something comic, spoken by the villains in the old mystery plays just for a laugh.

The seventeenth and eighteenth centuries, during which printing became established, saw the stabilization of spelling and, more important, the establishment of colonies in America. Immediately the language of the New World and that of the Old World began to draw apart; American speech developed its own rhythms and vigor, found or adapted special words for its own needs, and, in western areas, rioted with a sort of defiant exuberance. It became a language of the people, somewhat as Anglo-Saxon had been during the rule of the Norman overlords.

In writing, too, a change has taken place. The use of the colloquial in American writing is increasing rather than diminishing, although its opponents sometimes label it as "pandering to the masses" and a "debasement" of the language. The increasing use of the colloquial in our writing is an interesting change that is bound to have far-reaching consequences. Our common, informal speech has always been colloquial; that is what the word *colloquial* means. The sensible man speaks colloquially most of the time. When he tries to be formal or unusually impressive, he speaks the way he thinks he writes—and usually makes a fool of himself; worse, he often fails to convey his meaning. Yet whenever he stops to think, the common man feels guilty about his speech and feels that he ought to be more formal, that he ought not to use in writing (about which he retains a semiliterate awe) the expressions that just come naturally to his mind. Thus, when he sees a language form marked "colloq." in the dictionary, he thinks he ought not to use it at all, although actually the colloquial meaning of most words is the "real" meaning to him.

Opposed to the increased use of the colloquial is a minor but increasingly vocal group that insists on rules and correctness, basing that stand on a liking for absolutes; they may be motivated in part by a sense of insecurity produced by the rapidly changing social status of millions. At best, the demands of this group, if acceded to, will sacrifice vigor to propriety; at worst, they are producing a new kind of bad grammar—the uncertainty and pretentiousness that lead to the substitution of *myself* for *me* ("he gave it to John and myself"), to sticking ly on the ends of adverbs that don't need it ("our missile program is moving fastly"), to such vulgar elegances as "Whom shall I say is calling?"

The enormous enlargement of our vocabulary, the increasing use in our writing of the spoken idiom, and changes in our pronunciation are not the only changes that are taking place, however. There have also been significant grammatical alterations in our language. Such changes take place only by generations or decades, at the fastest, so they pass unnoticed by all but grammarians; yet even the layman can perceive them when he is told that something that seems "quite all

pander to to provide sth. that satisfies unreasonable wishes
debasement /dɪ'beɪsmənt/ *n.* reduction of the quality or value of something
far-reaching *adj.* having a wide influence
impressive /ɪm'presɪv/ *adj.* causing admiration
convey /kən'veɪ/ *v.* to express; make your feelings, ideas or thoughts know to other people
guilty /'gɪlti/ *adj.* a. having broken a law or disobeyed a moral or social rule b. having or showing a feeling of guilt c. uncomfortable
semiliterate /'semi'litərit/ *adj.* hardly able to read and write
vocal /'vəʊkəl/ *adj.* expressing yourself freely and noisily
motivate /'məʊtɪveɪt/ *v.* to provide someone with a reason for doing sth.
accede to to agree to do or accept sth.
propriety /prə'praɪəti/ *n.* correctness of social or moral behavior
pretentiousness /prɪ'tenʃəsnis/ *n.* the act of trying to be more important or clever than is really the case
vulgar /'vʌlgə/ *adj.* showing a lack of fine feeling or good judgment in the choice of what is beautiful
elegance /'elɪgəns/ *n.* pleasing and stylish appearance
layman /'leɪmən/ *n.* a person who is not trained in a particular profession or subject

right" to him was regarded as erroneous only a few years ago.

Take, for example, the extraordinary increase in the use of the infinitive, one of the characteristics of modern American speech and writing. Ask any educated American to point out what is wrong with "The government has a duty to protect the worker" or "We have a plan to keep the present tariff" and chances are he couldn't see anything wrong in either sentence. Yet in 1925 Fowler*, a noted grammarian, listed both of these sentences as ungrammatical, arguing that they should read "of protecting" and "of keeping."

A further example of change in our grammar is the great increase in the use of what are called "empty" verbs. Where people used to say "Let's drink" or "Let's swim," there is now a strong tendency to say "Let's have a drink" or "Let's take a swim." Where people formerly said "It snowed heavily," we are inclined to say "There was a heavy snowfall." Our fathers "decided"; we, on the other hand, more often "reach a decision."

Nobody knows why all these changes are being made; perhaps we are in the process of reducing our verbs to a few basic words, like those handy household tools where one handle serves as a blade, screwdriver, hammer, corkscrew, and a dozen other things. If this is so, it may mark a change as significant as that which took place after the Norman conquest.

Whatever the reasons for the changes that are taking place, the vocabulary will probably continue to expand, because the expansion of our knowledge and experience requires the invention of new words or the adaptation of old ones. Meaning will depend more and more upon word order and context, and spelling will become simpler, with fewer common variants. Pronunciation, because of the great mobility of our population and the spread of radio and television, will tend to become more uniform.

One thing by now seems certain—that the speech of the men who lost to the Norman invaders will not die; that language, preserved by the sturdy, surly, freedom-loving commoners who did not attempt to ingratiate themselves with their conquerors by learning their speech, will adapt and endure.

erroneous /ɪ'rəʊniəs/ *adj.* mistaken or incorrect
sturdy /'stɜːdi/ *adj.* strong and unlikely to break or be hurt
surly /'sɜːli/ *adj.* rude and unpleasant
ingratiate /ɪn'greɪʃieɪt/ *v.* to gain favor with someone by making yourself pleasant to them and saying things that will please them

Cultural Notes

1. **Bergen Evans** (1904—1978) was a well-known American expert on the English language. He taught English literature at Northwestern University for over forty years, hosted the CBS television show *The Last Word* (1957—1959), and wrote various books and short works.
2. **Rip van Winkle** is a character in the short story *Rip van Winkle* by American writer Washington Irving (1783—1859). Rip slept overnight before the War of Independence, woke up and found that twenty years had passed, during which big social changes had occurred.
3. **William Shakespeare** (1564—1616) was an English poet, dramatist and actor, often called the English national poet and considered by many to be the greatest dramatist of all time.
4. **The Norman Conquest** refers to the conquest by the French-speaking Normans under Duke William in 1066. After defeating the English at Hastings, William was crowned as King of England.
5. **Anglo-Saxon,** the original Germanic element in the English language, is plain, simple, blunt, monosyllabic, and often rude or vulgar.
6. Nicknamed **Richard the Lion-hearted,** Richard I (1157—1199) was king of England during the years 1189—1199.
7. ***Ivanhoe*** (1820) is a historical novel written by British writer Sir Walter Scott (1771—1832). The novel is set in the late 12th century, when the English people, or Anglo-Saxons, led a hard life under the rule of their Norman conquerors.
8. **Henry Watson Fowler** (1858—1933) was an English lexicographer. Together with his brother, he worked on *The King's English* (1906), a trenchant and witty book of modern English usage and misusage, and on *The Concise Oxford Dictionary of Current English* (1911) and *The Pocket Oxford Dictionary* (1924). After the death of his brother in 1918, H. W. Fowler completed *A Dictionary of Modern English Usage* (1926) alone. These works became invaluable reference books for writers, editors, and all those interested in the usage of modern English.

Comprehension Exercises

I. Please answer the following questions according to the text you have just read.

1. Why does the author mention Rip van Winkle at the beginning of the text?
2. Where have most new words come from? What does "adaptation of elements already in the language" mean?
3. What language did the Normans speak before 1066?
4. What language was established as the most important language in England after the Norman Conquest?
5. What changes had happened to English and Norman French by about three hundred years after the Norman Conquest?
6. Why did spelling become stabilized in the seventeenth and eighteenth centuries?
7. What changes happened to the English Language, with the establishment of colonies in America?
8. What is the author's opinion of colloquial language?
9. What conclusion might Evans draw in the text?

II. Are the following judgments correct according to the text? Write "T" if the judgment is correct, or "F" if the judgment is wrong.

1. Words such as egghead, mambo, microfilm, nylon, etc. appeared in the twentieth century.
2. Most new words are borrowed from other languages.
3. Languages have been changing at the same speed.
4. The first truly significant period of change in the English language began in the eleventh century.
5. The Normans were those who had raided from the north and settled in France.
6. For more than two hundred years after the Norman Conquest, people in England spoke Norman French.
7. Formal language is better than colloquial language.
8. If rigid rules are imposed on a language, it will lose its vigor.
9. There have been no great grammatical changes in English.

III. Please paraphrase the following sentences:

1. For more than two centuries nobody who was anybody spoke Anglo-Saxon.
2. Never did a language become more "corrupted" by alterations, foreign words, and errors.

3. The seventeenth and eighteenth centuries, during which printing become established, saw the stabilization of spelling and, more important, the establishment of colonies in America.
4. The use of the colloquial in American writing is increasing rather than diminishing, although its opponents sometimes label it as "pandering to the masses" and a "debasement" of the language.
5. At best, the demands of this group, if acceded to, will sacrifice vigor to propriety.

IV. Please translate the following sentences into Chinese:

1. After their conquest of England they instituted Norman French as the dominant language—the language of the upper classes, of law, of government, and of such commerce as there was.
2. American speech developed its own rhythms and vigor, found or adapted special words for its own needs, and, in western areas, rioted with a sort of defiant exuberance.
3. The increasing use of the colloquial in our writing is an interesting change that is bound to have far-reaching consequences.
4. Opposed to the increased use of the colloquial is a minor but increasingly vocal group that insists on rules and correctness, basing that stand on a liking for absolutes; they may be motivated in part by a sense of insecurity produced by the rapidly changing social status of millions.

V. How would you respond to each of the following statements?

1. Something that was regarded as erroneous only a few years ago seems quite all right now.
2. Nobody knows why all the language changes are being made.
3. Whatever the reasons for the changes that are taking place, the vocabulary will probably continue to expand, because the expansion of our knowledge and experience requires the invention of new words or the adaptation of old ones.

VI. Please provide a text, which might support your view on one of the statements in *Exercise V*.

Text B

How to Talk about the World

*Peter Farb**

Most people assume that a text in one language can be accurately translated into another language, so long as the translator uses a good bilingual dictionary. But that is not so, because words that are familiar in one language may have no equivalent usage in another. The word *home*, for example, has special meaning for English speakers, particularly those who live in the British Isles. To an Englishman, a *home* is more than the physical structure in which he resides; it is his castle, no matter how humble, the place of his origins, fondly remembered, as well as his present environment of happy family relationships. *This is my home* says the Englishman, and he thereby points not only to a structure but also to a way of life. The same feeling, though, cannot be expressed even in a language whose history is as closely intertwined with English as is French. The closest a Frenchman can come is *Voilá ma maison* or *Voilá mon logis*—words equivalent to the English *house* but certainly not to the English *home*.

Mark Twain* humorously demonstrated the problems of translation when he published the results of his experiment with French. He printed the original version of his well-known story "The Celebrated Jumping Frog of Calaveras County," followed by a Frenchman's translation of it, and then a literal translation from the French back into English. Here are a few sentences from each version:

Twain's Original Version: "Well, there was a feller here once by the name of Jim Smiley, in the winter of'49—or maybe it was the spring of'50—I don't recollect exactly, somehow though what makes me think it was one or the other is because I remember the big flume wasn't finished when he first come to the camp."

French Version: (omitted)

bilingual /baɪˈlɪŋgwəl/ *adj.* spoken or written in two languages
reside /rɪˈzaɪd/ *v.* to live
intertwine /ˌɪntəˈtwaɪn/ *v.* to twine together
literal translation an exact, word-for-word translation
recollect /ˌrekəˈlekt/ *v.* to remember
flume /fluːm/ *n.* (in a gold-mining camp) an artificial channel or open pipe through which water passes

Literal Retranslation into English: "It there was one time here an individual known under the name of Jim Smiley; it was in the winter of '49, possibly well at the spring of '50, I no me recollect exactly. That which makes me to believe that it was one or the other, it is that I shall remember that the grand flume was no achieved when he arrives at the camp for the first time."

bizarre /bɪ'zɑː/ *adj.* very strange
ineptness /i'neptnis/ *n.* foolishness or a poor performance
disastrous /dɪ'zɑːstrəs/ *adj.* terrible
ultimatum /ˌʌltɪ'meɪtəm/ *n.* statement of final condition not open for discussion
laden /'leɪdn/ *adj.* loaded with; carrying
anecdote /'ænɪkdəʊt/ *n.* a short interesting story about a particular person or event
obligatory categories of grammar required grammatical classes of words
aspect /'æspekt/ *n.* a verb form, esp. related to sense of time, as in the English perfect with go in I have gone

Twain, of course, exaggerated his example of bizarre translation—but sometimes such ineptness can have disastrous consequences. At the end of July 1945, Germany and Italy had surrendered and the Allies* issued an ultimatum to Japan to surrender also. Japan's premier called a press conference at which he stated that his country would *mokusatsu* the Allied ultimatum. The word *mokusatsu* was an extremely unfortunate choice. The premier apparently intended it to mean that the cabinet would "consider" the ultimatum. But the word has another meaning, "take no notice of," and that was the one the English-language translators at Domei, Japan's overseas broadcasting agency, used. The world heard that Japan had rejected the ultimatum—instead of that Japan was still considering it. Domei's mistranslation led the United States to send B-29s, laden with atomic bombs, over Hiroshima* and Nagasaki*. Apparently, if *mokusatsu* had been correctly translated, the atomic bomb need never have been dropped.

Such anecdotes about failures in translation do not get at the heart of the problem, because they concern only isolated words and not the resistance of an entire language system to translation. For example, all languages have obligatory categories of grammar that may be lacking in other languages. Russian—like many languages but not like English—has an obligatory category for gender which demands that a noun, and often a pronoun, specify whether it is masculine, feminine, or neuter. Another obligatory category, similarly lacking in English, makes a verb state whether or not an action has been completed. Therefore, a Russian finds it impossible to translate accurately the English sentence *I hired a worker* without having much more information. He would have to know whether the *I* who was speaking was a man or a woman, whether the action of *hired* had a completive or noncompletive aspect ("already hired" as opposed to "was in the process of hiring"), and whether the *worker* was a man or a woman.

Or imagine the difficulty of translating into English a Chinese story in which a character identified as a *biaomei* appears. The obligatory categories to which this word belongs require that it tell whether it refers to a male or a female, whether the character is older or younger than the speaker, and whether the character belongs to the family of the speaker's father or mother. *biaomei* therefore can be translated into English only by the unwieldy statement "a female cousin on my mother's side and younger than myself." Of course, the translator might simply establish these facts about the character the first time she appears and thereafter render the words as "cousin," but that would ignore the significance in Chinese culture of the repetition of these obligatory categories.

unwieldy /ʌn'wiːldi/ *adj.* large, heavy, and awkward to move
render /'rendə/ *v.* to translate
rip /rɪp/ to tear
intersection /ˌintə'sekʃən/ *n.* a place where roads or lines cross
thoroughfare /'θʌrəfeə/ *n.* main road or street (usu. busy)
eccentricity /eksen'trɪsɪti/ *n.* peculiarity; strangeness

The Russian and Chinese examples illustrate the basic problem in any translation. No matter how skilled the translator is, he cannot rip language out of the speech community that uses it. Translation obviously is not a simple two-way street between two languages. Rather, it is a busy intersection at least five thoroughfares meet—the two languages with all their eccentricities, the cultures of the two speech communities, and the speech situation in which the statement was uttered.

Cultural Notes

1. **Peter Farb** (1925—1980) was a naturalist, linguist, anthropologist, and a free-lance writer on many topics, spanning from human culture to the geological formation of North America. His *Face of America: The Natural History of a Continent* (1964) became so popular that President Kennedy presented it to the heads of one hundred foreign governments.
2. **Mark Twain** (1835—1910) was an American writer, journalist, and humorist. The short story "The Celebrated Jumping Frog of Calaveras County" (1865) marked the beginning of his literary career. He won a worldwide audience for his novels *Tom Sawyer* and *Huckleberry Finn*. Sensitive to the sound of language, Twain introduced colloquial speech into American fiction. According to Ernest Hemingway, "All modern American literature comes from one book by Mark Twain called *Huckleberry Finn....*"
3. **The Allies** of World War II were mainly the United Kingdom, the United States, the Soviet Union, and France. Other allied nations included Australia, Canada, China, Denmark, New Zealand, Poland, Yugoslavia and so on. The involvement of many of the Allies in World War II was natural and inevitable,

because they were either invaded or under the direct threat of invasion by the Axis.

4. **Hiroshima** and **Nagasaki** are two seaport cities of Japan. In early August 1945, two atomic bombs made by the allied powers (USA and UK) were dropped on Hiroshima and Nagasaki respectively. These brought the long Second World War to a sudden end.

Comprehension Exercises

I. Please answer the following questions according to the text you have just read.

1. How is the English word "home" different from the French equivalent in connotations or associations?
2. What does the experiment Mark Twain made demonstrate?
3. What example does Farb use to show that inaccurate translation may have very serious consequences?
4. Why does Farb say that the anecdotes such as Domei mistranslation "do not get at the heart of the problem"?
5. What would the translator have to know in order to translate "I hired a worker" into Russian?
6. Why is the English translation of Chinese "*biaomei*" unsatisfactory?
7. What does Farb mean to say by "five thoroughfares"?
8. What conclusion does Farb intend to draw?

II. Are the following judgments correct according to the text? Write "T" if the judgment is correct, or "F" if the judgment is wrong.

1. A text in one language can be accurately translated into another language.
2. Words familiar in one language always have equivalent usage in another language.
3. Poor translation can cause very serious consequences.
4. Momei's mistranslation was solely responsible for the atomic bombings in Hiroshima and Nagasaki.
5. Russian nouns have a gender category while English nouns don't.

III. Please paraphrase the following sentences:

1. Twain, of course, exaggerated his example of bizarre translation—but sometimes such ineptness can have disastrous consequences.
2. Such anecdotes about failures in translation do not get at the heart of the problem, because they concern only isolated words and not the resistance of an entire

language system to translation.

3. No matter how skilled the translator is, he cannot rip language out of the speech community that uses it.
4. Of course, the translator might simply establish these facts about the character the first time she appears and thereafter render the words as "cousin," but that would ignore the significance in Chinese culture of the repetition of these obligatory categories.

IV. Please translate the following sentences into Chinese:

1. The same feeling, though, cannot be expressed even in a language whose history is as closely intertwined with English as is French.
2. Apparently, if *mokusatsu* had been correctly translated, the atomic bomb need never have been dropped.
3. All languages have obligatory categories of grammar that may be lacking in other languages.
4. Translation obviously is not a simple two-way street between two languages. Rather, it is a busy intersection at least five thoroughfares meet—the two languages with all their eccentricities, the cultures of the two speech communities, and the speech situation in which the statement was uttered.
5. Russian—like many languages but not like English—has an obligatory category for gender which demands that a noun, and often a pronoun, specify whether it is masculine, feminine, or neuter.

V. How would you respond to each of the following statements?

1. Words with the same denotative meanings may have different connotations in different languages.
2. One problem in translation is that different languages have different obligatory categories.
3. It takes much more than a dictionary to be a good translator.
4. The service that translators render to enhance cultures and nurture languages has been significant throughout history.
5. The translator's task is to create conditions under which the source language and the target language can interact with one another.
6. The act of translating takes place in the social-cultural context.

VI. Please provide a text, which might support your view on one of the statements in *Exercise V*.

Unit Four

Text A

The Art of Living Simply

*Richard Wolkomir**

We paddled down Maine's Saco River that September afternoon, five couples in canoes, basking in the summer's last golden sunlight. Grazing deer, fluttering their white tails, watched our flotilla pass. That evening we pitched tents, broiled steaks and sprawled around the campfire, staring sleepily at the stars. One man, strumming his guitar, sang an old Shaker* song: "'Tis the gift to be simple. 'Tis the gift to be free."

Our idyll ended, of course, and we drove back to the world of loan payments, jobs and clogged washing machines. "'Tis the gift to be simple," I found myself humming at odd moments, "'Tis the gift to be free." How I longed for that simplicity. But where could I find it?

"Our life is frittered away by detail. Simplify, simplify." That dictum of Henry David Thoreau*'s, echoing from the days of steamboats and ox-drawn plows, had long haunted me. Yet Thoreau himself was able to spend only two years in the cabin he built beside Walden Pond. And Henry—wifeless, childless, jobless—never had to tussle with such details as variable-rate mortgages.

My life attracted detail, as if my motto were: "Complicate, complicate." And I've found I'm not alone. But one day my thinking about simplicity turned upside down.

I was visiting a physicist in his office tower jutting from his Illinois farmlands. We looked through his window at the laboratory's miles-around particle accelerator, an immense

paddle /ˈpædl/ *v.* to move a small light boat through water, using one or more paddles

bask /bɑːsk/ *v.* to enjoy sitting or lying in the heat of the sun or a fire

flotilla /fləˈtɪlə/ *n.* a group of small ships

pitch /pɪtʃ/ *v.* to set up (a tent, camp, etc.) in position on open ground, esp. for a certain time only

broil /brɔil/ *v.* to grill (chicken, meat, or fish)

sprawl /sprɒːl/ *v.* to lie or sit with your arms or legs stretched out in a lazy or careless way

idyll /ˈɪdɪl/ *n.* a place or experience in which everything is peaceful and everyone is perfectly happy

fritter /ˈfrɪtə/ *v.* to waste time, money, or effort on sth. small or unimportant

dictum /ˈdɪktəm/ *n.* a short phrase that expresses a general rule or truth

haunt /hɔːnt/ *v.* to make someone worry or make them sad

tussle /ˈtʌsəl/ *v.* to fight or struggle without using any weapons, by pulling or pushing someone rather than hitting them

mortgage /ˈmɔːgɪdʒ/ *n.* a legal arrangement by which you borrow money from a bank in order to buy a house, and pay back the money over a period of years

jut /dʒʌt/ *v.* to stick out, or make sth. stick out, esp. beyond the surface or edge of sth.

particle accelerator a device in physics used to accelerate charged elementary particles to high energies

circle in the prairie far below. "It's a kind of time machine," he said, explaining that the accelerator enables physicists to study conditions like those shortly after Creation*'s first moment. The universe was simpler then, he noted, a mere dot comprising perhaps only one kind of force and one kind of particle. Now it has many kinds of forces, scores of different particles, and contains everything from stars and galaxies to dandelions, elephants and the poems of Keats*.

Complexity, I began to see from that tower, is part of God's plan.

prairie /ˈpɑːrɪkəl/ *n.* a wide open area of fairly flat land in North America which is covered in grass or wheat
galaxy /ˈgæləksi/ *n.* one of the large groups of stars that make up the universe
dandelion /ˈdændɪlaɪən/ *n.* a wild plant with a bright yellow flower
disparage /dɪsˈpærɪdʒ/ *v.* to speak without respect of; make (someone or sth.) sound of little value or importance —disparagingly *adv.*
simpleton /ˈsɪmpəltən/ *n.* (old) someone who has a very low level of intelligence
defect /diˈfekt/ *n.* sth. lacking or imperfect; fault
insulation /ˌɪnsjʊˈleɪʃən/ *n.* covering sth. with a material that stops electricity, sound, heat etc. from getting in or out
septic system sewage system
albatross /ˈælbətrɒs/ *n.* sth. that causes problems for you and prevents you from succeeding
a gaggle of a noisy group of
divert /daɪˈvɜːt/ *v.* **a.** to change the direction in which sth. travels **b.** to deliberately take someone's attention from sth. by making them think about other things **c.** (formal) to entertain someone
incipient /ɪnˈsɪpiənt/ *adj.* starting to happen or exist

Deep down, we sense that we speak, disparagingly, of a "simpleton." Nobody wants to be guilty of "simplistic" thinking.

But blinding ourselves to complexity can be dangerous. Once I bought a home. I liked its setting so much I unconsciously avoided probing into its possible defects. After it was mine, I found it needed insulation, roofing, a new heating system, new windows, a new septic system—everything. That old house became an albatross, costing far more than I could afford, the cost in stress was even higher, I had refused to look at the complexities.

Even ordinary finances are rarely simple—what does your insurance policy actually cover? Yet, economics is simplicity itself compared with moral questions.

One afternoon when I was ten, I found myself the leader of an after-school gaggle of boys. I had to divert them quickly, I knew, or my career as leader would be brief. And then I saw Joe.

Joe was an Eiffel Tower* of a kid, an incipient giant. His family had emigrated from Europe, and he had a faint accent.

"Let's get him!" I said.

My little troop of Goths swarmed upon Joe. Somebody snatched his hat and we played catch with it. Joe ran home, and I took his hat as a trophy.

That night, our doorbell rang. Joe's father, a worried-looking farmer with a thick accent, asked for Joe's hat. I returned it sheepishly. "Please don't upset Joe," he said earnestly. "He has asthma. When he has an attack, it is hard for him to get better."

I felt a lead softball in my chest. The next evening I walked to Joe's house. He was in the garden, tilling the soil, he watched me warily as I walked up. I asked if I could help. "Okay," he said. After that I went often to help him and we became best friends.

I had taken a step toward adulthood. Inside myself I had seen possibilities, like a tangle of wires. This red wire was the possibility for evil, which requires no more than ignoring another's pain. And here was the white wire of sympathy. I could have a hand in connecting all those wires—it was a matter of the decisions I made. I had discovered complexity, and found in it an opportunity to choose, to grow. Its price is responsibility.

Perhaps, that is one reason we yearn for the simple life. In a way, we want to be children, to let someone else carry the awkward backpack of responsibility.

Not long ago I attended a college seminar where a U.S. State Department officer talked about international negotiation. Afterward he asked for questions. One student demanded: "Why don't you just get rid of all these terrible nuclear weapons?" The diplomat looked at her blankly, then said, "That's the problem of our times—some of the world's best minds are struggling with it." "Well, just get rid of them," the student said. After a silence, he sighed and said, "If only it were that simple." Behind that sigh were the teeming complexities of national security, of international politics, of the inability to "disinvent" an existing technology. For me, their exchange had a message: in a complex world, to insist upon simplicity is foolish.

Goth /gɒθ/ *adj.* ignorant, uncivilized and brutal man
trophy /ˈtrəufi/ *n.* sth. that you keep to prove your success in sth., esp. in war or hunting
sheepish /ˈʃiːpɪʃ/ *adj.* uncomfortable, as from being slightly ashamed or fearful of others —sheepishly *adv.*
asthma /ˈæsmə/ *n.* a medical condition that causes difficulties in breathing
till /tɪl/ *v.* to prepare land for growing crops; cultivate
wary /weəri/ showing watchfulness or suspicion —warily *adv.*
tangle /ˈtæŋɡəl/ *n.* a. a confused mass b. a confused disordered state
seminar /ˈsemɪnɑː/ *n.* a class at a university or college for a small group of students and a teacher to study or discuss a particular subject
teeming /ˈtiːmɪŋ/ *adj.* full of people, animals etc. that are all moving around
disinvent /ˌdisinˈvent/ *v.* to undo the invention of sth.; to make sth. cease to exist

We are like wheat, here on earth to ripen. We ripen intellectually by letting in as much of the universe's complexity as we can. Morally we ripen by making our choices. And we ripen spiritually by opening our eyes to Creation's endless detail.

One afternoon I picked up a fallen leaf from the sugar maple in our yard. Up close it was yellow, with splashes of red. At arm's length it was orange. Its color depends on how I looked at it.

I knew a little about how this leaf had spent its life, transforming sunlight and carbon dioxide into nutrients, and I knew that we animals breathe that oxygen that such plants emit, while they thrive upon the carbon dioxide we exhale. And I knew that each cell of the leaf has a nucleus containing a chemical—DNA*—upon which is inscribed all the instructions for making and operating a sugar maple. Scientists know far more about this than I. But even their knowledge extends only a short way into the sea of complexity that is a sugar maple.

I'm beginning to understand, I think, what simplicity means. It does not mean blinding ourselves to the world's stunning complexity or avoiding the choices that ripen us. By "simplify, simplify," Thoreau meant simplifying ourselves.

To accomplish this, we can:

Focus on deeper things. The simple life is not necessarily living in a cabin, cultivating beans. It is refusing to let our lives be "frittered away by detail." A professor taught me a secret for focusing: Turn off the TV and read great books. They open doors in your brain.

Undertake life's journey one step at a time. I once met a young couple both blind since birth. They had a three-year-old daughter and an infant, both fully sighted. For those parents, everything was complex: bathing the baby, monitoring their daughter, mowing the lawn. Yet they were full of smiles and laughter. I asked the mother how she kept track of their lively daughter. "I tie

nutrient /ˈnjuːtriənt/ *n.* a chemical or food that provides what is needed for plants or animals to live and grow
emit /ɪˈmɪt/ *v.* to send out gas, heat, light, sound
nucleus /ˈnjuːkliəs/ *n.* the central part of almost all the cells of living things
inscribe /ɪnˈskraɪb/ *v.* to carefully cut, print, or write words on sth., esp. on the surface of a stone or coin
mow /məu/ *v.* to cut grass using a machine

little bells in her shoes," she said with a laugh. "What will you do when the infant walks too?" I asked. She smiled. "Everything is so complicated that I don't try to solve a problem until I have to. I take one thing at a time!"

pare down to reduce sth., esp. by making a lot of small reductions
nibble /ˈnɪbəl/ *v.* to eat small amounts of food by taking very small bites
snarl /snɑːl/ *n.* a confused, complicated, or tangled situation; a predicament
slouch /slaʊtʃ/ *v.* to stand, sit, or walk with your shoulders bent forward that makes you look tired or lazy
shrivel /ˈʃrivl/ *v.* to become wrinkled smaller or cause somebody to become so esp. from drying out or aging
well /wel/ *v.* to rise or flow to the surface from inside the ground or the body, or cause sth. to do this
bewilder /bɪˈwɪldə/ to confuse, esp. by the presence of lots of different things at the same time —bewilderment *n.*
savor /ˈseɪvə/ *v.* to fully enjoy the taste or smell of sth.
brim /brɪm/ *v.* to fill sth., or be full, to the top edge

Pare down your desires. English novelist and playwright Jerome Klapka Jerome* caught the spirit of that enterprise when he wrote, "Let your boat of life be light, packed only with what you need—a homely home and simple pleasure, one or two friends, worth the name, someone to love and someone to love you, a cat, a dog and a pipe or two, enough to eat and enough to wear and a little more than enough to drink, for thirst is a dangerous thing."

Not long ago I flew home to see my father in the hospital. He has a disease that nibbles away the mind. I was a snarl of worries. Treatments? Nursing homes? Finances?

He was slouched in a wheelchair, a shriveled, whitened remnant of the father I had known. As I stood there, hurt and confused, he looked up and saw me. And then I saw something unexpected and wonderful in his eyes: recognition and love. It welled up and filled his eyes with tears. And mine.

That afternoon, my father came back from wherever his illness had taken him. He joked and laughed, once again the man I had known. And then he tired, and we put him to bed. The next day, he did not remember I had come. And the next night he died.

Every death is a door opening on Creation's mystery. The door opens, but we see only darkness. In that awful moment, we realize how vast the universe is, complexity upon complexity, beyond us. But that is the true gift of simplicity: to accept the world's infinite complication, to accept bewilderment.

And then, especially, we can savor simple things. A face we love, perhaps, eyes brimming with love.

It is the simplest of things. But it is more than enough.

Cultural Notes

1. **Richard Wolkomir** is an editor with the McGrawHill Publishing Company in New York. Together with his wife, Joyce Rogers Wolkomir, he writes essays and articles for magazines ranging from *Smithsonian* and *Reader's Digest* to *Wildlife Conservation, Playboy,* and *National Geographic Magazine.*
2. **Shaker** is a name applied to the United Society of Believers in Christ's Second Coming, a sect first heard of about 1750 in Great Britain. The name Shaking Quakers or Shakers came from the peculiar trembling of the secessionists at their meetings. Shaker communities held property in common, practiced asceticism, and honored celibacy above marriage. The movement diminished after 1860.
3. **Henry David Thoreau:** see Page 53.
4. **Creation** means the origin of the universe. Big Bang Theory proposes that the universe was once extremely compact, dense, and hot. Some original event, a cosmic explosion called the big bang, occurred about 13.7 billion years ago, and the universe has since been expanding and cooling.
5. **John Keats** (1795—1821) was a British poet and considered among the greatest in English. His works, melodic and rich in classical imagery, include *The Eve of St. Agnes, Ode on a Grecian Urn,* and *To Autumn.*
6. **Eiffel Tower** is a wrought iron tower in Paris. It was designed and built by the French civil engineer Alexandre Gustave Eiffel for the Paris World's Fair of 1889.
7. **DNA:** see Page 97
8. **Jerome Klapka Jerome** (1859—1927) was an English novelist and playwright. Two books, *Idle Thoughts of an Idle Fellow* (1886) and *Three Men in a Boat* (1889), represent his greatest success as a novelist.

Comprehension Exercises

I. Please answer the following questions according to the text you have just read.

1. How do you understand Thoreau's dictum about simplicity and the author's motto about complexity?
2. Do you think the author finally understood what Thoreau means by "simplify, simplify"?

3. What does the author mean by "complicate, complicate"? How does he prove the complexity of human morality, life, nature and the universe?
4. How are such topics as morality, growth, choice, responsibility, nuclear weapons, love, etc. relevant to the theme of the essay? How do they contribute to the final conclusion?
5. How does the author adopt the first-person point of view and share with us some episodes in his life?

II. Are the following judgments correct according to the text? Write "T" if the judgment is correct, or "F" if the judgment is wrong.

1. The brief escape from the stressful city life made the author long for simplicity and follow Thoreau's example.
2. Modern people, burdened with work, family and finance, cannot afford a complete retreat from them.
3. Compared with its original form, the present universe is far more complicated, comprising many kinds of particles, forces, stars, plants, animals, and civilizations.
4. The experience of buying the house further proves the danger of simplifying things, because complexity is the true nature of the universe.
5. Joe was tall and therefore not an ideal prospect for fight.
6. Joe came from a rich family in Europe and knew much about Eiffel Tower.
7. Growth is complicated because you may make mistakes, have to make decisions and take responsibility.
8. Jerome advised to take a little more than enough to drink.
9. The death of the author's father convinces him that the universe is complicated and life is not a simple journey.

III. Please paraphrase the following sentences:

1. After a silence, he sighed and said, "If only it were that simple."
2. That afternoon, my father came back from wherever his illness had taken him. He joked and laughed, once again the man I had known.
3. Every death is a door opening on Creation's mystery. The door opens, but we see only darkness.
4. It is the simplest of things. But it is more than enough.

IV. Please translate the following sentences into Chinese:

1. That dictum of Henry David Thoreau's, echoing from the days of steamboats and ox-drawn plows, had long haunted me.

2. Deep down, we sense that we speak, disparagingly, of a "simpleton." Nobody wants to be guilty of "simplistic" thinking.
3. Inside myself I had seen possibilities, like a tangle of wires. This red wire was the possibility for evil, which requires no more than ignoring another's pain. And here was the white wire of sympathy. I could have a hand in connecting all those wires—it was a matter of the decisions I made.
4. We ripen intellectually by letting in as much of the universe's complexity as we can. Morally we ripen by making our choices. And we ripen spiritually by opening our eyes to Creation's endless detail.
5. Scientists know far more about this than I. But even their knowledge extends only a short way into the sea of complexity that is a sugar maple.
6. He has a disease that nibbles away the mind. I was a snarl of worries. Treatments? Nursing homes? Finances?
7. He was slouched in a wheelchair, a shriveled, whitened remnant of the father I had known.
8. In that awful moment, we realize how vast the universe is, complexity upon complexity, beyond us.

V. How would you respond to each of the following statements?

1. Physical maturity is not enough.
2. Complexity is part of God's plan.
3. Blinding ourselves to complexity can be dangerous.
4. Simple life is not necessarily living in a cabin, cultivating beans.

VI. Please provide a text, which might support your view on one of the statements in *Exercise V*.

Text B

Holy Dying

*Jeremy Taylor**

Neither must we think that the life of a man begins when he can feed himself, or walk alone, when he can fight, or beget his like; for so he is contemporary with a camel or a cow; but he is first a man, when he comes to a certain steady use of reason, according to his proportion; and when that is, all the world of men cannot tell precisely.

beget his like to become the father of a child

Some men are called *at age* at fourteen, some at one-and-twenty, some never; but all men late enough, for the life of a man comes upon him slowly and insensibly. But as when the sun approaches towards the gates of the morning, he first opens a little eye of heaven, and sends away the spirits of darkness, and gives light to a cock, and calls up the lark to matins, and by and by gilds the fringes of a cloud, and peeps over the eastern hills, thrusting out his golden horns, like those which decked the brows of Moses* when he was forced to wear a veil because himself had seen the face of God; and still while a man tells the story, the sun gets up higher, till he shows a fair face and a full light, and then he shines one whole day, under a cloud often, and sometimes weeping great and little showers and sets quickly; so is a man's reason and his life. He first begins to perceive himself, to see or taste, making little reflections upon his actions of sense, and can discourse of flies and dogs, shells and play, horses and liberty; but when he is strong enough to enter into arts and little institutions, he is at first entertained with trifles and impertinent things, not because he needs them, but because his understanding is no bigger, and little images of things are laid before him, like a cock-boat to a whale, only to play withal; but before a man comes to be wise, he is half dead with gouts and consumption, with catarrhs and aches, with sore eyes and a worn-out body. So that if we must not reckon the life of a man but by the accounts of his reason, he is long before his soul be dressed; and he is not to be called a man without a wise and an adorned soul, a soul at least furnished with what is necessary towards his well-being; but by that time his soul is thus furnished, his body is decayed; and then you can hardly reckon him to be alive, when his body is possessed by so many degrees of death.

matins /ˈmætɪnz/ *n.* the first prayers of the day in the Christian religion; fig. the morning song
thrust /θrʌst/ *v.* to push sth. somewhere roughly
deck /dek/ *v.* to decorate
discourse /disˈkɔːs/ *v.* to talk
impertinent /ɪmˈpɜːtɪnənt/ *adj.* not pertaining to the matter in hand
cock-boat small boat
withal /wiˈðɔːl/ *prep.* with
gout /gaʊt/ *n.* a disease that makes your toes, fingers, and knees swollen and painful
consumption /kənˈsʌmpʃən/ *n.* (old) tuberculosis
catarrh /kəˈtɑː/ *n.* inflammation of mucous membranes, esp. of the nose and throat
arrest /əˈrest/ *n.* imprisonment
ten to one very likely
impediment /ɪmˈpedɪmənt/ *n.* a situation that makes it difficult for someone or sth. to succeed or make progress
want /wɒnt/ *v.* **a.** to suffer from the lack of **b.** to lack; to be without

But there is yet another arrest. At first he wants strength of body, and then he wants the use of reason, and when that is come, it is ten to one but he stops by the impediments of vice, and wants the strength of the *spirit*; and we know that *body*, and *soul*, and *spirit*, are the constituent parts of every Christian man. And now let us consider what that thing is which we call *years* of discretion. The young man is past his tutors, and arrived at the bondage of a caitiff spirit; he is run from discipline, and is let loose to passion; the man by this time hath wit enough to choose his vice, to act his lust, to court his mistress, to talk confidently, and ignorantly, and perpetually. To despise his betters, to deny nothing to his appetite, to do things that when he is indeed a man he must for ever be ashamed of; for this is all the discretion that most men show in the first stage of their manhood; they can discern good from evil; and they prove their skill by leaving all that is good; and wallowing in the evils of folly and an unbridled appetite. And by this time the young man hath contracted vicious habits, and is a beast in manners, and therefore it will not be fitting to reckon the beginning of his life; he is a fool in his understanding, and that is a sad death; and he is dead in trespasses and sins, and that is a sadder; so that he hath no life but a natural, the life of a beast, or a tree; in all other capacities he is dead; he neither hath the intellectual nor the spiritual life, neither the life of a man nor of a Christian; and this sad truth lasts too long. For old age seizes upon most men while they still retain the minds of boys and vicious youth, doing actions from principles of great folly and a mighty ignorance, admiring things useless and hurtful, and filling up all the dimensions of their abode with businesses of empty affairs, being at leisure to attend no virtue. They cannot pray, because they are busy, and because they are passionate. They cannot communicate, because they have quarrels and intrigues of perplexed causes, complicated hostilities, and things of the world; and therefore they cannot attend to the things of God; little considering that they must find a time to die in, when death comes they must be at leisure for that. Such men are like sailors loosing from a port, and tossed immediately with a perpetual tempest, lasting till their cordage crack, and either they sink or return back again to the same place; they did not make a voyage, though they were long at sea. The business and impertinent affairs of most men steal all their time, and they are restless in a foolish motion; but this is not the progress of a man; he is no farther advanced in the course of a life, though he reckon many years; for still his soul is childish and trifling, like an untaught boy.

discretion /dɪs'kreʃən/ *n.* the ability and right to decide exactly what should be done in a particular situation
caitiff /'keitif/ *adj.* extremely bad, immoral, or cruel
hath /hæθ/ *v.* (old use) has
better /'betə/ *n.* sth. or someone better
wallow /'wɒləu/ *v.* to indulge unrestrainedly in vice, sensuality, etc.
unbridled /ʌn'braɪdld/ *adj.* not controlled and too extreme or violent
trespass /'trespəs/ *n.* sth. you have done that is morally wrong
natural /'nætʃərəl/ *n.* (old) a person with a weak mind; idiot
abode /ə'bəud/ *n.* (formal) someone's home
intrigue /ɪn'triːg/ *n.* a plan to do sth. bad
perpetual /pə'petʃuəl/ *adj.* permanent; continuing all the time without changing or stopping
tempest /'tempɪst/ *n.* a violent storm
cordage /'kɔːdɪdʒ/ *n.* rope or cord in general, esp. on a ship

Cultural Notes

1. **Jeremy Taylor** (1613—1667) was an Anglican clergyman and writer. Taylor was educated at the University of Cambridge and was ordained in 1633. By 1655 he had written his enduring works: *The Rule and Exercises of Holy Living* (1650) and *The Rule and Exercises of Holy Dying* (1651). These devotional handbooks were written to help members of the Church of England who were deprived of a regular ministry during the disturbances of the Commonwealth. The books' beauty and spiritual insight made them popular with all denominations. The text is taken from his *The Rule and Exercises of Holy Dying* (1651).
2. **Moses:** see Page 141.

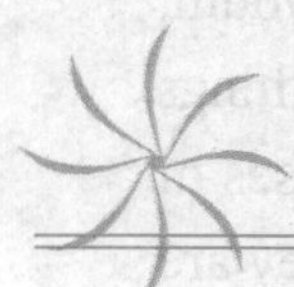

Comprehension Exercises

I. Please answer the following questions according to the text you have just read.

1. What enables a person to enter the state of man?
2. In what case does a person want the strength of the spirit?
3. What actions should be taken to attain the rank of true humanity?
4. What gets in the way of our appreciation of the meaning of life and its permanent spiritual values?
5. Faced with the reality of the vanity and shortness of his life, what should a man do to lengthen his days and to improve the quality of life?

II. Are the following judgments correct according to the text? Write "T" if the judgment is correct, or "F" if the judgment is wrong.

1. A well-disposed mind can distinguish a man from a beast or a tree.
2. A person with a furnished soul is reckoned to be alive, even if his body is decayed.
3. A wise man can look upon death, and see its face with the same countenance with which he hears its story.
4. A man can endure all the labors of his life so long as his soul supports his body.
5. It can be inferred that a man's humanity is directly proportional to the purity of his mind.
6. If a person's youth is chaste and temperate, modest and industrious, proceeding through a prudent and sober manhood to a religious old age, then he has the life of a man.

IV. Please translate the following sentences into Chinese:

1. He is first a man, when he comes to a certain steady use of reason, according to his proportion.
2. If we must not reckon the life of a man but by the accounts of his reason, he is long before his soul be dressed.
3. The young man is past his tutors, and arrived at the bondage of a caitiff spirit.
4. They fill up all the dimensions of their abode with businesses of empty affairs, being at leisure to attend no virtue.
5. They prove their skill by leaving all that is good; and wallowing in the evils of folly and an unbridled appetite.

V. How would you respond to each of the following statements?

1. Neither must we think that the life of a man begins when he can feed himself, or walk alone, when he can fight, or beget his like; for so he is contemporary with a camel or a cow.
2. All men late enough, for the life of a man comes upon him slowly and insensibly.
3. He first begins to perceive himself, to see or taste, making little reflections upon his actions of sense, and can discourse of flies and dogs, shells and play, horses and liberty.
4. When the sun approaches towards the gates of the morning, he first opens a little eye of heaven, and sends away the spirits of darkness, and gives light to a cock, and calls up the lark to matins.
5. At first he wants strength of body, and then he wants the use of reason, and when that is come, it is ten to one but he stops by the impediments of vice, and wants the strength of the spirit.
6. He is a fool in his understanding, and that is a sad death; and he is dead in trespasses and sins, and that is a sadder; so that he hath no life but a natural, the life of a beast, or a tree.
7. The business and impertinent affairs of most men steal all their time, and they are restless in a foolish motion; but this is not the progress of a man; he is no farther advanced in the course of a life, though he reckon many years; for still his soul is childish and trifling, like an untaught boy.

VI. Please provide a text, which might support your view on one of the statements in *Exercise V.*

Unit Five

Text A

Solitude

*Henry David Thoreau**

This is a delicious evening, when the whole body is one sense, and imbibes delight through every pore. I go and come with a strange liberty in Nature, a part of herself. As I walk a long the stony shore of the pond in my shirt-sleeves, though it is cool as well as cloudy and windy, and I see nothing special to attract me, all the elements are unusually congenial to me. The bullfrogs trump to usher in the night, and the note of the whip- poor-will is borne on the rippling wind from over the water. Sympathy with the fluttering alder and poplar leaves almost takes away my breath; yet, like the lake, my serenity is rippled but not ruffled. These small waves raised by the evening wind are as remote from storm as the smooth reflecting surface. Though it is now dark, the wind still blows and roars in the wood, the waves still dash, and some creatures lull the rest with their notes. The repose is never complete. The wildest animals do not repose, but seek their prey now; the fox, and skunk, and rabbit, now roam the fields and woods without fear. They are Nature's watchmen—links which connect the days of animated life.

I find it wholesome to be alone the greater part of the time. To be in company, even with the best, is soon wearisome and dissipating. I love to be alone. I never found the companion that was so companionable as solitude. We are for the

imbibe /ɪm'baɪb/ *v.* to drink sth., esp. alcohol

congenial /kən'dʒiːniəl/ *adj.* pleasant in a way that makes you feel comfortable and relaxed

trump /trʌmp/ *v.* to blow a trumpet

whip-poor-will common American bird, of the goatsucker family, named for its whip-poor-will call

ripple /'rɪpəl/ *v.* to make a noise like water flowing gently

alder /'ɔːldə(r)/ *n.* common name for a group of shrubs and trees native to cold and temperate climates

serene /sɪ'riːn/ *adj.* completely calm and peaceful —serenity *n.*

ruffle /'rʌfəl/ *v.* to make a smooth surface uneven

lull /lʌl/ *v.* to make someone feel calm or want to sleep

repose /rɪ'pəuz/ *n.* state of calm or comfortable rest

prey /preɪ/ *n.* an animal, bird etc. that is hunted and eaten by another animal

skunk /skʌŋk/ *n.* a small black and white North American animal that produces a strong unpleasant smell if it is attacked or afraid

wholesome /'həulsəm/ *adj.* likely to make you healthy

wearisome /'wɪərisəm/ making you feel bored, tired, or annoyed

dissipate /'dɪsɪpeɪt/ *v.* to gradually become less or weaker before disappearing completely, or to make sth. do this

most part more lonely when we go abroad among men than when we stay in our chambers. A man thinking or working is always alone, let him be where he will. Solitude is not measured by the miles of space that intervene between a man and his fellows. The really diligent student in one of the crowded hives of Cambridge College is as solitary as a dervish in the desert. The farmer can work alone in the field or the woods all day, hoeing or chopping, and not feel lonesome, because he is employed; but when he comes home at night he cannot sit down in a room alone, at the mercy of his thoughts, but must be where he can "see the folks," and recreate, and, as he thinks, remunerate himself for his day's solitude; and hence he wonders how the student can sit alone in the house all night and most of the day without ennui and "the blues"; but he does not realize that the student, though in the house, is still at work in his field, and chopping in his woods, as the farmer in his, and in turn seeks the same recreation and society that the latter does, though it may be a more condensed form of it.

intervene /ˌɪntə'viːn/ *v.* to become involved in an argument, fight, or other difficult situation in order to change what happens
hive /haiv/ *n.* a place that is full of busy people
dervish /'dɜːvɪʃ/ *n.* a member of a Muslim religious group, some of whom dance fast and spin around as part of a religious ceremony
remunerate /rɪ'mjuːnəreɪt/ *v.* to pay someone for goods or services, or compensate somebody for losses or inconvenience
ennui /'ɒnwiː/ *n.* a feeling of being tired, bored, and unsatisfied with your life
musty /'mʌsti/ *adj.* tasting old, stale, and moldy
etiquette /'etɪket/ *n.* the formal rules for polite behavior in society or in a particular group
suffice /sə'fais/ *v.* to be enough
loon /luːn/ *n.* a large North American bird that eats fish and makes a long high sound
azure /'æʒə/ *adj.* having a bright blue color like the sky
tint /tɪnt/ *n.* a small amount of a particular color

Society is commonly too cheap. We meet at very short intervals, not having had time to acquire any new value for each other. We meet at meals three times a day, and give each other a new taste of that old musty cheese that we are. We have had to agree on a certain set of rules, called etiquette and politeness, to make this frequent meeting tolerable and that we need not come to open war. We meet at the post-office, and at the sociable, and about the fireside every night; we live thick and are in each other's way, and stumble over one another, and I think that we thus lose some respect for one another. Certainly less frequency would suffice for all important and hearty communications. Consider the girls in a factory—never alone, hardly in their dreams. It would be better if there were but one inhabitant to a square mile, as where I live. The value of a man is not in his skin, that we should touch him.

I have a great deal of company in my house; especially in the morning, when nobody calls. Let me suggest a few comparisons, that some one may convey an idea of my situation. I am no more lonely than the loon in the pond that laughs so loud, or than Walden Pond itself. What company has that lonely lake, I pray? And yet it has not the blue devils, but the blue angels in it, in the azure tint of its waters. The sun is alone, except in thick weather, when there sometimes appear to be two, but one is a mock sun. God is alone—but the devil, he is far from being alone; he sees a great deal of company; he is legion. I am no more lonely than a single mullein or dandelion in a pasture, or a bean leaf, or sorrel, or a horse-fly, or a bumblebee. I am no more lonely than the Mill Brook, or a weathercock, or the north star, or the south wind, or an April shower, or a January thaw, or the first spider in a new house.

I have occasional visits in the long winter evenings, when the snow falls fast and the wind howls in the wood, from an old settler and original proprietor, who is reported to have dug Walden Pond, and stoned it, and fringed it with pine woods; who tells me stories of old time and of new eternity; and between us we manage to pass a cheerful evening with social mirth and pleasant views of things, even without apples or cider—a most wise and humorous friend, whom I love much, who keeps himself more secret than ever did Goffe or Whalley*; and though he is thought to be dead, none can show where he is buried. An elderly dame, too, dwells in my neighborhood, invisible to most persons, in whose odorous herb garden I love to stroll sometimes, gathering simples and listening to her fables; for she has a genius of unequalled fertility, and her memory runs back farther than mythology, and she can tell me the original of every fable, and on what fact every one is founded, for the incidents occurred when she was young. A ruddy and lusty old dame, who delights in all weathers and seasons, and is likely to outlive all her children yet.

The indescribable innocence and beneficence of Nature—of sun and wind and rain, of summer and winter—such health, such cheer, they afford forever! And such sympathy have they ever with our race, that all Nature would be affected, and the sun's brightness fade, and the winds would sigh humanely, and the clouds rain tears, and the woods shed their leaves and put on mourning in

mock /mɒk/ *adj.* not real, but intended to be very similar to a real situation, substance etc.
legion /ˈliːdʒən/ *n.* a large group of soldiers, esp. in ancient Rome
mullein /ˈmʌlɪn/ *n.* a flowering tall plant with hairy leaves native to Europe and Asia, naturalized in the United States
sorrel /ˈsɒrəl/ *n.* a plant with leaves that taste bitter, sometimes used in cooking
horse-fly a large fly that bites horses and cattle
bumblebee /ˈbʌmbəlˌbiː/ *n.* a large hairy bee
weathercock /ˈweðəkɒk/ *n.* a weather vane in the shape of a male chicken to show the direction the wind coming from
thaw /θɔː/ *n.* a period of warm weather during which snow and ice melt
proprietor /prəˈpraɪətə/ *n.* an owner of a business
fringe /frɪndʒ/ *v.* to be around the edge of sth.
eternity /ɪˈtɜːnɪti/ *n.* the whole of time without any end
mirth /mɜːθ/ *n.* happiness and laughter
cider /ˈsaɪdə/ *n.* an alcoholic drink made from apples, or a glass of this drink
dame /deɪm/ *n.* (American English, old-fashioned, informal) a woman
dwell /dwel/ *v.* (literary) to live in a particular place
stroll /strəʊl/ *v.* to walk in a slow relaxed way
simple /ˈsɪmpəl/ *n.* (old) a wild plant used as medicine
fertility /fəːˈtɪlɪti/ *n.* the ability of the land or soil to produce good crops or of a person, animal, or plant to produce babies, young animals, or seeds
ruddy /ˈrʌdi/ *adj.* with a healthy and reddish glow
lusty /ˈlʌsti/ *adj.* strong and healthy, powerful
outlive /aʊtˈliv/ *v.* to live longer than; to remain alive after someone else has died
beneficence /bɪˈnefisəns/ *n.* kindness and generosity
humane /hjuːˈmeɪn/ *adj.* showing the better aspects of the human character, esp. kindness and compassion —humanely *adv.*

midsummer, if any man should ever for a just cause grieve. Shall I not have intelligence with the earth? Am I not partly leaves and vegetable mould myself?

What is the pill which will keep us well, serene, contented? Not my or thy great-grandfather's, but our great-grandmother Nature's universal, vegetable, botanic medicines, by which she with their decaying fatness. For my panacea, instead of one of those quack vials of a mixture dipped from Acheron* and the Dead Sea, which come out of those long shallow black-schooner-looking wagons which we sometimes see made to carry bottles, let me have a draught of undiluted morning air. Morning air! If men will not drink of this at the fountainhead of the day, why, then, we must even bottle up some and sell it in the shops, for the benefit of those who have lost their subscription ticket to morning time in this world. But remember, it will not keep quiet till noonday even in the coolest cellar, but drive out the stopples long ere that and follow westward the steps of Aurora*. I am no worshipper of Hygeia*, who was the daughter of that old herb-doctor Aesculapius*, and who is represented on monuments holding a serpent in one hand, and in the other a cup out of which the serpent sometimes drinks; but rather of Hebe*, cup-bearer to Jupiter*, who was the daughter of Juno* and wild lettuce, and who had the power of restoring gods and men to the vigor of youth. She was probably the only thoroughly sound-conditioned, healthy, and robust young lady that ever walked the globe, and wherever she came it was spring.

thy /ðaɪ/ *pron.* (old) your
botanic /bəˈtænik/ *adj.* relating to plants or the scientific study of plants
panacea /ˌpænəˈsɪə/ *n.* a supposed cure for all diseases and problems
quack /kwæk/ *adj.* relating to the activities or medicines of someone who pretends to be a doctor
vial /ˈvaɪəl/ *n.* a very small bottle used for medicine
schooner /ˈskuːnə/ *n.* a fast sailing ship with two sails
undiluted /ˌʌndaɪˈluːtɪd/ *adj.* (of a feeling) very strong and not mixed with any other feelings; (of a liquid) not made weaker by adding water
fountainhead /ˈfaʊntɪnˌhed/ *n.* the place from which sth. originates
subscription /səbˈskrɪpʃən/ *n.* an amount of money you pay, usu. once a year, to receive copies of a newspaper or magazine, or receive a service
stopple /ˈstɔpl/ *n.* (same as stopper) cork or plug that is put into an opening in order to close it
ere /eə/ *prep.* (old use or literary) before

Cultural Notes

1. **Henry David Thoreau** (1817—1862) was an American writer, philosopher, and a member of the Transcendentalist Club in Boston and a close associate with Ralph Waldo Emerson. Thoreau's best-known work is *Walden; or, Life in the Woods* (1854), of which "Solitude" is Chapter 5. It records Thoreau's experiences in a hand-built cabin at Walden Pond near Concord, Massachusetts, where he spent two years in partial seclusion.

2. **Goffe or Whalley** refers to William Goffe (died c.1679) and his father-in-law, Edward Whalley (1615?—1675?), two of the Puritan "regicides" of King Charles I, who fled to America at the Restoration. Goffe lived in hiding in the forest.
3. **Old Parr** refers to Thomas Parr, an Englishman, who reputedly lived 152 years.
4. **Acheron,** a river in the Greek Epirus, passed through several caves and was said to lead to Hades.
5. **Aurora** is the goddess of the dawn in Roman mythology. In Greek mythology her name is Eos.
6. **Hygeia** is the goddess of health in Greek mythology, the daughter of Aesculapius. She is often represented as a maiden feeding a snake.
7. **Aesculapius** is the god of healing in Greek mythology. He became so skilled that he attempted to resurrect dead, thus angering Zeus, who struck him dead with a thunderbolt. The medical profession has adopted his symbol, a staff entwined by a snake.
8. **Hebe** is daughter of Zeus and Hera, and in Greek mythology goddess of youth. She served youth-giving nectar to the gods and goddesses of Mount Olympus and was wife of Hercules, a hero known for his very great strength and for performing the twelve Labors. Hebe was believed to have been conceived not by the agency of her father, but because her mother ate a surfeit of wild lettuce.
9. **Jupiter** is the king of the gods in Roman mythology. The Greek equivalent is Zeus. **Juno** is the queen of the gods and wife of Jupiter in Roman mythology. The Greek equivalent is Hera.

Comprehension Exercises

I. Please answer the following questions according to the text you have just read.

1. How is "solitude" different from "being alone, lonely or lonesome"? How does Thoreau enjoy being alone?
2. What's the difference between the farmer and the student? Why can't the farmer sit down in the room alone?
3. What are Thoreau's attitudes towards society, meeting friends and etiquette? What does he mean by "open war"?
4. What is his company in his house? What kind of situation is conveyed by the comparisons?
5. How does Thoreau describe his two friends, an old settler and an elderly dame? Why do they keep themselves secret and invisible to most persons?

6. What is our pill to keep us well, according to Thoreau? What does "subscription ticket to morning time" mean?

II. Are the following judgments correct according to the text? Write "T" if the judgment is correct, or "F" if the judgment is wrong.

1. "Delicious" in the first sentence is an example of transferred epithet.
2. Thoreau likes to walk along the river bank in fine weathers and feel attracted by the animated Nature: bullfrog cries, birds singing, wind roaring, leaves fluttering, waves rippling, sound and movement and darkness.
3. Thoreau believes that people feel more lonely when they go abroad because there are strangers everywhere.
4. A farmer cannot stand being unemployed and being alone in the house because he seldom thinks.
5. Thoreau believes that the farmer and the student share a lot in common and thinks highly of them because they work alone in their own fields.
6. Girls in a factory meet and talk so frequently that they hardly have any rich and full spiritual life.
7. Thoreau is as lonely as the loon, the pond, the plant and the creature in the woods.
8. Thoreau believes that nature is kind and sympathetic to human beings and shows her sorrow when man grieves.
9. Everyone, including Thoreau, longs for getting a cure-for-all magic pill and enjoys a long, serene and contented life.
10. Handled properly, the fresh air can be bottled for those who are too busy to breathe it in the morning.

III. Please paraphrase the following sentences:

1. They are Nature's watchmen—links which connect the days of animated life.
2. Solitude is not measured by the miles of space that intervene between a man and his fellows. The really diligent student in one of the crowded hives of Cambridge College is as solitary as a dervish in the desert.
3. Certainly less frequency would suffice for all important and hearty communications. Consider the girls in a factory—never alone, hardly in their dreams.
4. What company has that lonely lake, I pray? And yet it has not the blue devils, but the blue angels in it, in the azure tint of its waters.
5. Shall I not have intelligence with the earth? Am I not partly leaves and vegetable mould myself?

IV. Please translate the following sentences into Chinese:

1. This is a delicious evening, when the whole body is one sense, and imbibes delight through every pore. I go and come with a strange liberty in Nature, a part of herself.
2. Sympathy with the fluttering alder and poplar leaves almost takes away my breath; yet, like the lake, my serenity is rippled but not ruffled.
3. And such sympathy have they ever with our race, that all Nature would be affected, and the sun's brightness fade, and the winds would sigh humanely, and the clouds rain tears, and the woods shed their leaves and put on mourning in midsummer, if any man should ever for a just cause grieve.
4. Not my or thy great-grandfather's, but our great-grandmother Nature's universal, vegetable, botanic medicines, by which she has kept herself young always, outlived so many old Parrs in her day, and fed her health with their decaying fatness.
5. For my panacea, instead of one of those quack vials of a mixture dipped from Acheron and the Dead Sea, which come out of those long shallow black-schooner-looking wagons which we sometimes see made to carry bottles, let me have a draught of undiluted morning air.

V. How would you respond to each of the following statements?

1. The value of a man is not in his skin, that we should touch him.
2. Loneliness is the poverty of self; solitude is the richness of self. (May Sarton)
3. The person who tries to live alone will not succeed as a human being. His heart withers if it does not answer another heart. His mind shrinks away if he hears only the echoes of his own thoughts and finds no other inspiration. (Pearl S. Buck)
4. In this age of alienation, what's really blocking our joy in relationships, our creativity, and our peace of mind, is a lack of solitude. (Ester Buchholz)

VI. Please provide a text, which might support your view on one of the statements in *Exercise V*.

Text B

Once More to the Lake

*E. B. White**

One summer, along about 1904, my father rented a camp on a lake in Maine and took us all there for the month of August. The vacation was a success and from then on none of us ever thought there was any place in the world like that lake in Maine. We returned summer after summer—always on August 1st for one month. I have since become a salt-water man, but sometimes in summer there are days when the restlessness of the tides and the fearful cold of the sea water and the incessant wind which blows across the afternoon and into the evening make me wish for the placidity of a lake in the woods. A few weeks ago this feeling got so strong I bought myself a couple of bass hooks and a spinner and returned to the lake where we used to go, for a week's fishing and to revisit old haunts.

I took along my son, who had never had any fresh water up his nose and who had seen lily pads only from train windows. On the journey over to the lake I began to wonder what it would be like. I wondered how time would have marred this unique, this holy spot—the coves and streams, the hills that the sun set behind, the camps and the paths behind the camps. I was sure that the tarred road would have found it out and I wondered in what other ways it would be desolated. It is strange how much you can remember about places like that once you allow your mind to return into the grooves which lead back. You remember one thing, and that suddenly reminds you of another thing. I guess I remembered clearest of all the early mornings, when the lake was cool and motionless, remembered how the bedroom smelled of the lumber it was made of and of the

incessant /ɪnˈsesənt/ *adj.* constant; continuing without stopping
placidity /plæˈsɪdɪti/ *n.* the state of being calm and not easily excited, upset, or disturbed
bass /bæs/ *n.* a fish that can be eaten and lives in both rivers and the sea
spinner /ˈspɪnə/ *n.* a thing used for catching fish that spins when pulled through the water
haunt /hɔːnt/ *n.* a place that someone likes to go to often
pad /pæd/ *n.* here the leaf of a water lily
mar /mɑː/ *v.* to spoil; to make sth. less attractive or enjoyable
cove /kəuv/ *n.* bay; part of the coast where the land curves round so that the sea is partly surrounded by land
tar /tɑː/ *v.* to cover a surface with tar, a black substance used esp. for making road surfaces
desolate /ˈdesələt/ *v.* to make someone feel very sad and lonely

wet woods whose scent entered through the screen. The partitions in the camp were thin and did not extend clear to the top of the rooms, and as I was always the first up I would dress softly so as not to wake the others, and sneak out into the sweet outdoors and start out in the canoe, keeping close along the shore in the long shadows of the pines. I remembered being very careful never to rub my paddle against the gunwale for fear of disturbing the stillness of the cathedral.

We went fishing the first morning. I felt the same damp moss covering the worms in the bait can, and saw the dragonfly alight on the tip of my rod as it hovered a few inches from the surface of the water. It was the arrival of this fly that convinced me beyond any doubt that everything was as it always had been, that the years were a mirage and there had been no years. The small waves were the same, chucking the rowboat under the chin as we fished at anchor, and the boat was the same boat, the same color green and the ribs broken in the same places, and under the floor-boards the same freshwater leavings and debris—the dead hellgrammite, the wisps of moss, the rusty discarded fishhook, the dried blood from yesterday's catch. We stared silently at the tips of our rods, at the dragonflies that came and wells. I lowered the tip of mine into the water, tentatively, pensively dislodging the fly, which darted two feet away, poised, darted two feet back, and came to rest again a little farther up the rod. There had been no years between the ducking of this dragonfly and the other one—the one that was part of memory.

It seemed to me, as I kept remembering all this, that those times and those summers had been infinitely precious and worth saving. There had been jollity and peace and goodness. The arriving (at the beginning of August) had been so big a business in itself, at the railway station the farm wagon drawn up, the first smell of the pine-laden air, the first glimpse of the smiling farmer, and the great importance of the trunks and your father's enormous authority in such matters, and the feel of the

partition /pɑːˈtɪʃən/ *n.* a thin wall that separates one part of a room from another
gunwale /ˈɡʌnəl/ *n.* the upper edge of the side of a boat or small ship
cathedral /kəˈθiːdrəl/ *n.* a church of a particular area under the control of a bishop
hover /ˈhɒvə/ *v.* to float or flutter in the air without moving very far from the same spot
mirage /ˈmɪrɑːʒ/ *n.* a. an effect caused by hot air in a desert, which makes you think that you can see objects when they are not actually there b. illusion; a dream, hope, or wish that cannot come true
chuck sb. under the chin to gently touch someone under the chin in a friendly way
debris /ˈdebriː/ *n.* pieces of waste material, paper etc.
hellgrammite a large, stout-bodied, net-winged aquatic insect used as fishing bait
wisp /wɪsp/ *n.* a. a small separate untidy piece b. a small thin twisting bit (of smoke or steam)
tentative /ˈtentətɪv/ *adj.* made or done only as a suggestion to see the effect; not certain —tentatively *adv.*
pensive /ˈpensɪv/ *adj.* thoughtful; thinking a lot about sth., esp. because you are worried or sad —pensively *adv.*
dislodge /dɪsˈlɒdʒ/ *v.* to force or knock sth. out of its position
poise /pɔiz/ *v.* to put or hold sth. in a carefully balanced position, esp. above sth. else
duck /dʌk/ *v.* to lower your head or body very quickly, esp. to avoid being seen or hit
jollity /ˈdʒɒlɪti/ *n.* fun; cheerful, joking, or celebratory behavior

wagon under you for the long ten-mile haul, and at the top of the last long hill catching the first view of the lake after eleven months of not seeing this cherished body of water. The shouts and cries of the other campers when they saw you, and the trunks to be unpacked, to give up their rich burden.

We had a good week at the camp. The bass were biting well and the sun shone endlessly, day after day. We would be tired at night and lie down in the accumulated heat of the little bedrooms after the long hot day and the breeze would stir almost imperceptibly outside and the smell of the swamp drift in through the rusty screens. Sleep would come easily and in the morning the red squirrel would be on the roof, tapping out his gay routine. I kept remembering everything, lying in bed in the mornings—the small steamboat that had a long rounded stern like the lip of a Ubangi*, and how quietly she ran on the moonlight sails, when the older boys played their mandolins and the girls sang and we ate doughnuts dipped in sugar, and how sweet the music was on the water in the shining night, and what it had felt like to think about girls then. After breakfast we would go up to the store and the things were in the same place—the minnows in a bottle, the plugs and spinners disarranged and pawed over by the youngsters from the boys' camp. Outside, the road was tarred and cars stood in front of the store. Inside, all was just as it had always been, except there was more Coca Cola and not so much Moxie* and root beer* and birch beer* and sarsaparilla*. We would walk out with a bottle of pop apiece and sometimes the pop would backfire up our noses and hurt. We explored the streams, quietly, where the turtles slid off the sunny logs and dug their way into the soft bottom; and we lay on the town wharf and fed worms to the tame bass. Everywhere we went I had trouble making out which was I, the one walking at my side, the one walking in my pants.

One afternoon while we were there at that lake a thunderstorm came up. It was like the revival of an old melodrama that I had seen long ago with childish awe. The second-act climax of the drama of the electrical disturbance over a lake in America had not changed in any important respect. This was the big scene, still the big scene. The whole thing was so familiar, the first feeling of

imperceptible /ˌimpəˈseptəbəl/ *adj.* unable to be noticed because of smallness or slightness —imperceptibly *adv.*

tap out to hit sth. lightly, esp. with your fingers or foot, in order to make a pattern of sounds

stern /stɜːn/ *n.* the back end of a ship

mandolin /ˌmændəˈlɪn/ *n.* a musical instrument with eight metal strings and a round back, played with a plectrum (small piece of plastic, metal etc.)

doughnut /ˈdəʊnʌt/ *n.* a small round cake, often in the form of a ring

minnow /ˈmɪnəʊ/ *n.* a very small fish that lives in rivers and lakes used as fishing baits

paw /pɔː/ *v.* to touch somebody or sth., or caress somebody, roughly or rudely with the hands

apiece /əˈpiːs/ *adv.* to, for, or from each person or thing; each

backfire /bækˈfaɪə/ *v.* to have an effect opposite to the one intended

tame /teɪm/ *adj.* no longer wild; changed from a wild or uncultivated state to one suitable for domestic use or life

melodrama /ˈmelədrɑːmə/ *n.* a play with a sensational or romantic plot

oppression and heat and a general air around camp of not wanting to go very far away. In mid-afternoon (it was all the same) a curious darkening of the sky, and a lull in everything that had made life tick; and then the way the boats suddenly swung the other way at their moorings with the coming of a breeze out of the new quarter, and the premonitory rumble. Then the kettle drum, then the snare, then the bass drum and cymbals, then crackling light against the dark, and the gods grinning and licking their chops in the hills. Afterward the calm, the rain steadily rustling in the calm lake, the return of light and hope and spirits, and the campers running out in joy and relief to go swimming in the rain, their bright cries perpetuating the deathless joke about how they were getting simply drenched, and the children screaming with delight at the new sensation of bathing in the rain, and the joke about getting drenched linking the generations in a strong indestructible chain.

lull /lʌl/ *n.* a short period of time when there is less activity or less noise than usual
tick /tɪk/ *v.* to function well or in the right way
moorings *n.* the ropes, chains, anchors etc. used to fasten a ship or boat to the land or the bottom of the sea
premonitory /ˌprɪˈmɒnɪtə ri/ *adj.* giving a warning that sth. unpleasant is going to happen
rumble /ˈrʌmbəl/ *n.* a series of long low sounds, esp. a long distance away from you
snare /sneə/ *n.* a trap for catching an animal
cymbal /ˈsɪmbəl/ *n.* a musical instrument in the form of a thin round metal plate, which you play by hitting it with a stick or by hitting two of them together
rustle /ˈrʌsəl/ *v.* to make slight sounds like papers, dry leaves, silk, etc. moving or being rubbed together
perpetuate /pəˈpetʃueɪt/ *v.* to make a situation, attitude etc, esp. a bad one, continue to exist for a long time
drench /drentʃ/ *v.* to make sth. or someone extremely wet
trunks /trʌŋk/ *n.* shorts worn by men for boxing or swimming
wring /rɪŋ/ *v.* to squeeze to remove water
languid /ˈlæŋgwɪd/ *adj.* lacking strength or will; slow and weak —languidly *adv.*
wince /wɪns/ *v.* to suddenly change the expression on your face as a reaction to sth. painful or upsetting
vitals /ˈvaɪtlz/ *n.* the parts of your body that are necessary to keep you alive, e.g. your heart and lungs
soggy /ˈsɒgi/ *adj.* unpleasantly wet and soft
groin /grɔin/ *n.* the place where the tops of your legs meet the front of your body

When the others went swimming my son said he was going in too. He pulled his dripping trunks from the line where they had hung all through the shower, and wrung them out. Languidly, and with no thought of going in, I watched him, his hard little body, skinny and bare, saw him wince slightly as he pulled up around his vitals the small, soggy, icy garment. As he buckled the swollen belt, suddenly my groin felt the chill of death.

Cultural Notes

1. **E. B. White** (1899—1985) was an American writer, famous for his essays and children's literature. Born in Mount Vernon, New York, and educated at Cornell University, White joined the staff of the magazine *The New Yorker* in 1926, when it had just been founded, and remained a regular contributor for many

years. White's elegantly written essays gently satirize the complexities and difficulties of modern civilization.

2. **Ubangi**, also called the Oubangui, is a river of central Africa, the chief tributary of the Congo River.
3. **Moxie** is a brand of soft drink originally marketed as a "nerve tonic" in mid twentieth century. In American informal English, Moxie means courage and determination.
4. **Root beer** is an American staple for centuries, quenching the thirst and aiding the digestion and came into commercial marketplace in the late nineteenth century. It is sweet brown carbonated non-alcoholic drink made from the roots or the extracts of various roots and herbs.
5. **Birch beer** is derived from the sap (plant fluid) of the birch tree, a carbonated soft drink made from herbal extracts, usually from birch bark. It was once very popular and has a taste similar to yet distinct from root beer.
6. **Sarsaparilla** is a sweet carbonated drink without alcohol, made from the root of the sassafras plant, similar to root beer.

Comprehension Exercises

I. Please answer the following questions according to the text you have just read.

1. How does White express his love of the lake and its surroundings?
2. How does White perceive the change of his identity from a son to a father?
3. What does White benefit most from his return to the lake?
4. What makes the thunderstorm a good ending?
5. What does White imply by the last sentence?

II. Are the following judgments correct according to the text? Write "T" if the judgment is correct, or "F" if the judgment is wrong.

1. *Once More to the Lake* is autographical and intensely personal.
2. It has been years since White's last visit to the lake. He didn't go there because no father took him there, because he was trapped by work and family, and also because he became a salt-water man and lived far away from the lake.
3. What White remembered clearest of his past in the lake was to go boating alone in the early morning to the cathedral.
4. The theme of the text is the passage of time and the changes that it brings. Revisiting the lake, White struggles with the illusion that the idyllic world of his childhood and his present existence within it remains the same.

5. Despite his claim that "there had been no years", White confronted several changes that had occurred since his last visit as a child.
6. As the thunderstorm was approaching, White heard the drumming of the kettle, snare, bass and cymbals.
7. The change in the drink catalog of the local store suggests the replacement of the rural and local with the homogenized and the commonplace. Although the store is essentially unchanged, the outside world is intruding.

III. Please paraphrase the following sentences:

1. It was the arrival of this fly that convinced me beyond any doubt that everything was as it always had been, that the years were a mirage and there had been no years.
2. I was sure that the tarred road would have found it out and I wondered in what other ways it would be desolated.
3. Everywhere we went I had trouble making out which was I, the one walking at my side, the one walking in my pants.
4. Then the kettle drum, then the snare, then the bass drum and cymbals, then crackling light against the dark, and the gods grinning and licking their chops in the hills.

IV. Please translate the following sentences into Chinese:

1. I have since become a salt-water man, but sometimes in summer there are days when the restlessness of the tides and the fearful cold of the sea water and the incessant wind which blows across the afternoon and into the evening make me wish for the placidity of a lake in the woods.
2. I lowered the tip of mine into the water, tentatively, pensively dislodging the fly, which darted two feet away, poised, darted two feet back, and came to rest again a little farther up the rod.
3. We would be tired at night and lie down in the accumulated heat of the little bedrooms after the long hot day and the breeze would stir almost imperceptibly outside and the smell of the swamp drift in through the rusty screens.
4. In mid-afternoon (it was all the same) a curious darkening of the sky, and a lull in everything that had made life tick; and then the way the boats suddenly swung the other way at their moorings with the coming of a breeze out of the new quarter, and the premonitory rumble.
5. Afterward the calm, the rain steadily rustling in the calm lake, the return of light and hope and spirits, and the campers running out in joy and relief to go swimming in the rain, their bright cries perpetuating the deathless joke about how

they were getting simply drenched and the children screaming with delight at the new sensation of bathing in the rain, and the joke about getting drenched linking the generations in a strong indestructible chain.

V. How would you respond to each of the following statements?

1. The day has its morning, noon and sunset, and the year has its seasons. No one can say that a life with childhood, manhood and old age is not a beautiful arrangement. (Lin Yutang)
2. We do not inherit the earth from our ancestors; we borrow it from our children.
3. The best remedy for those who are afraid, lonely or unhappy is to go outside, somewhere where they can be quiet, alone with the heavens, nature and God. Because only then does one feel that all is as it should be and that God wishes to see people happy, amidst the simple beauty of nature. (Anne Frank)
4. You remember one thing, and that suddenly reminds you of another thing.

VI. Please provide a text, which might support your view on one of the statements in *Exercise V.*

Unit Six

Text A

A Vindication of the Rights of Woman

*Mary Wollstonecraft**

My own sex, I hope, will excuse me, if I treat them like rational creatures, instead of flattering their *fascinating* graces, and viewing them as if they were in a state of perpetual childhood, unable to stand alone. I earnestly wish to point out in what true dignity and human happiness consists—I wish to persuade women to endeavor to acquire strength, both of mind and body, and to convince them that the soft phrases, susceptibility of heart, delicacy of sentiment, and refinement of taste, are almost synonymous with epithets of weakness, and that those beings who are only the objects of pity and that kind of love, which has been termed its sister, will soon become objects of contempt.

Dismissing then those pretty feminine phrases, which the men condescendingly use to soften our slavish dependence, and despising that weak elegancy of mind, exquisite sensibility, and sweet docility of manners, supposed to be the sexual characteristics of the weaker vessel, I wish to show that elegance is inferior to virtue, that the first object of laudable ambition is to obtain a character as a human being, regardless of the distinction of sex; and that secondary views should be brought to this simple touchstone.

This is a rough sketch of my plan; and should I express my conviction with the energetic emotions that I feel whenever I think of the subject, the dictates of experience and reflection

vindicate /ˈvɪndɪkeɪt/ *v.* a. to show that charges made against someone or sth. are untrue b. to prove (sth. that was in doubt) to be true or right —vindication *n.*

rational /ˈræʃənəl/ *adj.* endowed with the faculty of reason; having or exercising reason, sound judgment, or good sense

perpetual /pəˈpetjuəl/ *adj.* lasting forever or for a long time

susceptibility /səˌseptəˈbɪlɪti/ *n.* capacity for receiving mental or moral impressions; tendency to be emotionally affected

epithet /ˈepɪθet/ *n.* an adjective or descriptive phrase, esp. of praise or blame used of a person

condescend /kɒndɪˈsend/ *v.* to act in a patronizing manner —condescendingly *adv.*

exquisite /ˈɪkskwɪzɪt/ a. very finely made or done; almost perfect b. sensitive and delicate

docile /ˈdəʊsaɪl/ *adj.* easily taught or led —docility *n.*

weaker vessel a woman

laudable /ˈlɔːdəbəl/ *adj.* deserving commendation; praiseworthy

touchstone /ˈtʌtʃstəʊn/ *n.* anything used as a test or standard; criterion

conviction /kənˈvɪkʃən/ *n.* a fixed or firm belief

dictate /ˈdikteit/ *n.* an order which should be obeyed

will be felt by some of my readers. Animated by this important object, I shall disdain to cull my phrases or polish my style—I aim at being useful, and sincerity will render me unaffected; for, wishing rather to persuade by the force of my arguments, than dazzle by the elegance of my language, I shall not waste my time in rounding periods, nor in fabricating the turgid bombast of artificial feelings, which, coming from the head, never reach the heart. I shall be employed about things, not words! and, anxious to render my sex more respectable members of society, I shall try to avoid that flowery diction which has slided from essays into novels, and from novels into familiar letters and conversation.

These pretty nothings, these caricatures of the real beauty of sensibility, dropping glibly from the tongue, vitiate the taste, and create a kind of sickly delicacy that turns away from simple unadorned truth; and a deluge of false sentiments and over-stretched feelings, stifling the natural emotions of the heart, render the domestic pleasures insipid, that ought to sweeten the exercise of those severe duties, which educate a rational and immortal being for a nobler field of action.

The education of women has, of late, been more attended to than formerly; yet they are still reckoned a frivolous sex, and ridiculed or pitied by the writers who endeavor by satire or instruction to improve them. It is acknowledged that they spend many of the first years of their lives in acquiring a smattering of accomplishments: meanwhile, strength of body and mind are sacrificed to libertine notions of beauty, to the desire of establishing themselves, the only way women can rise in the world—by marriage. And this desire making mere animals of them, when they marry, they act as such children may be expected to act—they dress; they paint, and nickname God's creatures. Surely these weak beings are only fit for the seraglio!—Can they govern a

animate /ˈænɪmeɪt/ *v.* to fill with courage or boldness; to move or stir to action; motivate

disdain /dɪsˈdeɪn/ *v.* to look upon or treat with contempt; despise; scorn

cull /kʌl/ *v.* to choose; select; pick

render /ˈrendə/ *v.* to cause to be or become; make

dazzle /ˈdæzəl/ *v.* to amaze, overwhelm, or bewilder with spectacular display

period /ˈpɪəriəd/ *n.* a sentence of several carefully balanced clauses in formal writing

fabricate /ˈfæbrɪkeɪt/ *v.* to make by art or skill; construct

turgid /ˈtɜːdʒɪd/ *adj.* inflated, overblown, or pompous; bombastic

bombast /ˈbɔmbæst/ *n.* speech too pompous for an occasion; pretentious words

glib /glɪb/ *adj.* (of a person) able to speak well, whether speaking the truth or not —glibly *adv.*

vitiate /ˈvɪʃieɪt/ *v.* to impair the quality of; make faulty; spoil

unadorned /ˈʌnəˈdɔːnd/ *adj.* not decorated with sth. to increase its beauty or distinction

deluge /ˈdeljuːdʒ/ *n.* anything that overwhelms like a flood

stifle /ˈstaɪfəl/ *v.* to keep in or hold back; repress

insipid /ɪnˈsɪpɪd/ *adj.* lacking qualities that excite, stimulate, or interest; dull

sweeten /ˈswiːtn/ *v.* to make sweet or sweeter; to make more pleasant or agreeable

frivolous /ˈfrɪvələs/ *adj.* characterized by lack of seriousness or sense

smattering /ˈsmætərɪŋ/ *n.* a slight, superficial, or introductory knowledge of sth.

libertine /ˈlɪbətiːn/ *adj.* morally unrestrained; dissolute

seraglio /seˈrɑːliəu/ *n.* the part of a Muslim house or palace in which the wives and concubines are secluded; harem

family, or take care of the poor babes whom they bring into the world?

If then it can be fairly deduced from the present conduct of the sex, from the prevalent fondness for pleasure, which takes place of ambition and thosc nobler passions that open and enlarge the soul; that the instruction which women have received has only tended, with the constitution of civil society, to render them insignificant objects of desire—mere propagators of fools!—if it can be proved that in aiming to accomplish them, without cultivating their understandings, they are taken out of their sphere of duties, and made ridiculous and useless when the short-lived bloom of beauty is over, I presume that *rational* men will excuse me for endeavoring to persuade them to become more masculine and respectable.

Indeed the word masculine is only a bugbear: there is little reason to fear that women will acquire too much courage or fortitude; for their apparent inferiority with respect to bodily strength, must render them, in some degree, dependent on men in the various relations of life; but why should it be increased by prejudices that give a sex to virtue, and confound simple truths with sensual reveries?

Women are, in fact, so much degraded by mistaken notions of female excellence, that I do not mean to add a paradox when I assert, that this artificial weakness produces a propensity to tyrannize, and gives birth to cunning, the natural opponent of strength,which leads them to play off those contemptible infantile airs that undermine esteem even whilst they excite desire. Let them becomemore chaste and modest, and if women do not grow wiser in the same ratio, it will be clear that they have weaker understandings. It seems scarcely necessary to say that I now speak of the sex in general. Many individuals have more sense than their male relatives; and, as nothing preponderates where there is a constant struggle for an equilibrium, without it has naturally more gravity, some women govern their husbands without degrading themselves , because intellect will always govern.

deduce /dɪ'djuːs/ *v.* to derive as a conclusion from sth. known or assumed; infer

propagator /'prɒpəgeɪtə/ *n.* producer

bugbear /'bʌgbeə/ *n.* any source, real or imaginary, of needless fright or fear

fortitude /'fɔːtɪtjuːd/ *n.* mental and emotional strength in facing difficulty, adversity, danger, or temptation courageously

reverie /'revəri/ *n.* a fantastic, visionary, or impractical idea

propensity /prə'pensɪti/ *n.* natural inclination or tendency

tyrannize /'tɪrənaɪz/ *v.* to exercise absolute power

cunning /'kʌnɪŋ/ *n.* skill in deception; guile

play off to set (one individual or party) in opposition to another so as to advance one's own interests

infantile /'ɪnfəntaɪl/ *adj.* displaying or suggesting a lack of maturity; childish; of or relating to infants or infancy

preponderate /prɪ'pɒndəreɪt/ *v.* to exceed sth. else in weight

equilibrium /ˌiːkwɪ'lɪbriəm/ *n.* a state of rest or balance due to the equal action of opposing forces

Cultural Notes

Mary Wollstonecraft (1759—1797) was an English author and feminist. She was an early proponent of educational equality between men and women, and her *Vindication of the Rights of Women* (1792), from which this text is taken, is the first great feminist document.

Comprehension Exercises

I. Please answer the following questions according to the text you have just read.

1. What are the worries of the author when she decides to write this article?
2. What is the rough sketch of her plan to justify the rights of woman?
3. In what manner is the author going to state her opinion?
4. Why is female inferiority assumed without question?
5. What are the basic ideas of the text?
6. What might be a better title for the text?

II. Are the following judgments correct according to the text? Write "T" if the judgment is correct, or "F" if the judgment is wrong.

1. Soft phrases, susceptibility of heart, delicacy of sentiment, and refinement of taste are synonyms of epithets of weakness.
2. The author prefers flowery language to forceful argumentation.
3. Physical strength is related to natural pre-eminence.
4. Women are only fit for the seraglio because they dress, paint, and nickname God's creatures.
5. The ability to govern is not based on sex, but rather, the level at which the individual's reasoning has developed.

III. Please paraphrase the following sentences:

1. My own sex, I hope, will excuse me, if I treat them like rational creatures, instead of flattering their fascinating graces, and viewing them as if they were in a state of perpetual childhood, unable to stand alone.
2. This is a rough sketch of my plan; and should I express my conviction with the energetic emotions that I feel whenever I think of the subject, the dictates of experience and reflection will be felt by some of my readers.

3. Anxious to render my sex more respectable members of society, I shall try to avoid that flowery diction which has slided from essays into novels, and from novels into familiar letters and conversation.
4. The education of women has, of late, been more attended to than formerly, yet they are still reckoned a frivolous sex, and ridiculed or pitied by the writers who endeavor by satire or instruction to improve them.
5. If it can be proved, that in aiming to accomplish them, without cultivating their understandings, they are taken out of their sphere of duties, and made ridiculous and useless when the short lived bloom of beauty is over, I presume that rational men will excuse me for endeavoring to persuade them to become more masculine and respectable.

IV. Please translate the following sentences into Chinese:

1. I earnestly wish to point out in what true dignity and human happiness consists—I wish to persuade women to endeavor to acquire strength, both of mind and body, and to convince them, that the soft phrases, susceptibility of heart, delicacy of sentiment, and refinement of taste, are almost synonymous with epithets of weakness, and that those beings who are only the objects of pity and that kind of love, which has been termed its sister, will soon become objects of contempt.
2. Dismissing then those pretty feminine phrases, which the men condescendingly use to soften our slavish dependence, and despising that weak elegancy of mind, exquisite sensibility, and sweet docility of manners, supposed to be the sexual characteristics of the weaker vessel, I wish to show that elegance is inferior to virtue, that the first object of laudable ambition is to obtain a character as a human being, regardless of the distinction of sex; and that secondary views should be brought to this simple touchstone.
3. Animated by this important object, I shall disdain to cull my phrases or polish my style—I aim at being useful, and sincerity will render me unaffected; for wishing rather to persuade by the force of my arguments, than dazzle by the elegance of my language, I shall not waste my time in rounding periods, nor in fabricating the turgid bombast of artificial feelings, which, coming from the head, never reach the heart.
4. A deluge of false sentiments and over-stretched feelings, stifling the natural emotions of the heart, render the domestic pleasures insipid, that ought to sweeten the exercise of those severe duties, which educate a rational and immortal being for a nobler field of action.
5. Women are, in fact, so much degraded by mistaken notions of female excellence,

that I do not mean to add a paradox when I assert, that this artificial weakness produces a propensity to tyrannize, and gives birth to cunning, the natural opponent of strength, which leads them to play off those contemptible infantile airs that undermine esteem even whilst they excite desire.

V. How would you respond to each of the following statements?

1. Those women who are only the objects of pity will soon become objects of contempt.
2. The desire of establishing themselves by marriage makes mere animals of women.
3. The first object of laudable ambition is to obtain a character as a human being, regardless of the distinction of sex.
4. The word "masculine" is only a bugbear.
5. Intellect will always govern.
6. Elegance is inferior to virtue.

VI. Please provide a text, which might support your view on one of the statements in *Exercise V.*

Text B

Men Are Very Delicate

*Barbara Cawthorne Crafton**

I think I have to fire a man. I have tried warnings and changes in the job description and other changes in the work location and God knows what else. But it has become clear that he has no intention of working at the level of excellence of which he is capable and which his colleagues maintain, that he may be less than candid in his reporting of the work he does do, and that his fellow employees see all this and are wondering how long it's going to go on. So do my superiors, who also, then, wonder about *me*.

He has had detractors for years. People have been telling on this guy ever since I became his supervisor. I have suspected that some of the snitching is racist, and I still think that. I have suspected that some of the misgivings I myself

maintain /meɪn'teɪn/ *v.* to hold; to keep up

candid /'kændɪd/ *adj.* open; frank; ingenuous; outspoken

detractor /dɪ'træktə/ *n.* one who criticize or belittles the worth of sth. or somebody

snitching /snɪtʃ/ *n.* the act of giving away information about somebody

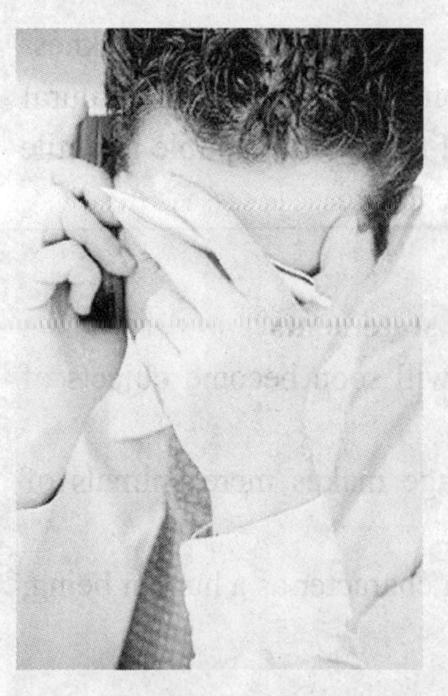

havc had about his work may be racist, too, the impatience of a WASP who hits the ground running with a person of another, more leisurely culture, one that was producing masterpieces of literature and sculpturc when my ancestors were sitting around a campfire painting themselves blue. But dammit, I say to myself, I didn't paint myself blue, and he didn't write those poems. We're just trying to do a job here, and I don't think he's trying very hard. I have kept him on too long for the good of the group already.

He has a wife and two children. Can I put a father out of his job? When should I do it? Before Christmas so his unemployment can start the first of January? Or should I let him get through the holidays in innocence? What if he argues with me? What if he begs me to keep him on? What if he hates me? What if he drew my name for the office Christmas party?

I have known for a long time that one of my biggest enemies is my own desire to make men feel good. I threw spelling bees so that boys could win them. I remember one that I did not throw, and I am *still* cut by the hate in the glance Patrick Reeves shot me thirty years ago as I spelled "foreign" correctly and won. I have felt responsible for men's inadequacies all my life, it seems, and have expended a fair amount of energy shoring them up, patching them together so well that the stitches barely show. I have felt responsible for helping them to conceal the areas in which they fall short, creating distractions from these unpleasantnesses by serving as a loud cheerleader for the smallest of their virtues.

This makes me a very kind boss. I love everything they do. If I don't love it, I feel it's somehow my fault. In a way that I now think emasculating, I have wanted to pick up after them, cleaning up their messes, following them with an invisible whisk broom and dust pan into which I sweep their mistakes so that nobody else will see them. In doing this, I deny them the opportunity to learn from the consequences of their errors, the painful but educational road people have to travel to advance. I have to fight myself—hard—to avoid showing these hurtful kindnesses.

WASP White Anglo-Saxon Protestant
throw /θrəu/ *v.* to lose deliberately
spelling bee a contest in which you are eliminated if you fail to spell a word correctly
cut /kʌt/ *v.* hurt
inadequacy /ɪn'ædɪkwɪəsi/ *n.* a lack of competence
shore (up) /ʃɔː/ *v.* to support by placing against sth. solid or rigid
emasculate /'mæskjʊleɪt/ *v.* to deprive of masculine vigor or spirit; to weaken
whisk broom a small short-handled broom used to brush clothes

I am not alone in this. Generations of women have made sure men looked smart and strong, and have made sure *they* didn't appear too smart and strong in the presence of the Other Kind. The male ego, we were told, simply couldn't tolerate the threat. It was only recently that we gave ourselves political permission to stop doing this. At last, we said, we can be what we are. What shocked me—continues to shock me—is how reflexive a thing it is for me, still, to try and smooth their paths. I still feel an obligation to support men in their work.

ego /'iːgəʊ/ *n.* your consciousness of your own identity
reflexive /rɪ'fleksɪv/ *adj.* automatic
up to one's ears busy
hunt-and-peck an act of typing on a keyboard using only one or two fingers of each hand
stereotypical /ˌsteriə'tipikəl/ *adj.* lacking spontaneity or originality or individuality
spare /speə/ *v.* **a.** to use frugally or carefully **b.** to refrain from harming
threshold /'θreʃhəʊld/ *n.* an amount, level, or limit on a scale
frazzled /'fræzəld/ *adj.* exhausted
trauma /'trɔːmə/ *n.* any physical damage to the body caused by violence or accident or fracture etc.
tuck /tʌk/ *v.* to insert; to fit into

I type for a colleague when something has to get finished and all the secretaries are up to their ears. I made my living as a secretary once upon a time, and I'm fast. He uses a slow hunt-and-peck. I offer to help, and am proud of my speed. I love him. And I feel happy to have helped him meet his deadline. But I am also aware that what I have just done is a very stereotypical thing. I've put aside my work to help him finish his. I'll get mine done somehow. I always do.

Why aren't there more famous women composers and rocket scientists? One reason is that men are usually the ones who decide who's going to be famous. The other one is that men can usually find women to help arrange their worlds so they can do their work. Nobody does that for us. Men are encouraged from childhood to be single-minded about their work, not to allow any distractions. And women are encouraged from childhood to set things up for them so that they don't have any. Don't make so much noise; your father is working. And when do we do our work? Late at night, when everyone is sleeping. Or early in the morning, before anyone else is up.

As a result of being spared like this, men have a low threshold for distraction. They are *delicate*. They are made nervous by having to do more than one thing at a time. They feel frazzled and angry if they have to answer three phone calls, and have a hard time settling back to work after the trauma. Women, on the other hand, develop the skill of doing many things at once. They tuck the phone in between their shoulders and their ears, hold a baby on one hip, stir a pot on the stove, all the while thinking about an idea for a story. They don't think it's unfair to have to do this. They think it's normal.

Women are just more complex than men about work. We've learned how to be that way. We've learned to love our ambidextrousness, our snatches of solitary time, and to make the most of them. For years I got up at five so I could write with no kids around. The kids are grown up now, but I still do that. It has become my most creative time. I wouldn't give it up for anything. It's not particularly fair that it was necessary, but there you are. Men do their jobs brilliantly when they have little else to do. I should think they would. If they contended with the additional jobs many women have, they'd measure success differently. And they'd be stronger.

The goddess Kali*, friend of Hindu women, is depicted with nine arms. That's about how many you need. She's not as affirming to men as we tend to be; she rains down death and destruction on those who treat women unjustly, and she doesn't care who they are. I don't know about that. There's got to be a middle ground between our colluding in men's privileging themselves and wanting to kill them. Marrying later may help—more brides today go into marriage with established careers and work habits than used to be the case. They have negotiating skills that ought to help them get a fair shake. Their husbands carry their babies around in canvas slings and shop at the same time. That's progress. But even now, even with babies in slings, the burden of home and child care is not equitably distributed in most marriages.

But it's an imperfect world. Things usually *aren't* equitable. Somebody usually has to give. It's usually the woman, and it usually makes her mad if she has time to think about it, and then she usually gets over being mad and makes the best of it, and grows in complexity as a result. Life is short, and most people don't want to fight their way through it. So couples point out to each other from time to time that things aren't fair, and a fairness that fits is found. It may be a little lopsided, and it's irritating when people pretend it's perfectly symmetrical. It's not. But it fits. That's the important thing.

ambidextrousness /ˌæmbiˈdekstrəsnis/ *n.* the ability to use both hands with equal ease; versatility

snatch /snætʃ/ *n.* **a.** a small piece, fragment, or quantity. **b.** a broken part

contend /kənˈtend/ *v.* to compete for sth.; engage in a contest

affirm /əˈfɜːm/ *v.* **a.** to declare or assert positively **b.** to make firm; to confirm, or ratify

collude /kəˈluːd/ *v.* to act together secretly to achieve a goal

privilege /ˈprɪvɪlɪdʒ/ *n.* a special right or advantage limited to a few people of a particular kind; *v.* to grant a privilege to

shake /ʃeɪk/ *n.* treatment; chance

sling /slɪŋ/ an object made of ropes, straps, or cloth that is used for carrying things

equitable /ˈekwɪtəbəl/ *adj.* just, fair. —equitably *adv.*

get over to deal with successfully

lopsided /ˈlɒpˈsaɪdɪd/ *adj.* turned or twisted toward one side

symmetrical /sɪˈmetrɪkəl/ *adj.* having similarity in size, shape, and relative posit

Cultural Notes

1. **Barbara Cawthorne Crafton** is an Episcopal priest living in New York City. Her work has taken her from Trinity Church on Wall Street to the New York waterfront. She is now on the staff of Seamen's Church Institute, serving merchant sailors. Crafton has published essays in magazines and newspapers, including *New Woman, Family Circle,* and the "Hers" column of the *New York Times*. The selection here comes from Crafton's book *The Sewing Room: Uncommon Reflections on Life, Love and Work* (1993).
2. **Kali** is a complex Hindu goddess. She is sometimes identified as the wife of Shiva. She is death and destruction, but, to some she is the instrument of rebirth, too. In Tantric Hinduism, she comes to be the Supreme divinity.

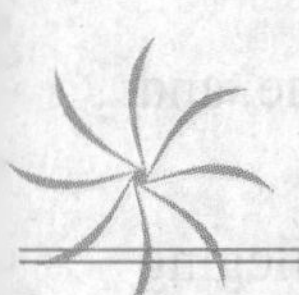

Comprehension Exercises

I. Please answer the following questions according to the text you have just read.

1. Why does the author want to fire her employee?
2. Why does the author hesitate to fire her employee?
3. Why aren't there more famous women composers and rocket scientists?
4. In what way does the author mean "men are very delicate"?
5. How are women different from men according to the author?
6. What might be the author's tone of voice throughout the text?

II. Are the following judgments correct according to the text? Write "T" if the judgment is correct, or "F" if the judgment is wrong.

1. The man the author wants to fire works as hard as his colleagues after receiving some warnings.
2. The author is a kind, helpful and considerate boss.
3. The author is a WASP.
4. The author feels satisfied with what she did for men in her work.
5. The author was once an efficient secretary.
6. With social progress, the burden of home and child care is now equitably distributed in most marriages now.

III. Please paraphrase the following sentences:

1. I have kept him on too long for the good of the group already.
2. Should I let him get through the holidays in innocence?
3. Generations of women have made sure *they* didn't appear too smart and strong in the presence of the Other Kind.
4. As a result of being spared like this, men have a low threshold for distraction.
5. They have negotiating skills that ought to help them get a fair shake.

IV. Please translate the following sentences into Chinese:

1. I have tried warnings and changes in the job description and other changes in the work location and God knows what else.
2. In doing this, I deny them the opportunity to learn from the consequences of their errors, the painful but educational road people have to travel to advance.
3. Women are encouraged from their childhood to set things up for them so that they don't have any.
4. We've learned to love our ambidextrousness, our snatches of solitary time, and to make the most of them.
5. There's got to be a middle ground between our colluding in men's privileging themselves and wanting to kill them.

V. How would you respond to each of the following statements?

1. The hand that rocks the cradle rules the world.
2. Behind every successful man there is a woman.
3. Women always worry about the things that men forget; men always worry about the things women remember.
4. Generations of women have made sure men looked smart and strong.
5. Life is short, and most people don't want to fight their way through it.

VI. Please provide a text, which might support your view on one of the statements in *Exercise V.*

Unit Seven

Text A

Beauty

*Susan Sontag**

For the Greeks, beauty was a virtue: a kind of excellence. Persons then were assumed to be what we now have to call—lamely, enviously—whole persons. If it did occur to the Greeks to distinguish between a person's "inside" and "outside," they still expected that inner beauty would be matched by beauty of the other kind. The well-born young Athenians who gathered around Socrates* found it quite paradoxical that their hero was so intelligent, so brave, so honorable, so seductive—and so ugly. One of Socrates' main pedagogical acts was to be ugly—and teach those innocent, no doubt splendid-looking disciples of his how full of paradoxes life really was.

They may have resisted Socrates' lesson. We do not. Several thousand years later, we are more wary of the enchantments of beauty. We not only split off—with the greatest facility—the "inside" (character, intellect) from the "outside" (looks); but we are actually surprised when someone who is beautiful is also intelligent, talented, good.

It was principally the influence of Christianity that deprived beauty of the central place it had in classical ideals of human excellence. By limiting excellence (*virtus* in Latin) to moral virtue only, Christianity set beauty adrift — as an alienated, arbitrary, superficial enchantment. And beauty has continued to lose prestige.

lamely /ˈleɪmli/ *adv.* in a way that does not sound very confident

paradox /ˈpærədɒks/ *n.* a situation that seems to have contradictory or inconsistent qualities. —paradoxical *adj.*

seductive /sɪˈdʌktɪv/ *adj.* a. tending to seduce, or lead astray b. tempting; enticing; interesting

pedagogical /pedəˈgɒdʒɪkəl/ *adj.* of or characteristic of teachers or teaching

disciple /dɪˈsaɪpəl/ *n.* a pupil or follower of any teacher or school of religion, learning, art, etc.

wary /ˈweəri/ cautious

facility /fəˈsɪlɪti/ *n.* a. ease of doing or making b. a ready ability

adrift /əˈdrɪft/ *adj.* a. floating freely without being steered b. without any particular aim or purpose

alienate /ˈeɪliəneɪt/ *v.* to make it difficult for someone to belong to a particular group

arbitrary /ˈɑːbɪtrəri/ *adj.* not fixed by rules but left to one's judgment or choice

prestige /preˈstiːʒ/ *n.* a. the power to impress. b. reputation; renown

For close to two centuries it has become a convention to attribute beauty to only one of the two sexes: the sex which, however Fair, is always Second. Associating beauty with women had put beauty even further on the defensive, morally.

compliment /'kɒmplɪmənt/ *n.* **a.** an act or expression of courtesy or respect **b.** sth. said in admiration, praise, or flattery
demean /dɪ'miːn/ *v.* to lower in status or character; degrade; humble
overtone /'əuvətəun/ *n.* an implication; nuance
vestige /'vestɪdʒ/ *n.* a trace or sign of sth. that once existed but has passed away
pagan /'peɪgən/ *n.* not Christian, Moslem, or Jewish
detriment /'detrɪmənt/ *n.* damage; injury; harm
in the throes of in the act of struggling with a problem, a decision, task, etc.
narcissism /'nɑːsɪsɪzəm/ *n.* excessive self-love
stereotype /'steriəutaɪp/ *n.* a fixed or conventional notion or conception of a person, group, idea, etc.
administer /əd'mɪnɪstə/ *v.* to give out or dispense punishment or justice
fretful /'fretfəl/ *adj.* irritable and discontented; peevish
scrutiny /'skruːtɪni/ *n.* a close examination; minute inspection
pass muster to be accepted as good enough

A beautiful woman, we say in English. But a handsome man. "Handsome" is the masculine equivalent of—and refusal of—a compliment which has accumulated certain demeaning overtones, by being reserved for women only. That one can call a man "beautiful" in French and in Italian suggests that Catholic countries—unlike those countries shaped by the Protestant version of Christianity—still retain some vestiges of the pagan admiration for beauty. But the difference, if one exists, is of degree only. In every modern country that is Christian or post-Christian, women are the beautiful sex—to the detriment of the notion of beauty as well as of women.

To be called beautiful is thought to name something essential to women's character and concerns. (In contrast to men—whose essence is to be strong, or effective, or competent.) It does not take someone in the throes of advanced feminist awareness to perceive that the way women are taught to be involved with beauty encourages narcissism, reinforces dependence and immaturity. Everybody (women and men) knows that. For it is "everybody," a whole society, that has identified being feminine with caring about how one *looks*. (In contrast to being masculine—which is identified with caring about what one is and *does* and only secondarily, if at all, about how one looks.) Given these stereotypes, it is no wonder that beauty enjoys, at best, a rather mixed reputation.

It is not, of course, the desire to be beautiful that is wrong but the obligation to be—or to try. What is accepted by most women as a flattering idealization of their sex is a way of making women feel inferior to what they actually are—or normally grow to be. For the ideal of beauty is administered as a form of self-oppression. Women are taught to see their bodies in parts, and to evaluate each part separately. Breasts, feet, hips, waistline, neck, eyes, nose, complexion, hair, and so on—each in turn is submitted to an anxious, fretful, often despairing scrutiny. Even if some pass muster, some will always be found wanting. Nothing less than perfection will do.

In men, good looks is a whole, something taken in at a glance. It does not need to be confirmed by giving measurements of different regions of the body; nobody encourages a man to dissect his appearance, feature by feature. As for perfection, that is considered trivial—almost unmanly. Indeed, in the ideally good-looking man a small imperfection or blemish is considered positively desirable. According to one movie critic (a woman) who is a declared Robert Redford* fan, it is having that cluster of skin-colored moles on one cheek that saves Redford from being merely a "pretty face." Think of the depreciation of women—as well as of beauty—that is implied in that judgment.

"The privileges of beauty are immense," said Cocteau*. To be sure, beauty is a form of power. And deservedly so. What is lamentable is that it is the only form of power that most women are encouraged to seek. This power is always conceived in relation to men; it is not the power to do but the power to attract. It is a power that negates itself. For this power is not one that can be chosen freely—at least, not by women—or renounced without social censure.

To preen, for a woman, can never be just a pleasure. It is also a duty. It is her work. If a woman does real work—and even if she has clambered up to a leading position in politics, law, medicine, business, or whatever—she is always under pressure to confess that she still works at being attractive. But in so far as she is keeping up as one of the Fair Sex, she brings under suspicion her very capacity to be objective, professional, authoritative, thoughtful. Damned if they do—women are. And damned if they don't.

One could hardly ask for more important evidence of the dangers of considering persons as split between what is "inside" and what is "outside" than that interminable half-comic half-tragic tale, the oppression of women. How easy it is to start off by defining women as caretakers of their surfaces, and then to disparage them (or find them adorable) for

dissect /dɪ'sekt/ *v.* **a.** to cut up the body in order to study it **b.** to examine carefully
trivial /'trɪviəl/ *adj.* not serious, important, or valuable
blemish /'blemɪʃ/ *n.* a small mark on the surface of an object that spoils its appearance
depreciation /dɪˌpriːʃi'eɪʃən/ *n.* a reduction in the value or price of sth.
lamentable /'læməntəbəl/ *adj.* very unsatisfactory or disappointing; terrible
negate /nɪ'geɪt/ *v.* **a.** to prevent sth. from having any effect **b.** to state that sth. does not exist or is untrue
renounce /rɪ'naʊns/ *v.* to give up by a formal public statement
censure /'senʃə/ *n.* a condemning as wrong; strong disapproval
preen /priːn/ *v.* **a.** to clean and trim (the feathers) with the beak **b.** to make oneself trim; dress up or adorn oneself
clamber /'klæmbə/ *v.* to climb with effort or clumsily
confess /kən'fes/ *v.* **a.** to admit a fault **b.** to acknowledge an opinion or view. **c.** to declare one's faith in
interminable /ɪn'tɜːmɪnəbəl/ *adj.* forever; endless
disparage /dɪs'pærɪdʒ/ *v.* to speak slightingly of; show disrespect for; belittle

being "superficial." It is a crude trap, and it has worked for too long. But to get out of the trap requires that women get some critical distance from that excellence and privilege which is beauty, enough distance to see how much beauty itself has been abridged in order to prop up the mythology of the "feminine." There should be a way of saving beauty *from* women—and *for them*.

abridge /ə'brɪdʒ/ to reduce in scope, extent, etc.; to lessen or curtail rights, authority, etc.

Cultural Notes

1. **Susan Sontag** (1933—2004) was an American essayist, novelist, human rights activist and leading commentator on modern culture. Her innovative essays on such diverse subjects as camp, pornographic literature, fascist aesthetics, photography, AIDS, and revolution have gained a wide attention. Sontag also writes screenplays and directed films. She has a great impact on experimental art in the 1960s and 1970s, and has introduced many new stimulating ideas to American culture.
2. **Socrates** (470 BC—399 BC) was a classical Greek philosopher. He is best known for the creation of Socratic Irony and the Socratic Method. Specifically, he is renowned for developing the practice of a philosophical type of pedagogy in which the teacher asks students questions to elicit the best answer and fundamental insight. Socrates is credited with exerting a powerful influence upon the founders of Western philosophy, most particularly Plato and Aristotle, and while Socrates' principal contribution to philosophy is in the field of ethics, he also makes important and lasting contributions to the fields of epistemology and logic. His willingness to call everything into question and his determination to accept nothing less than an adequate account of the nature of things make him the first clear exponent of critical philosophy.
3. **Charles Robert Redford, Jr.** (1936—) is among the biggest American movie stars of the 1970s. In spite of an increasingly rare onscreen presence in subsequent years, he remains a powerful motion-picture industry force as an Academy Award-winning director as well as a highly visible champion of American independent filmmaking.
4. **Jean Maurice Eugène Clément Cocteau** (1889—1963) was a French poet, novelist, dramatist, playwright and filmmaker. Like Victor Hugo and Charles Baudelaire, he intended his artistic work to serve a dual purpose—to be entertaining and political. His versatile, unconventional approach and enormous output brought him international acclaim.

Comprehension Exercises

I. Please answer the following questions according to the text you have just read.

1. What does Sontag want to say most in the text?
2. Why is beauty associated with women and why does it enjoy a mixed reputation?
3. How does beauty mean differently to the Greeks, Socrates and Christians?
4. How was Socrates different from other Greeks?
5. What might be an ideal woman like, according to Sontag?
6. What does Sontag suggest women to do?

II. Are the following judgments correct according to the text? Write "T" if the judgment is correct, or "F" if the judgment is wrong.

1. Susan Sontag disagrees with Socrates.
2. Susan Sontag means that people don't have to be wary of the enchantment of beauty.
3. It is possible for someone to be beautiful, intelligent and good at once.
4. Christian culture is hostile to both beauty and women.
5. Catholic countries are more prejudiced against beauty than Protestant countries.
6. Susan Sontag favors feminism.
7. Susan Sontag believes that external beauty does not matter for a woman.
8. Susan Sontag believes that women are taught in a wrong way.

III. Please paraphrase the following sentences:

1. If it did occur to the Greeks to distinguish between a person's "inside" and "outside," they still expected that inner beauty would be matched by beauty of the other kind.
2. It was principally the influence of Christianity that deprived beauty of the central place it had in classical ideals of human excellence.
3. Associating beauty with women had put beauty even further on the defensive, morally.
4. What is accepted by most women as a flattering idealization of their sex is a way of making women feel inferior to what they actually are—or normally grow to be.
5. Nothing less than perfection will do.
6. To get out of the trap requires that women get some critical distance from that

excellence and privilege which is beauty, enough distance to see how much beauty itself has been abridged in order to prop up the mythology of the "feminine."

7. There should be a way of saving beauty *from* women—and *for them.*

IV. Please translate the following sentences into Chinese:

1. The well-born young Athenians who gathered around Socrates found it quite paradoxical that their hero was so intelligent, so brave, so honorable, so seductive—and so ugly.
2. By limiting excellence (*virtus* in Latin) to moral virtue only, Christianity set beauty adrift—as an alienated, arbitrary, superficial enchantment.
3. "Handsome" is the masculine equivalent of—and refusal of—a compliment which has accumulated certain demeaning overtones, by being reserved for women only.
4. In every modern country that is Christian or post-Christian, women are the beautiful sex—to the detriment of the notion of beauty as well as of women.
5. It does not take someone in the throes of advanced feminist awareness to perceive that the way women are taught to be involved with beauty encourages narcissism, reinforces dependence and immaturity.
6. The ideal of beauty is administered as a form of self-oppression.
7. If a woman does real work—and even if she has clambered up to a leading position in politics, law, medicine, business, or whatever—she is always under pressure to confess that she still works at being attractive.

V. How would you respond to each of the following statements?

1. It is not the desire to be beautiful that is wrong but the obligation to be.
2. The privileges of beauty are immense.
3. What is lamentable is that beauty is the only form of power that most women are encouraged to seek.
4. For a woman it is a duty to preen.
5. It is easy to start off by defining women as caretakers of their surfaces, and then to disparage them (or find them adorable) for being "superficial."

VI. Please provide a text, which might support your view on one of the statements in *Exercise V.*

Text B

Cinderella's Stepsisters

*Toni Morrison**

Let me begin by taking you back a little. Back before the days at college. To nursery school, probably, to a once-upon-a-time time when you first heard, or read, or, I suspect, even saw "Cinderella*." Because it is Cinderella that I want to talk about; because it is Cinderella who causes me a feeling of urgency. What is unsettling about that fairy tale is that it is essentially the story of household — a world, if you please — of women gathered together and held together in order to abuse another woman. There is, of course, a rather vague absent father and a nick-of-time prince with a foot fetish. But neither has much personality. And there are the surrogate "mothers," of course (god- and step-), who contribute both to Cinderella's grief and to her release and happiness. But it is her stepsisters who interest me. How crippling it must have been for those young girls to grow up with a mother, to watch and imitate that mother, enslaving another girl.

I am curious about their fortunes after the story ends. For contrary to recent adaptations, the stepsisters were not ugly, clumsy, stupid girls with outsize feet. The Grimm collection* describes them as "beautiful and fair in appearance." When we are introduced to them they are beautiful, elegant, women of status, and clearly women of power. Having watched and participated in the violent dominion of another woman, will they be any less cruel when it comes their turn to enslave other children, or even when they are required to take care of their own mother?

It is not a wholly medieval problem. It is quite a contemporary one: feminine power when directed at other women has historically been wielded in what has been described as a "masculine" manner. Soon

abuse /ə'bjuːz/ *v.* to treat in a harmful, injurious, or offensive way; to speak insultingly, harshly, and unjustly to or about

nick-of-time the critical moment, the exact instant at which sth. has to take place

fetish /'fetɪʃ/ *n.* (in psychology) an object whose presence is necessary for sexual satisfaction

surrogate /'sʌrəgit/ *n.* a substitute

crippling /'krɪplɪŋ/ *adj.* having a severe adverse effect on; weakening seriously

dominion /də'mɪnjən/ *n.* the power or right to rule

medieval /ˌmedi'iːvəl/ *adj.* of, pertaining to, characteristic of, or in the style of the Middle Ages; (*Informal*) extremely old-fashioned; primitive

feminine /'femɪnɪn/ *adj.* pertaining to a woman or girl; belonging to the female sex; female

wield /wiːld/ *v.* to exercise (power, authority, influence, etc.), as in ruling or dominating

you will be in a position to do the very same thing. Whatever your background—rich or poor—whatever the history of education in your family—five generations or one—you have taken advantage of what has been available to you at Barnard* and you will therefore have both the economic and social status of the stepsisters *and* you will have their power.

I want not to *ask* you but to *tell* you not to participate in the oppression of your sisters. Mothers who abuse their children are women, and another woman, not an agency, has to be willing to stay their hands. Mothers who set fire to school buses are women, and another woman, not an agency, has to tell them to stay their hands. Women who stop the promotion of other women in careers are women, and another woman must come to the victim's aid. Social and welfare workers who humiliate their clients may be women, and other women colleagues have to deflect their anger.

agency /'eɪdʒənsi/ *n.* an organization, company, or bureau that provides some service for another; a governmental bureau, or an office that represents it
stay one's hand to cease action; to stop or halt; check
deflect /dɪ'flekt/ *v.* to turn aside or cause to turn aside; turn aside and away from an initial or intended course
decency /'diːsənsi/ *n.* the quality of being socially acceptable
killing floor /'wɪðə/ the slaughtering room of an abattoir, a slaughter house
wither /'wɪðə/ *v.* to cause (esp. plant) to become reduced in size, color, etc.
deserving /dɪ'zɜːvɪŋ/ *adj.* qualified for or having a claim to reward, assistance, etc.
expendable /ɪks'pendəbəl/ *adj.* not strictly necessary; dispensable
first-order first-class
rainbow /'reɪnbəu/ *n.* a visionary goal; any brightly multicolored arrangement or display

I am alarmed by the violence that women do to each other: professional violence, competitive violence, emotional violence. I am alarmed by the willingness of women to enslave other women. I am alarmed by a growing absence of decency on the killing floor of professional women's worlds. You are the women who will take your place in the world where *you* can decide who shall flourish and who shall wither; you will make distinctions between the deserving poor and the undeserving poor; where you can yourself determine which life is expendable and which is indispensable. Since you will have the power to do it, you may also be persuaded that you have the right to do it. As educated women the distinction between the two is first-order business.

I am suggesting that we pay as much attention to our nurturing sensibilities as to our ambition. You are moving in the direction of freedom and the function of freedom is to free somebody else. You are moving toward self-fulfillment, and the consequences of that fulfillment should be to discover that there is something just as important as you are and that just-as-important thing may be Cinderella—or your stepsister.

In your rainbow journey toward the realization of personal goals, don't make choices based only on your security and your safety. Nothing is safe. That is not to say that anything ever was, or that anything worth achieving ever should be. Things of value seldom are. It is not safe to have a child. It is not safe to challenge the status quo. It is not safe to choose work that has not been done before, or to do old work in a new way. There will always be someone there to stop you. But in pursuing your highest ambitions, don't let your personal safety diminish the safety of your stepsister. In wielding the power that is deservedly yours, don't permit it to enslave your stepsisters. Let your might and your power emanate from that place in you that is nurturing and caring.

status quo the existing state or condition, also status in quo
diminish /dɪˈmɪnɪʃ/ *v.* to make or cause to seem smaller, less important; lessen; reduce
emanate /ˈeməneɪt/ *v.* to flow out, issue, or proceed, as from a source or origin; come forth; originate
abstraction /əbˈstrækʃən/ *n.* an abstract or general idea or term; the act of considering sth. as a general quality or characteristic, apart from concrete realities, specific objects, or actual instances

Women's rights is not only an abstraction, a cause; it is also a personal affair. It is not only about "us"; it is also about me and you. Just the two of us.

Cultural Notes

1. **Toni Morrison** (1931—) is the first African American woman to receive the Nobel Prize for Literature (1993). She is widely recognized for her epic power, unerring ear for dialogue, and her poetically-charged and richly-expressive depictions of Black America. In her novels she focuses on the experience of black Americans, particularly emphasizing black women's experience in a racist and male-dominated society and their search for cultural identity. She uses fantasy and mythic elements along with realistic depiction of racial, gender and class conflict. "Cinderella's Stepsisters" is a speech given at **Barnard** College.
2. "**Cinderella**" is a fairy tale or folk tale written by the Grimm Brothers (Jacob and Wilhelm) and collected in ***The Grimm Fairy Tales***. In the story, the titular heroine is maltreated by a malevolent stepmother, but marries a prince and achieves happiness through the benevolent intervention of a fairy godmother.

Comprehension Exercises

I. Please answer the following questions according to the text you have just read.

1. Why is Morrison interested in the story of Cinderella?
2. What does Morrison mean when she says "I want not to ask you but to *tell* you not to participate in the oppression of your sisters"?
3. What is professional violence, competitive violence or emotional violence, according to Morrison?
4. What is the first-order business to educated women, according to Morrison?
5. Why does Morrison say that women's rights is a personal affair?
6. What does Morrison mean by the last sentence?
7. Does Morrison address any racial problems in the speech? If yes, how?

II. Are the following judgments correct according to the text? Write "T" if the judgment is correct, or "F" if the judgment is wrong.

1. There is a detailed description of man characters in "Cinderella".
2. Having watched and participated in the violent dominion of another woman, Cinderella's stepsisters will be as cruel when it comes their turn to enslave other children, or even when they are required to take care of their own mother.
3. The problem is that feminine power has always been used in a masculine manner when directed at women.
4. In professional women's worlds, the competition is fierce and violent, even at the price of decency.
5. According to Morrison, nurturing sensibilities are as important as ambition.

III. Please paraphrase the following sentences:

1. There is, of course, a rather vague absent father and a nick-of-time prince with a foot fetish.
2. It is quite a contemporary one: feminine power when directed at other women has historically been wielded in what has been described as a "masculine" manner.
3. I am alarmed by a growing absence of decency on the killing floor of professional women's worlds.
4. In your rainbow journey toward the realization of personal goals, don't make choices based only on your security and your safety.

5. Women's rights is not only an abstraction, a cause; it is also a personal affair.

IV. Please translate the following sentences into Chinese:

1. What is unsettling about that fairy tale is that it is essentially the story of household—a world, if you please—of women gathered together and held together in order to abuse another woman.
2. Whatever your background—rich or poor—whatever the history of education in your family—five generations or one—you have taken advantage of what has been available to you at Barnard and you will therefore have both the economic and social status of the stepsisters and you will have their power.
3. You are the women who will take your place in the world where you can decide who shall flourish and who shall wither; you will make distinctions between the deserving poor and the undeserving poor; where you can yourself determine which life is expendable and which is indispensable.
4. You are moving toward self-fulfillment, and the consequences of that fulfillment should be to discover that there is something just as important as you are and that just-as-important thing may be Cinderella—or your stepsister.
5. Nothing is safe. That is not to say that anything ever was, or that anything worth achieving ever should be. Things of value seldom are. It is not safe to have a child. It is not safe to challenge the status quo. It is not safe to choose work that has not been done before, or to do old work in a new way. There will always be someone there to stop you.

V. How would you respond to each of the following statements?

1. Let your might and your power emanate from that place in you that is nurturing and caring.
2. Mercy drops as the gentle rain from heaven, blesses him that gives and him that takes.
3. Beauty does not necessarily mean virtue.
4. Feminine power, like masculine power, might be abused.
5. Maternity/Femininity does not necessarily mean mercy.
6. In pursuing your highest ambitions, don't let your personal safety diminish the safety of your stepsister.

VI. Please provide a text, which might support your view on one of the statements in *Exercise V.*

Unit Eight

Text A

What Is Science?

*George Orwell**

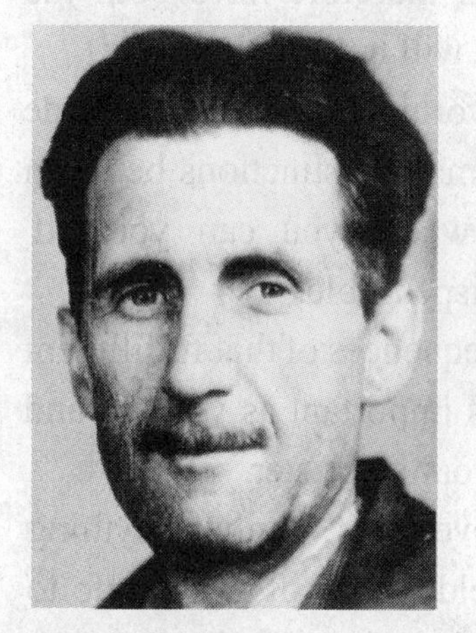

In last week's *Tribune**, there was an interesting letter from Mr. J. Stewart Cook, in which he suggested that the best way of avoiding the danger of a "scientific hierarchy" would be to see to it that every member of the general public was, as far as possible, scientifically educated. At the same time, scientists should be brought out of their isolation and encouraged to take a greater part in politics and administration.

As a general statement, I think most of us would agree with this, but I notice that, as usual, Mr. Cook does not define science, and merely implies in passing that it means certain exact sciences whose experiments can be made under laboratory conditions. Thus, adult education tends "to neglect scientific studies in favour of literary, economic and social subjects," economics and sociology not being regarded as branches of science, apparently. This point is of great importance. For the word science is at present used in at least two meanings, but the whole question of scientific education is obscured by the current tendency to dodge from one meaning to the other.

Science is generally taken as meaning either (a) the exact sciences, such as chemistry, physics, etc., or (b) a method of thought which obtains verifiable results by reasoning logically from observed fact.

If you ask any scientist, or indeed almost any educated person, "What is science?" you are likely to get an answer approximating to (b). In everyday life, however, both in speaking and in writing, when people say "science" they mean (a). Science means something that happens in a laboratory:

tribune /'trɪbjuːn/ *n.* **a.** an official elected by the people in ancient Rome to defend their rights; a popular leader **b.** a raised area that somebody stands on to make a speech in public

imply /ɪm'plaɪ/ *v.* to suggest that sth. is true

obscure /əb'skjʊə/ *v.* to make it difficult to see, hear or understand sth.

dodge /dɒdʒ/ *v.* to move quickly and suddenly to one side in order to avoid somebody or sth.

the very word calls up a picture of graphs, test-tubes, balances, Bunsen burners, microscopes. A biologist, an astronomer, perhaps a psychologist or a mathematician, is described as a "man of science": no one would think of applying this term to a statesman, a poet, a journalist or even a philosopher. And those who tell us that the young must be scientifically educated mean, almost invariably, that they should be taught more about radioactivity, or the stars, or the physiology of their own bodies, rather than that they should be taught to think more exactly.

graph /grɑːf/ *n.* a planned drawing, consisting of a line or lines, showing how two or more sets of numbers are related to each other
balance /ˈbæləns/ *n.* an instrument for weighing things, with a bar that is supported in the middle and has dishes hanging from each end
Bunsen burner /ˌbʌnsən ˈbɜːnə/ an instrument used in scientific work that produces a hot gas flame
invariably /ɪnˈveərɪəblɪ/ *adv.* always
radioactivity /ˈreɪdiəuækˈtɪvɪti/ *n.* the sending out of radiation when the nucleus of an atom has broken apart
approach /əˈprəʊtʃ/ *n.* a method of doing sth. or dealing with a problem
approach /əˈprəʊtʃ/ *v.* to begin to deal with a situation or problem in a particular way or with a particular attitude
scruple /ˈskruːpəl/ *n.* a belief about what is right and wrong that prevents you from doing bad things
synthetic /sɪnˈθetɪk/ *adj.* produced by combining different artificial substances, rather than being naturally produced
projectile /prəˈdʒektaɪl/ *n.* an object that is thrown at someone or is fired from a gun or other weapon, such as a bullet, stone, or shell

This confusion of meaning, which is partly deliberate, has in it a great danger. Implied in the demand for more scientific education is the claim that if one has been scientifically trained one's approach to *all* subjects will be more intelligent than if one had had no such training. A scientist's political opinions, it is assumed, his opinions on sociological questions, on morals, on philosophy, perhaps even on the arts, will be more valuable than those of a layman. The world, in other words, would be a better place if the scientists were in control of it. But a "scientist," as we have just seen, means in practice a specialist in one of the exact sciences. It follows that a chemist or a physicist, as such, is politically more intelligent than a poet or a lawyer, as such. And, in fact, there are already millions of people who do believe this.

But is it really true that a "scientist," in this narrower sense, is any likelier than other people to approach non-scientific problems in an objective way? There is not much reason for thinking so. Take one simple test — the ability to withstand nationalism. It is often loosely said that "Science is international," but in practice the scientific workers of all countries line up behind their own governments with fewer scruples than are felt by the writers and the artists. The German scientific community, as a whole, made no resistance to Hitler*. Hitler may have ruined the long-term prospects of German science, but there were still plenty of gifted men to do the necessary research on such things as synthetic oil, jet planes, rocket projectiles and the atomic bomb. Without them the German war machine could never have been built up.

On the other hand, what happened to German literature when the Nazis came to power? I believe no exhaustive lists have been published, but I imagine that the number of German scientists—Jews apart—who voluntarily exiled themselves or were persecuted by the régime was much smaller than the number of writers and journalists. More sinister than this, a number of German scientists swallowed the monstrosity of "racial science." You can find some of the statements to which they set their names in Professor Brady* 's *The Spirit and Structure of German Fascism.*

But, in slightly different forms, it is the same picture everywhere. In England, a large proportion of our leading scientists accept the structure of capitalist society, as can be seen from the comparative freedom with which they are given knighthoods, baronetcies and even peerages. Since Tennyson*, no English writer worth reading—one might, perhaps, make an exception of Sir Max Beerbohm*—has been given a title. And those English scientists who do not simply accept the status quo are frequently Communists, which means that, however intellectually scrupulous they may be in their own line of work, they are ready to be uncritical and even dishonest on certain subjects. The fact is that a mere training in one or more of the exact sciences, even combined with very high gifts, is no guarantee of a humane or sceptical outlook. The physicists of half a dozen great nations, all feverishly and secretly working away at the atomic bomb, are a demonstration of this.

But does all this mean that the general public should *not* be more scientificallly educated? On the contrary! All it means is that scientific education for the masses will do little good, and probably a lot of harm, if it simply boils down to more physics, more chemistry, more biology, etc. to the detriment of literature and history. Its probable effect on the average human being would be to narrow the range of his thoughts and make him more than ever contemptuous of such knowledge as he did not possess, and his political reactions would probably be somewhat less intelligent than those of an illiterate peasant who retained a few historical memories and a fairly sound aesthetic sense. Clearly, scientific education ought to mean the implanting of a rational, sceptical, experimental habit of mind. It ought to mean acquiring a *method*—a method that can be used on any problem that one meets—and not simply piling up a lot of facts. Put it in those words, and the apologist of scientific education will

exhaustive /ɪɡˈzɔːstɪv/ *adj.* extremely thorough and complete

persecute /ˈpɜːsɪkjuːt/ *v.* to treat someone cruelly or unfairly over a period of time, esp. because of their religious or political beliefs

sinister /ˈsɪnɪstə/ *adj.* making you feel that sth. evil, dangerous, or illegal is happening or will happen

monstrosity /mɒnsˈtrɒsɪti/ *n.* sth. large and ugly, esp. a building

baronetcy /ˈbærənɪtsi/ *n.* the rank of a baronet, i.e. a British lemight

peerage /ˈpɪərɪdʒ/ *n.* the rank of a British peer

sceptical /ˈskeptɪkəl/ *adj.* tending to disagree with what other people tell you

feverish /ˈfiːvərɪʃ/ *adj.* very excited or worried about something -feverishly *adv.*

contemptuous /kənˈtemptʃuəs/ *adj.* showing that you think someone or sth. deserves no respect

retain /rɪˈteɪn/ *v.* to keep sth.or continue to have sth.

usually agree. Press him further, ask him to particularize, and somehow it always turns out that scientific education means more attention to the exact sciences, in other words—more *facts*. The idea that science means a way of looking at the world, and not simply a body of knowledge, is in practice strongly resisted. I think sheer professional jealousy is part of the reason for this. For if science is simply a method or an attitude, so that anyone whose thought-processes are sufficiently rational can in some sense be described as a scientist—what then becomes of the enormous prestige now enjoyed by the chemist, the physicist, etc. and his claim to be somehow wiser than the rest of us?

particularize /pəˈtɪkjʊləraɪz/ *v.* to give the details of sth.
sheer /ʃɪə/ *adj.* pure
prestige /preˈstiːʒ/ *n.* the respect and admiration that someone or sth. gets because of their success or important position in society
smug /smʌg/ *adj.* showing too much satisfaction with your own cleverness or success —smugly *adv.*
pendulum /ˈpendjʊləm/ *n.* **a.** a long metal stick with a weight at the bottom that swings regularly from side to side to control the working of a clock **b.** the tendency of idea, beliefs etc. to change regularly to the opposite
sane /seɪn/ *adj.* able to think in a normal and reasonable way
lunatic /ˈluːnətɪk/ *n.* someone who behaves in a crazy or very stupid way
acquaintance /əˈkweɪntəns/ *n.* knowledge or experience of a particular subject

A hundred years ago, Charles Kingsley* described science as "making nasty smells in a laboratory". A year or two ago a young industrial chemist informed me, smugly, that he "could not see what was the use of poetry". So the pendulum swings to and fro, but it does not seem to me that one attitude is any better than the other. At the moment, science is on the up-grade, and so we hear, quite rightly, the claim that the masses should be scientifically educated: we do not hear, as we ought, the counter-claim that the scientists themselves would benefit by a little education. Just before writing this, I saw in an American magazine the statement that a number of British and American physicists refused from the start to do research on the atomic bomb, well knowing what use would be made of it. Here you have a group of sane men in the middle of a world of lunatics. And though no names were published, I think it would be a safe guess that all of them were people with some kind of general cultural background, some acquaintance with history or literature or the arts—in short, people whose interests were not, in the current sense of the word, purely scientific.

Cultural Notes

1. **George Orwell** (1903—1950) was an English novelist, essayist and critic. V.S. Pritchett called him "the wintry conscience of a generation." During World War II he worked as a literary editor for BBC, Obs*erver* and *Tribune*.

Toward the end of the war, he wrote *Animal Farm*, a satirical allegory of the Russian Revolution, and argued that writers have an obligation of fighting social injustice, oppression, and totalitarian regimes. He died from tuberculosis in London in 1950 soon after the publication of *Nineteen Eighty-Four*, a bitter protest against the nightmarish future and corruption of truth and free speech of the modern world.

2. ***Tribune*** is a democratic socialist weekly set up in London in early 1937 by two left-wing Labour Party Members of Parliament in attempt to secure an anti-fascist and anti-appeasement United Front between the Labour Party and socialist parties to its left. In 1948, after the Soviet rejection of Marshall Aid and the communist takeover of Czechoslovakia, *Tribune* endorsed the North Atlantic Treaty Organization and took an anti-communist line. *Tribune* changed format from newspaper to magazine in 2001.
3. **Adolf Hitler** (1889—1945) was the military and political leader of Germany (1933—1945). His invasion of Poland in September 1939 began World War II. The Jews in the conquered countries were rounded up and killed. Millions of others whom he considered racially inferior were also killed or worked to death. In December 1941, he declared war on America. The war on the eastern front drained Germany's resources and in June 1944, the British and Americans landed in France. With Soviet troops poised to take Berlin, Hitler committed suicide on 30 April 1945.
4. **Robert A. Brady** (1901—1963) was an American economist. In *The Sprit and Structure of German Fascism* (1937) and *Business as a System of Power* (1943), important works in historical and comparative economics, Brady traced the rise of bureaucratic centralism in Germany, France, Italy, Japan and the United States and the emergence of an authoritarian model of economic growth and development.
5. **Alfred Tennyson** (1809—1892) was an English poet often regarded as the chief representative of the Victorian poetry. Tennyson succeeded Wordsworth as Poet Laureate in 1850. Among Tennyson's major poetic achievements is the elegy mourning the death of his friend Arthur Hallam, "In Memoriam" (1850). The patriotic poem "Charge of the Light Brigade" is one of his best known works. In 1884 he was created a baron. He died in 1892 and was buried in the Poets' Corner in Westminster Abbey.
6. **Sir Max Beerbohm** (1872—1956) was an English essayist, caricaturist, and parodist. His works include *A Christmas Garland* (1912), a collection of parodies on such authors as Joseph Conrad and Thomas Hardy. He was knighted in 1939.

7. **Charles Kingsley** (1819—1875) was an English novelist. His concern for social reform is illustrated in his great classic, *The Water-Babies* (1863), a kind of fairytale about a boy chimney-sweep, which retained its popularity well into the 20th century.

Comprehension Exercises

I. Please answer the following questions according to the text you have just read.

1. How does the author distinguish scientists from ordinary people in everyday life?
2. What might the term "racial science" mean?
3. What is the essence of scientific education according to the author?
4. Is the word "jealousy" an accurate word in the text? What might be an alternative?
5. What might "a little education" specifically refer to according to the context?

II. Are the following judgments correct according to the text? Write "T" if the judgment is correct, or "F" if the judgment is wrong.

1. Mr. J. Stewart Cook does not define science, but specifically refers to chemistry and physics.
2. Mr. J. Stewart Cook means to say that those majoring in chemistry and physics should be the leaders of a society.
3. The author distinguishes those "scientifically educated" people from those "taught to think more exactly."
4. The author holds a negative attitude toward nationalism, and implies that scientific workers are less scrupulous than writers and artists.
5. The author regards Sir Max Beerbohm as a writer worth reading.
6. According to the author, how to look at the facts is much more important than how many facts are discovered.

III. Please paraphrase the following sentences:

1. Thus, adult education tends "to neglect scientific studies in favour of literary, economic and social subjects", economics and sociology not being regarded as branches of science, apparently. This point is of great importance.
2. More sinister than this, a number of German scientists swallowed the monstrosity of "racial science".

3. The number of German scientists—Jews apart—who voluntarily exiled themselves or were persecuted by the régime was much smaller than the number of writers and journalists.
4. Science ought to mean acquiring a *method*—a method that can be used on any problem that one meets—and not simply piling up a lot of facts.
5. Put it in those words, and the apologist of scientific education will usually agree. Press him further, ask him to particularize, and somehow it always turns out that scientific education means more attention to the exact sciences, in other words—more *facts*.

IV. Please translate the following sentences into Chinese:

1. Science is generally taken as meaning either (a) the exact sciences, such as chemistry, physics, etc., or (b) a method of thought which obtains verifiable results by reasoning logically from observed fact.
2. This confusion of meaning, which is partly deliberate, has in it a great danger. Implied in the demand for more scientific education is the claim that if one has been scientifically trained one's approach to *all* subjects will be more intelligent than if one had had no such training.
3. Hitler may have ruined the long-term prospects of German science, but there were still plenty of gifted men to do the necessary research on such things as synthetic oil, jet planes, rocket projectiles and the atomic bomb.
4. The idea that science means a way of looking at the world, and not simply a body of knowledge, is in practice strongly resisted.
5. And though no names were published, I think it would be a safe guess that all of them were people with some kind of general cultural background, some acquaintance with history or literature or the arts—in short, people whose interests were not, in the current sense of the word, purely scientific.

V. How would you respond to each of the following statements?

1. Science means something that happens in a laboratory.
2. A chemist or a physicist is politically more intelligent than a poet or a lawyer.
3. In practice the scientific workers of all countries line up behind their own governments with fewer scruples than are felt by the writers and the artists.
4. A mere training in one or more of the exact sciences, even combined with very high gifts, is no guarantee of a humane or sceptical outlook.
5. Scientific education for the masses will do little good, and probably a lot of harm, if it simply boils down to more physics, more chemistry, more biology,

etc. to the detriment of literature and history.

6. Scientific education ought to mean the implanting of a rational, sceptical, experimental habit of mind.

VI. Please provide a text, which might support your view on one of the statements in *Exercise V*.

Text B

To Err Is Human

*Lewis Thomas**

Everyone must have had at least one personal experience with a computer error by this time. Bank balances are suddenly reported to have jumped from $ 379 into the millions, appeals for charitable contributions are mailed over and over to people with crazy-sounding names at your address, department stores send the wrong bills, utility companies write that they're turning everything off, that sort of thing. If you manage to get in touch with someone and complain, you then get instantaneously typed, guilty letters from the same computer, saying, "Our computer was in error, and an adjustment is being made in your account."

These are supposed to be the sheerest, blindest accidents. Mistakes are not believed to be part of the normal behavior of a good machine. If things go wrong, it must be a personal, human error, the result of fingering, tampering, a button getting stuck, someone hitting the wrong key. The computer, at its normal best, is infallible.

I wonder whether this can be true. After all, the whole point of computers is that they represent an extension of the human brain, vastly improved upon but nonetheless human, superhuman maybe. A good computer can think clearly and quickly enough to beat you at chess, and some of them have even been programmed to write obscure verse. They can do anything we can do, and more besides.

It is not yet known whether a computer

balance /ˈbæləns/ *n.* money which remains or is left over

appeal /əˈpiːl/ *n.* an earnest request for aid, support, sympathy, mercy, etc.; entreaty; petition; plea

charitable /ˈtʃærɪtəbəl/ *adj.* of, for, or concerned with charity; generous in donations or gifts to relieve the needs of indigent, ill, or helpless persons, or of animals

utility /juːˈtɪlɪti/ *n.* a public service, as a telephone or electric-light system, a streetcar or railroad line, or the like

tamper /ˈtæmpə/ *v.* to touch or make changes to sth. without permission

infallible /ɪnˈfæləbəl/ *adj.* not fallible; exempt from liability to error, as persons, their judgment, or pronouncements; absolutely trustworthy or sure

has its own consciousness, and it would be hard to find out about this. When you walk into one of those great halls now built for the huge machines, and stand listening, it is easy to imagine that the faint, distant noises are the sound of thinking, and the turning of the spools gives them the look of wild creatures rolling their eyes in the effort to concentrate, choking with information. But real thinking, and dreaming, are other matters.

spool /spu:l/ *n.* any cylindrical piece or device on which sth. is wound; the material or quantity of material wound on such a device
equivalent /ɪ'kwɪvələnt/ *adj.* equal in value, measure, force, effect, significance, etc.
property /'prɒpəti/ *n.* a quality, power, or effect that belongs naturally to sth.
embed /ɪm'bed/ *v.* to fix into a surrounding mass; to incorporate or contain as an essential part or characteristic
nodule /'nɒdju:l/ *n.* (*Botany*) a small knoblike outgrowth, as those found on the roots of many leguminous plants
knack /næk/ *n.* a special skill, talent, or aptitude; a trick or ruse
by the book according to the correct or established form; in the usual manner
buffer /'bʌfə/ *n.* an apparatus at the end of a railroad car, railroad track, etc., for absorbing shock
decimal /'desɪməl/ *adj.* pertaining to tenths or to the number 10
protocol /'prəutəkɒl/ *n.* plan for carrying out a scientific study or a patient's treatment regimen; (Computers) a set of rules governing the format of messages that are exchanged between computers
screw up to mismanage; make an error

On the other hand, the evidences of something like an unconscious, equivalent to ours, are all around, in every mail. As extensions of the human brain, they have been constructed with the same property of error, spontaneous, uncontrolled, and rich in possibilities.

Mistakes are at the very base of human thought, embedded there, feeding the structure like root nodules. If we were not provided with the knack of being wrong, we could never get anything useful done. We think our way along by choosing between right and wrong alternatives, and the wrong choices have to be made as frequently as the right ones. We get along in life this way. We are built to make mistakes, coded for error.

We learn, as we say, by "trial and error." Why do we always say that? Why not "trial and rightness" or "trial and triumph"? The old phrase puts it that way because that is, in real life, the way it is done.

A good laboratory, like a good bank or a corporation or government, has to run like a computer. Almost everything is done flawlessly, by the book, and all the numbers add up to the predicted sums. The days go by. And then, if it is a lucky day, and a lucky laboratory, somebody makes a mistake: the wrong buffer, something in one of the blanks, a decimal misplaced in reading counts, the warm room off by a degree and a half, a mouse out of his box, or just a misreading of the day's protocol. Whatever, when the results come in, something is obviously screwed up, and then the action can begin.

The misreading is not the important error: it opens the way. The next step is the crucial one. If the investigator can bring himself to say, "But even so, look at that!" then the new finding, whatever it is, is ready for snatching. What is needed, for progress to be made, is the move based on the error.

Whenever new kinds of thinking are about to be accomplished, or new varieties of music, there has to be an argument beforehand. With two sides debating in the same mind, haranguing, there is an amiable understanding that one is right and the other wrong. Sooner or later the thing is settled, but there can be no action at all if there are not the two sides, and the argument. The hope is in the faculty of wrongness, the tendency toward error. The capacity to leap across mountains of information to land lightly on the wrong side represents the highest of human endowments.

harangue /hə'ræŋ/ *v.* to make a long or intense verbal attack; to deliver a long and vehement speech
amiable /'eɪmiəbəl/ *adj.* of a pleasant nature; good-tempered; friendly
faculty /'fækəlti/ *n.* a. the power or ability to do sth. particular b. a natural power or ability, esp. of the mind
endowment /in'daʊmənt/ *n.* the natural qualities that a person is endowed with
stipulate /'stɪpjʊleɪt/ *v.* to make an express demand or arrangement as a condition of agreement
jumble /'dʒʌmbəl/ *n.* a disorderly mixture
con /kɒn/ *v.* to swindle; trick; to persuade by deception, cajolery, etc.
stick fast to be hopelessly bogged
maladroit /ˌmælə'drɔɪt/ *adj.* lacking in adroitness; unskillful; awkward; bungling; tactless

It may be that this is a uniquely human gift, perhaps even stipulated in our genetic instructions. Other creatures do not seem to have DNA* sequences for making mistakes as a routine part of daily living, certainly not for programmed error as a guide for action.

We are at our human finest, dancing with our minds, when there are more choices than two. Sometimes there are ten, even twenty different ways to go, all but one bound to be the wrong, and the richness of selection in such situations can lift us onto totally new ground. This process is called exploration and is based on human fallibility. If we had only a single center in our brains, capable of responding only when a correct decision was to be made, instead of the jumble of different credulous, easily conned clusters of neurons that provide for being flung off into blind alleys, up trees, down dead ends, out into blue sky, along wrong turnings, around bends, we could only stay the way we are today, stuck fast.

The lower animals do not have this splendid freedom. They are limited most of them, to absolute infallibility. Cats, for all their good side, never make mistakes. I have never seen a maladroit, clumsy, or blundering cat. Dogs are sometimes fallible, occasionally able to make charming minor mistakes, but they get this way by trying

to mimic their masters. Fish are flawless in everything they do. Individual cells in a tissue are mindless machines, perfect in their performance, as absolutely inhuman as bees.

We should have this in mind as we become dependent on more complex computers for the arrangement of our affairs. Give the computers their heads, I say; let them go their way. If we can learn to do this, turning our heads to one side and wincing while the work proceeds, the possibilities for the future of mankind, and computerkind, are limitless. Your average good computer can make calculations in an instant which would take a lifetime of slide rules for any of us. Think of what we could gain from the near infinity of precise, machine-made miscomputation which is now so easily within our grasp. We would begin the solving of some of our hardest problems. How, for instance, should we go about organizing ourselves for social living on a planetary scale, now that we have become, as a plain fact of life, a single community? We can assume, as a working hypothesis, that all the right ways of doing this are unworkable. What we need, then, for moving ahead, is a set of wrong alternatives much longer and more interesting than the short list of mistaken courses that any of us can think up right now. We need, in fact, an infinite list, and when it is printed out we need the computer to turn on itself and select, at random, the next way to go. If it is a big enough mistake, we could find ourselves on a new level, stunned, out in the clear, ready to move again.

mimic /ˈmɪmɪk/ *v.* to imitate or copy in action, speech, etc., often playfully or derisively

wince /wɪns/ *v.* to draw back, as with fear or pain

slide rule an instrument for calculating numbers

hypothesis /haɪˈpɒθəsɪs/*n.* a proposition, or set of propositions, set forth as an explanation for the occurrence of some specified group of phenomena, either asserted merely as a provisional conjecture to guide investigation (working hypothesis) or accepted as highly probable in the light of established facts

stun /stʌn/ *v.* **a.** to make unconscious by hitting the head **b.** to cause to lose the sense of balance **c.** to shock into helplessness **d.** to delight

in the clear absolved of blame or guilt; free

Cultural Notes

1. **Lewis Thomas** (1913—1993) was an American physician and educator. Educated at Princeton and Harvard, he served as president of Memorial Sloan-Kettering Cancer Center from 1973 to 1980. The short essays which he began writing for fun in 1971 established him as a serious writer of prose who combined his knowledge and insights into science, especially microbiology and immunology, with meditative reflections on nature and the

human body in a style widely recognized as clear, graceful and witty. The title "To Err Is Human" is a parody of a poem line: "To err is human, to forgive divine" taken from *An Essay on Criticism* written by Alexander Pope (1688—1744).

2. **DNA,** or deoxyribonucleic acid, is a nucleic acid that contains the genetic instructions used in the development and functioning of all known living organisms and some viruses. The main role of DNA molecules is the long-term storage of information. DNA is often compared to a set of blueprints, since it contains the instructions needed to construct other components of cells, such as proteins and RNA molecules. The DNA segments that carry this genetic information are called genes, but other DNA sequences have structural purposes, or are involved in regulating the use of this genetic information.

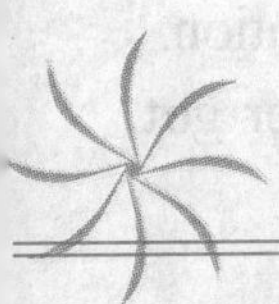

Comprehension Exercises

I. Please answer the following questions according to the text you have just read.

1. What is the author's tone of voice throughout the text? How could you prove this?
2. How would you summarize the author's opinions in your own words?
3. How does the author define a computer?
4. How is a human being different from an animal being?

II. Are the following judgments correct according to the text? Write "T" if the judgment is correct, or "F" if the judgment is wrong.

1. Computers are largely untrustworthy, so are human beings.
2. It is very common to be fooled by a computer.
3. It is almost impossible for a human being to make the right choice.
4. Wrong choices promote human progress.
5. It is certain that a computer has its own consciousness.
6. It is only human beings that seem to have DNA sequences for making mistakes as a routine part of daily living.
7. Absolute infallibility belongs to lower animals.

III. Please paraphrase the following sentences:

1. As extensions of the human brain, they have been constructed with the same property of error, spontaneous, uncontrolled, and rich in possibilities.
2. Mistakes are at the very base of human thought, embedded there, feeding the structure like root nodules.

3. Other creatures do not seem to have DNA sequences for making mistakes as a routine part of daily living, certainly not for programmed error as a guide for action.
4. Individual cells in a tissue are mindless machines, perfect in their performance, as absolutely inhuman as bees.
5. What we need, then, for moving ahead, is a set of wrong alternatives much longer and more interesting than the short list of mistaken courses that any of us can think up right now.

IV. Please translate the following sentences into Chinese:

1. When you walk into one of those great halls now built for the huge machines, and stand listening, it is easy to imagine that the faint, distant noises are the sound of thinking, and the turning of the spools gives them the look of wild creatures rolling their eyes in the effort to concentrate, choking with information.
2. If we were not provided with the knack of being wrong, we could never get anything useful done.
3. We are built to make mistakes, coded for error.
4. Whenever new kinds of thinking are about to be accomplished, or new varieties of music, there has to be an argument beforehand. With two sides debating in the same mind, haranguing, there is an amiable understanding that one is right and the other wrong.
5. If we had only a single center in our brains, capable of responding only when a correct decision was to be made, instead of the jumble of different credulous, easily conned clusters of neurons that provide for being flung off into blind alleys, up trees, down dead ends, out into blue sky, along wrong turnings, around bends, we could only stay the way we are today, stuck fast.
6. We are at our human finest, dancing with our minds, when there are more choices than two.

V. How would you respond to each of the following statements?

1. Cynicism leads to a tragic end.
2. DNA determines all.
3. Computers are an extension of human brain.
4. We learn by trial and error.
5. We are built to make mistakes, coded for error.
6. We leave traces of ourselves wherever we go, on whatever we touch.

VI. Please provide a text, which might support your view on one of the statements in *Exercise V*.

Unit Nine

Text A

On National Prejudice

*Oliver Goldsmith**

As I am one of that sauntering tribe of mortals who spend the greatest part of their time in taverns, coffeehouses, and other places of public resort, I have thereby an opportunity of observing an infinite variety of characters, which to a person of a contemplative turn is a much higher entertainment than a view of all the curiosities of art or nature. In one of these my late rambles I accidentally fell into a company of half a dozen gentlemen, who wereengaged in a warm dispute about some political affair, the decision of which, as they were equally divided in their sentiments, they thought proper to refer to me, which naturally drew me in for a share of the conversation.

Amongst a multiplicity of other topics, we took occasion to talk of the different characters of the several nations of Europe; when one of the gentlemen, cocking his hat, and assuming such an air of importance as if he had possessed all the merit of the English nation in his own person, declared, that the Dutch were a parcel of avaricious wretches; the French a set of flattering sycophants; that the Germans were drunken sots, and beastly gluttons; and the Spaniard proud, haughty, and surly tyrants; but that in

saunter /'sɔːntə/ *v.* to walk with a leisurely gait; stroll
mortal /'mɔːtl/ *n.* a human being
tavern /'tævən/ *n.* a public house, inn
resort /rɪ'zɔːt/ *n.* a place to which people frequently go for relaxation
turn /tɜːn/ *n.* character, disposition
ramble /'ræmbəl/ *n.* a walk without a definite route, taken merely for pleasure
amongst /ə'mʌŋst/ *prep.* among
cock /kɒk/ *v.* to set or turn up or to one side, often in an assertive, jaunty, or significant manner
merit /'merɪt/ *n.* sth. that deserves or justifies a reward or commendation; a commendable quality
avaricious /ˌævə'riʃəs/ *adj.* greedy for wealth
sycophant /'sɪkəfənt/ *n.* a flatterer
sot /sɒt/ *n.* a habitual drunkard
glutton /'glʌtn/ *n.* a. a person who eats and drinks voraciously. b. a person with a remarkable desire for sth.
haughty /'hɔːti/ *adj.* disdainfully proud; snobbish; scornfully arrogant

bravery, generosity, clemency, and in every other virtue, the English excelled all the world.

This very learned and judicious remark was received with a general smile of approbation by all the company—all, I mean, but your humble servant, who, endeavouring to keep my gravity as well as I could, and reclining my head upon my arm, continued for some time in a posture of affected thoughtfulness, as if I had been musing on something else, and did not seem to attend to the subject of conversation; hoping by this to avoid the disagreeable necessity of explaining myself, and thereby depriving the gentleman of his imaginary happiness.

clemency /'klemənsi/ *n.* mercy
excel /ɪk'sel/ *v.* to surpass others or be superior in some respect or area
judicious /dʒuː'dɪʃəs/ *adj.* discreet, prudent or politic
approbation /ˌæprə'beiʃən/ *n.* approval; commendation
gravity /'grævɪti/ *n.* dignity; serious conduct
muse /mjuːz/ *v.* to think or meditate in silence
suffrage /'sʌfrɪdʒ/ *n.* a. the right to vote b. a vote given in favor of a proposal
forward /'fɔːwəd/ *adj.* a. well-advanced b. ready, prompt, or eager
maxim /'mæksɪm/ *n.* a principle or rule of conduct
peremptory strain /pə'remptəri strein/ haughty air
scruple /'skruːpl/ *v.* to hesitate
frugal /'fruːgəl/ *adj.* a. economical in use or expenditure b. meager; scanty
staid /steɪd/ *adj.* sober, grave
sedate /sɪ'deɪt/ *adj.* calm, quiet, or composed
impetuous /ɪm'petʃuəs/ *adj.* impulsive
elated /ɪ'leɪtɪd/ *adj.* very happy or proud
despond /dis'pɔnd/ *v.* to be depressed by loss of hope
adversity /əd'vɜːsɪti/ *n.* a. adverse fortune or fate b. an adverse event or circumstance
jealous /'dʒeləs/ *adj.* hostile, resentful
observe /əb'zɜːv/ *v.* a. to follow b. to say or mention casually; remark c. to notice or perceive

But my pseudo-patriot had no mind to let me escape so easily. Not satisfied that his opinion should pass without contradiction, he was determined to have it ratified by the suffrage of every one in the company; for which purpose, addressing himself to me with an air of inexpressible confidence, he asked me if I was not of the same way of thinking. As I am never forward in giving my opinion, especially when I have reason to believe that it will not be agreeable; so, when I am obliged to give it, I always hold it for a maxim to speak my real sentiments. I therefore told him that, for my own part, I should not have ventured to talk in such a peremptory strain unless I had made the tour of Europe, and examined the manners of these several nations with great care and accuracy; that perhaps a more impartial judge would not scruple to affirm, that the Dutch were more frugal and industrious, the French more temperate and polite, the Germans more hardy and patient of labour and fatigue, and the Spaniards more staid and sedate, than the English; who, though undoubtedly brave and generous, were at the same time rash, headstrong, and impetuous; too apt to be elated with prosperity, and to despond in adversity.

I could easily perceive, that all the company began to regard me with a jealous eye before I had finished my answer, which I had no sooner done, than the patriotic gentleman observed, with a contemptuous sneer, that he was greatly surprised how some people could have the conscience to live in a country which they did not love, and to enjoy the protection of a government to which in their hearts they were inveterate enemies. Finding that by this modest declaration of my sentiments I had forfeited the good opinion of my companions, and given them occasion to call my political principles in question, and well knowing that it was in vain to argue with men who were so very full of themselves, I threw down my reckoning and retired to my own lodgings, reflecting on the absurd and ridiculous nature of national prejudice and prepossession.

Among all the famous sayings of antiquity, there is none that does greater honour to the author, or affords greater pleasure to the reader, (at least if he be a person of a generous and benevolent heart,) than that of the philosopher who, being asked what countryman he was, replied, that he was "a citizen of the world". How few are there to be found in modern times who can say the same, or whose conduct is consistent with such a profession! We are now become so much Englishmen, Frenchmen, Dutchmen, Spaniards, or Germans, that we are no longer citizens of the world; so much the natives of one particular spot, or members of one party society, that we no longer consider ourselves as the general inhabitants of the globe, or members of that grand society which comprehends the whole human kind.

Did these prejudices prevail only among the meanest and lowest of the people, perhaps they might be excused, as they have few, if any, opportunities of correcting them by reading, traveling, or conversing with foreigners; but the misfortune is, that they infect the minds, and influence the conduct, even of our gentlemen; of those, I mean, who have every title to this appellation but an exemption from prejudice, which, however, in my opinion, ought to be regarded as the characteristical mark of a gentleman; for let a man's birth be ever so high, his station ever so exalted, or his fortune ever so large, yet if he is not free from national and other prejudices, I should make bold to tell him, that he had a low and vulgar mind, and had no just claim to the character of a gentleman. And, in fact, you will always find that those are most apt to boast of national merit, who have little or no merit of their own to depend on; than which, to be sure, nothing is more natural; the slender vine twists around the sturdy oak, for no other reason in the world but because it has not strength sufficient to support itself.

inveterate /ɪn ˈvetə rɪt/ *adj.* firmly established over a long period; of long standing; deep-rooted
forfeit /ˈfɔːfit/ *v.* to lose or be deprived of for some crime, fault, etc.
reckoning /ˈrekənɪŋ/ *n.* bill in the public house
prepossess /ˌpriːpəˈzes/ *v.* a. to occupy beforehand b. to prejudice or bias, esp. favorably —prepossession. *n.*
comprehend /ˌkɒmprɪˈhend/ *v.* a. to grasp mentally; understand b. to include; comprise
station /ˈsteɪʃən/ *n.* social standing, position, or rank
exalt /ɪgˈzɔːlt/ *v.* to raise in status, dignity, power, honor, wealth, etc.
sturdy /ˈstɜːdi/ *adj.* physically strong; vigorous; hardy

Should it be alleged in defence of national prejudice, that it is the natural and necessary growth of love to our country, and that therefore the former cannot be destroyed without hurting the latter, I answer that this is a gross fallacy and delusion. That it is the growth of love to our country, I will allow; but that it is the natural and necessary growth of it, I absolutelydeny. Superstition and enthusiasm, too, are the growth of religion; but who ever took it in his head to affirm, that they are the necessary growth of this noble principle? They are, if you will, the bastard sprouts of this heavenly plant, but not its natural and genuine branches, and may safely enough be lopped off, without doing any harm to the parent stock; nay, perhaps, till once they are lopped off, this goodly tree can never flourish in perfect health and vigour.

gross /grəus/ *adj.* a. big b. total, entire
fallacy /'fæləsi/ *n.* an error in reasoning; defect in argument
enthusiasm /ɪn'θjuːzɪæzəm/ *n.* a. intense interest; zeal; fervor b. (archaic) religious fanaticism
lop off to trim (a tree, etc.) by cutting off branches, twigs, or stems
nay /neɪ/ *adv.* no
undaunted /ʌn'dɔːntɪd/ *adj.* not faltering or hesitating because of fear or discouragement; intrepid
resolution /ˌrezə'luːʃən/ *n.* a. a resolute quality of mind b. a formal statement of opinion or determination
poltroon /pɔl'truːn/ *n.* spiritless coward
own /əun/ *v.* a. to possess b. to admit; recognize; acknowledge
viz /vɪz/ *adv.* that is; namely

Is it not very possible that I may love my own country, without hating the natives of other countries? that I may exert the most heroic bravery, the most undaunted resolution, in defending its laws and liberty, without despising all the rest of the world as cowards and poltroons? Most certainly it is; and if it were not—But why need I suppose what is absolutely impossible? —But if it were not, I must own I should prefer the title of the ancient philosopher, viz, a citizen of the world, to that of an Englishman, a Frenchman, a European, or to any other appellation whatever.

Cultural Notes

Oliver Goldsmith (1728—1774) was an Anglo-Irish writer, poet, and physician known for his novel *The Vicar of Wakefield* (1766), his pastoral poem "The Deserted Village" (1770), and his plays *The Good-natur'd Man* (1768) and *She Stoops to Conquer* (1771). He belonged to the circle of Samuel Johnson, Edmund Burke, Joshua Reynolds, and was one of "The Club." His carelessness, intemperance, and habit of gambling constantly brought him into debt. Broken in health and mind, he died in 1774.

Comprehension Exercises

I. Please answer the following questions according to the text you have just read.

1. What does Goldsmith want to express most in the text?
2. How does Goldsmith define English nationality?
3. What is Goldsmith's standard for a real gentleman?
4. How does Goldsmith define the relationship between religion and superstition?
5. How did the English gentleman think of the Spaniard?

II. Are the following judgments correct according to the text? Write "T" if the judgment is correct, or "F" if the judgment is wrong.

1. Goldsmith does not love England.
2. Goldsmith loves drinking and constantly goes to the taverns.
3. Goldsmith compares religion to a heavenly plant.
4. Goldsmith would rather be called a citizen of the world than an Englishman.
5. Goldsmith was very disputatious.
6. The English gentlemen were prejudiced against almost all the European nations other than the English.

III. Please paraphrase the following sentences:

1. In one of these my late rambles I accidentally fell into a company of half a dozen gentlemen, who were engaged in a warm dispute about some political affair, the decision of which, as they were equally divided in their sentiments, they thought proper to refer to me, which naturally drew me in for a share of the conversation.
2. Finding that by this modest declaration of my sentiments I had forfeited the good opinion of my companions, and given them occasion to call my political principles in question, and well knowing that it was in vain to argue with men who were so very full of themselves, I threw down my reckoning and retired to my own lodgings, reflecting on the absurd and ridiculous nature of national prejudice and prepossession.
3. How few are there to be found in modern times who can say the same, or whose conduct is consistent with such a profession!
4. Did these prejudices prevail only among the meanest and lowest of the people, perhaps they might be excused, as they have few, if any, opportunities of correcting them by reading, traveling, or conversing with foreigners.

5. Should it be alleged in defence of national prejudice, that it is the natural and necessary growth of love to our country, and that therefore the former cannot be destroyed without hurting the latter, I answer that this is a gross fallacy and delusion. That it is the growth of love to our country, I will allow; but that it is the natural and necessary growth of it, I absolutely deny.

IV. Please translate the following sentences into Chinese:

1. As I am one of that sauntering tribe of mortals who spends the greatest part of their time in taverns, coffeehouses, and other places of public resort, I have thereby an opportunity of observing an infinite variety of characters, which to a person of a contemplative turn is a much higher entertainment than a view of all the curiosities of art or nature.
2. This very learned and judicious remark was received with a general smile of approbation by all the company—all, I mean, but your humble servant, who, endeavouring to keep my gravity as well as I could, and reclining my head upon my arm, continued for some time in a posture of affected thoughtfulness, as if I had been musing on something else, and did not seem to attend to the subject of conversation; hoping by this to avoid the disagreeable necessity of explaining myself, and thereby depriving the gentleman of his imaginary happiness.
3. Not satisfied that his opinion should pass without contradiction, he was determined to have it ratified by the suffrage of every one in the company; for which purpose, addressing himself to me with an air of inexpressible confidence, he asked me if I was not of the same way of thinking.
4. I could easily perceive, that all the company began to regard me with a jealous eye before I had finished my answer, which I had no sooner done, than the patriotic gentleman observed, with a contemptuous sneer, that he was greatly surprised how some people could have the conscience to live in a country which they did not love, and to enjoy the protection of a government to which in their hearts they were inveterate enemies.
5. Among all the famous sayings of antiquity, there is none that does greater honour to the author, or affords greater pleasure to the reader, (at least if he be a person of a generous and benevolent heart) than that of the philosopher who, being asked what countryman he was, replied, that he was "a citizen of the world".

V. How would you respond to each of the following statements?

1. The Germans are hardy and patient of labour and fatigue.
2. We are so much the natives of one particular spot, or members of one party society, that we no longer consider ourselves as the general inhabitants of the globe, or members of that grand society which comprehends the whole human kind.
3. If one is not free from national and other prejudices, he has a low and vulgar mind, and has no just claim to the character of a gentleman.
4. It is possible that one may love his own country, without hating the natives of other countries.

VI. Please provide a text, which might support your view on one of the statements in *Exercise V*.

Text B

Shall We Choose Death?

*Bertrand Russell**

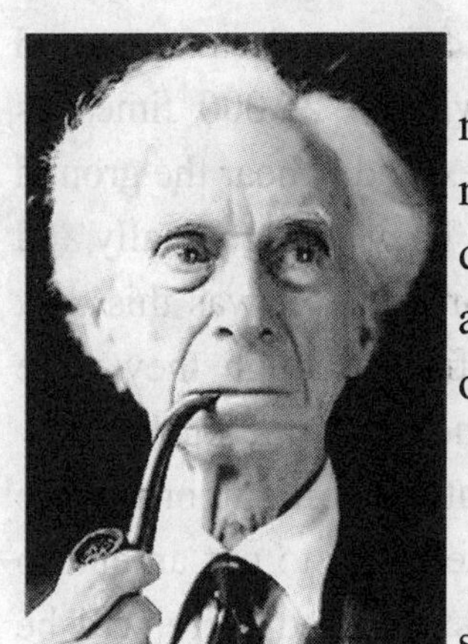

I am speaking not as a Briton, not as a European, not as a member of a western democracy, but as a human being, a member of the species Man, whose continued existence is in doubt. The world is full of conflicts: Jews and Arabs; Indians and Pakistanis; white men and Negroes in Africa; and, overshadowing all minor conflicts, the titanic struggle between communism and anticommunism.

Almost everybody who is politically conscious has strong feelings about one or more of these issues; but I want you, if you can, to set aside such feelings for the moment and consider yourself only as a member of a biological species which has had a remarkable history and whose disappearance none of us can desire. I shall try to say no single word which should appeal to one group rather than to another. All, equally, are in peril, and, if the peril is understood, there is hope that they may collectively avert it. We have to learn to think in a new way. We have to learn to ask ourselves not what steps can be taken to give military victory to

titanic /taɪ'tænɪk/ *adj.* very big, strong, impressive

peril /'perɪl/ *n.* great danger, esp. of being harmed or killed

avert /ə'vɜːt/ *v.* to prevent sth. unpleasant from happening

whatever group we prefer, for there no longer are such steps. The question we have to ask ourselves is: What steps can be taken to prevent a military contest of which the issue must be disastrous to all sides?

The general public, and even many men in positions of authority, have not realized what would be involved in a war with hydrogen bombs. The general public still thinks in terms of the obliteration of cities. It is understood that the new bombs are more powerful than the old and that, while one atomic bomb could obliterate Hiroshima, one hydrogen bomb could obliterate the largest cities such as London, New York, and Moscow. No doubt in a hydrogen-bomb war great cities would be obliterated. But this is one of the minor disasters that would have to be faced. If everybody in London, New York, and Moscow were exterminated, the world might, in the course of a few centuries, recover from the blow. But we now know, especially since the Bikini* test, that hydrogen bombs can gradually spread destruction over a much wider area than had been supposed. It is stated on very good authority that a bomb can now be manufactured which will be 25,000 times as powerful as that which destroyed Hiroshima. Such a bomb, if exploded near the ground or under water, sends radioactive particles into the upper air. They sink gradually and reach the surface of the earth in the form of a deadly dust or rain. It was this dust which infected the Japanese fishermen and their catch of fish although they were outside what American experts believed to be the danger zone. No one knows how widely such lethal radioactive particles might be diffused, but the best authorities are unanimous in saying that a war with hydrogen bombs is quite likely to put an end to the human race. It is feared that if many hydrogen bombs are used there will be universal death—sudden only for a fortunate minority, but for the majority a slow torture of disease and disintegration.

Here, then, is the problem which I present to you, stark and dreadful and inescapable: Shall we put an end to the human race or shall mankind renounce war? People will not face this alternative because it is so difficult to abolish war. The abolition of war will demand distasteful limitations of national sovereignty. But what

issue /'ɪsjuː/ *n.* a subject or problem that is often discussed or argued about, esp. a social or political matter that affects the interests of a lot of people

hydrogen /'haidrəudʒən/ *n.* a colorless gas that is the lightest of all gases

obliterate /ə'blɪtəreɪt/ *v.* to destroy sth. completely so that nothing remains —obliteration *n.*

exterminate /ɪk'stɜːmɪneɪt/ *v.* to kill large numbers of people or animals of a particular type so that they no longer exist.

infect /ɪn'fekt/ *v.* to give someone a disease

lethal /'liːθəl/ *adj.* causing death, or able to cause death

diffuse /dɪ'fjuːz/ *v.* to make heat, light, liquid etc. spread through sth. or to spread like this

unanimous /juˈnænɪməs/ *adj.* a. (of people) all agreeing b. (of agreements) supported by everyone in the same way

stark /stɑːk/ *adj.* very plain in appearance; unpleasantly clear and impossible to avoid

renounce /rɪ'naʊns/ *v.* to publicly say or show that you give up or reject sth.

perhaps impedes understanding of the situation more than anything else is that the term "mankind" feels vague and abstract. People scarcely realize in imagination that the danger is to themselves and their children and their grandchildren, and not only to a dimly apprehended humanity. And so they hope that perhaps war may be allowed to continue provided modern weapons are prohibited. I am afraid this hope is illusory. Whatever agreements not to use hydrogen bombs had been reached in time of peace, they would no longer be considered binding in time of war, and both sides would set to work to manufacture hydrogen bombs as soon as war broke out, for if one side manufactured the bombs and the other did not, the side that manufactured them would inevitably be victorious.

impede /ɪm'piːd/ *v.* to make it difficult for someone or sth. to move forward or make progress
apprehend /ˌæpri'hend/ *v.* to understand sth.
illusory /ɪ'luːsərɪ/ *adj.* false but seeming to be real or true
binding /'baɪndɪŋ/ *adj.* imposing or commanding adherence to a commitment, an obligation, or a duty
reckon /'rekən/ *v.* to calculate an amount
utterly /'ʌtəlɪ/ *adv.* completely
cosmos /'kɒzmɒs/ *n.* the whole universe
wax /wæks/ *v.* to grow bigger
wane /weɪn/ *v.* to grow smaller or less after being full or complete
unveil /ʌn'veɪl/ *v.* to remove a veil or covering from; to reveal
sublimity /sə'blimiti/ *n.* the state or quality of being noble, majestic, exalted, etc.
trivial /'trɪviəl/ *adj.* not serious, important, or valuable
destitute /'destɪtjuːt/ *adj.* having no money, no food, no home etc.; to be completely without sth.
dictate /dɪk'teɪt/ *n.* an order, rule, or principle that you have to obey
perish /'perɪʃ/ *v.* to die, esp. in a terrible or sudden way
reflect /rɪ'flekt/ *v.* to think carefully about sth., or to say sth. that you have been thinking about
immeasurable /ɪ'meʒərəbəl/ *adj.* used to emphasize that sth. is too big or too extreme to be measured —immeasurably *adv.*

As geological time is reckoned, Man has so far existed only for a very short period one million years at the most. What he has achieved, especially during the last 6,000 years, is something utterly new in the history of the Cosmos, so far at least as we are acquainted with it. For countless ages the sun rose and set, the moon waxed and waned, the stars shone in the night, but it was only with the coming of Man that these things were understood. In the great world of astronomy and in the little world of the atom, Man has unveiled secrets which might have been thought undiscoverable. In art and literature and religion, some men have shown a sublimity of feeling which makes the species worth preserving. Is all this to end in trivial horror because so few are able to think of Man rather than of this or that group of men? Is our race so destitute of wisdom, so incapable of impartial love, so blind even to the simplest dictates of self-preservation, that the last proof of its silly cleverness is to be the extermination of all life on our planet?—for it will be not only men who will perish, but also the animals, whom no one can accuse of communism or anticommunism.

I cannot believe that this is to be the end. I would have men forget their quarrels for a moment and reflect that, if they will allow themselves to survive, there is every reason to expect the triumphs of the future to exceed immeasurably the triumphs of the past. There lies before us, if we choose, continual progress in happiness, knowledge, and wisdom. Shall we, instead, choose death, because we cannot forget our quarrels? I appeal, as a human being to human beings: remember your humanity, and forget the rest. If you can do so, the way lies open to a new Paradise; if you cannot, nothing lies before you but universal death.

Cultural Notes

1. **Bertrand Russell** (1872—1970) was a British scholar in almost every field: philosophy, logic, mathematics, science, sociology, education, history, religion, and politics. Yet it was for literature that he won the Nobel Prize in 1950. He was a pacifist, an advocate of social justice, and a proponent of nuclear disarmament. Russell campaigned against World War I. His opposition led him to be sent to prison for six months in 1918. When nuclear weapons were developed he became one of the earliest supporters of CND (the Campaign for Nuclear Disarmament). He established the Bertrand Russell Peace Foundation in 1963. The text is adapted from a speech he made on December 30, 1954.
2. **Bikini** is an island in the Pacific Ocean. After World War II, Bikini, because of its location away from regular air and sea routes, was chosen to be the scene where the US performed nuclear weapons tests from 1946 until the 1960s. On March 1, 1954, the United States tested an H-bomb on Bikini Atoll that unexpectedly turned out to be the largest U.S. nuclear test ever exploded, more than a thousand times bigger than the bomb dropped on Hiroshima. Many nearby landers, exposed to the fallout from the hydrogen bomb test, suffered severe radiation sickness.

Comprehension Exercises

I. Please answer the following questions according to the text you have just read.

1. What are the two alternatives open to the species Man?
2. Why do people hardly realize the perils that have arisen as a result of the development of weapons of mass destruction?
3. What makes the human race worth preserving?
4. Why is it so difficult to abolish war?
5. What actions can avert nuclear danger?

II. Are the following judgments correct according to the text? Write "T" if the judgment is correct, or "F" if the judgment is wrong.

1. The author spoke for his compatriots.
2. Even the average people were fully aware of the danger caused by weapons of mass destruction.
3. Even if an agreement not to use hydrogen bombs had been reached in time of peace, nuclear weapons would still be employed as soon as war broke out.
4. The obliteration of cities is the only disaster that would be caused by a hydrogen-bomb war.
5. The hydrogen-bomb test can cause destruction in the area outside the danger zone.
6. War may be allowed to continue provided modern weapons are prohibited.
7. The elimination of weapons of mass destruction will lead to the abolishment of war.

III. Please paraphrase the following sentences:

1. What perhaps impedes understanding of the situation more than anything else is that the term "mankind" feels vague and abstract.
2. Whatever agreements not to use hydrogen bombs had been reached in time of peace, they would no longer be considered binding in time of war.
3. What he has achieved, especially during the last 6,000 years, is something utterly new in the history of the Cosmos, so far at least as we are acquainted with it.
4. In art and literature and religion, some men have shown a sublimity of feeling which makes the species worth preserving.
5. Is all this to end in trivial horror because so few are able to think of Man rather than of this or that group of men?

IV. Please translate the following sentences into Chinese:

1. I want you, if you can, to set aside such feelings for the moment and consider yourself only as a member of a biological species which has had a remarkable history and whose disappearance none of us can desire.
2. It is feared that if many hydrogen bombs are used there will be universal death—sudden only for a fortunate minority, but for the majority a slow torture of disease and disintegration.
3. People scarcely realize in imagination that the danger is to themselves and their children and their grandchildren, and not only to a dimly apprehended humanity.
4. For countless ages the sun rose and set, the moon waxed and waned, the stars shone in the night, but it was only with the coming of Man that these things

were understood.

5. In the great world of astronomy and in the little world of the atom, Man has unveiled secrets which might have been thought undiscoverable.
6. Is our race so destitute of wisdom, so incapable of impartial love, so blind even to the simplest dictates of self-preservation, that the last proof of its silly cleverness is to be the extermination of all life on our planet?
7. I would have men forget their quarrels for a moment and reflect that, if they will allow themselves to survive, there is every reason to expect the triumphs of the future to exceed immeasurably the triumphs of the past.
8. There lies before us, if we choose, continual progress in happiness, knowledge, and wisdom.
9. I appeal, as a human being to human beings: remember your humanity, and forget the rest. If you can do so, the way lies open to a new Paradise; if you cannot, nothing lies before you but universal death.

V. How would you respond to each of the following statements?

1. We shall choose death if we cannot forget our quarrels.
2. At a time when science plays such a powerful role in the life of society, scientists should be fully conscious of their social responsibility to humanity.
3. Ideological bias should not be an obstacle in the struggle for world peace and security.
4. People in today's world are still in peril, but the peril is radically different and more difficult to confront.
5. Man has unveiled the essence of the universe and humanity so far.
6. It is art, literature and religion which show the sublimity of human beings and make the species worth preserving.
7. So few are able to think of Man rather than of this or that group of men.
8. Our human race is so destitute of wisdom, so incapable of impartial love, so blind even to the simplest dictates of self-preservation that the last proof of its silly cleverness is to be the extermination of all life on our planet.

VI. Please provide a text, which might support your view on one of the statements in *Exercise V*.

Unit Ten

Text A

Daydreams of What You'd Rather Be

*Lance Morrow**

Kierkegaard* once confided to his journal that he would have been much happier if he had become a police spy rather than a philosopher. Richard Nixon* always wanted to be a sportswriter. If one considers these fantasies together, they seem to have got weirdly crossed. It is Nixon who should have been the police spy. On the other hand, Kierkegaard would probably have made an extraordinarily depressing sportswriter *(Fear and Trembling: The Angst of Bucky Dent)*.

We have these half-secret old ambitions—to be something else, to be someone else, to leap out of the interminable self and into another skin, another life. It is usually a brief out-of-body phenomenon, the sort of thing that we think when our gaze drifts away in the middle of a conversation. Goodbye. The imagination floats through a window into the conjectural and finds there a kind of bright blue antiself. The spirit stars itself in a brief hypothesis, an alternative, a private myth. What we imagine at such moments can suggest peculiar truths of character.

One rummages in closets for these revelations. Kierkegaard's fancy about being a police spy is a dark, shiny little item: a melancholic's impulse toward sneaking omnipotence, the intellectual furtively collaborating with state power,

confide /kən'faɪd/ *v.* to impart secrets trustfully

weird /wɪəd/ *adj.* a. involving or suggesting the supernatural; unearthly or uncanny b. fantastic; bizarr —weirdly *adv.*

cross /krɒs/ *v.* a. to mark with a cross b. to lie or pass across; intersect c. to mix

interminable /ɪn'tɜːmɪnəbəl/ *adj.* incapable of being terminated; unending

conjectural /kən'dʒektʃərəl/ *adj.* a. involving conjecture, problematical b. given to making conjectures

hypothesis /hai'pɒθisis/ *n.* a. a proposition set forth as an explanation b. a premise in an argument

rummage /'rʌmɪdʒ/ *v.* to search thoroughly (a place, receptacle, etc.)

melancholic /ˌmelən'kɒlɪk/ *n.* a person disposed to or affected with melancholy

omnipotent /ɒm'nɪpətənt/ *adj.* almighty or infinite in power, as God—omnipotence: the quality or state of being omnipotent

furtive /'fɜːtɪv/ *adj.* taken, done, used, etc. surreptitiously or by stealth —furtively *adv.*

committing sins of betrayal in police stations in the middle of the night. It is not far from another intellectual's fantasy: Norman Mailer* once proposed that Eugene McCarthy*, the dreamboat of the late '60s moderate left, might have made an ideal director of the FBI. McCarthy agreed. But of course, McCarthy had a sardonic genius for doubling back double back his public self and vanish . He did magic tricks of self-annihilation. Nixon's imaginary career—wholesome, all-American, unimpeachable—may suggest both a yearning for blamelessness (what could possibly be tainted in his writing about baseball?) and an oblique, pre-emptive identification with an old enemy: the press.

The daydream of an alternative self is a strange, flittingthing. This wistful speculation often occurs in summer, when a vacation loosens the knot of one's vocational identity. Why, dammit, says the refugee from middle management on his 13th day on the lake, why not just stay here all year? Set up as a fishing guide. Open a lodge. We'll take the savings and ... The soul at odd moments (the third trout, the fourth beer) will make woozy rushes at the pipe dream. Like a gangster who has cooperated with the district attorney, we want a new name and a new career and a new house in a different city—and maybe a new nose from the D.A.'s cosmetic surgeon.

Usually, the impulse passes. The car gets packed and pointed back toward the old reality. The moment dissolves, like one of those instants when one falls irrevocably in love with the face of a stranger through the window as the bus pulls away.

Sometimes, the urge does not vanish. The results are alarming. This month Ferdinand Waldo Demara Jr.* died. That was his final career change. His obituary listed nearly as many metamorphoses as Ovid* did. Demara, "the Great Imposter,"

dreamboat /ˈdriːmbəʊt/ *n.* a. a highly attractive or desirable person b. anything considered as highly desirable of its kind

sardonic /sɑːˈdɒnɪk/ *adj.* characterized by bitter or scornful derision; mocking; cynical; sneering

double back to turn back on a course or reverse direction

vanish /ˈvænɪʃ/ *v.* a. to disappear from sight, esp. quickly; become invisible b. to go away, esp. furtively or mysteriously

yearning /ˈjɜːnɪŋ/ *adj.* deep longing, esp. when accompanied by tenderness or sadness

taint /teɪnt/ *v.* a. to infect, contaminate, corrupt, or spoil b. to tarnish (a person's name, reputation, etc.)

oblique /əˈbliːk/ *adj.* a. indirectly stated or expressed; not straight-forward b. morally or mentally wrong

pre-emptive /priːˈemptive/ *adj.* taken as a measure against sth. possible, anticipated, or feared

flit /flit/ *v.* a. to move lightly and swiftly b. to flutter, as a bird; c. to pass quickly, as time

wistful /ˈwɪstfəl/ *adj.* a. characterized by melancholy; longing; yearning b. pensive, esp. in a melancholy way

speculation /ˌspekjʊˈleɪʃən/ *n.* a. the contemplation b. a single instance or process of consideration

refugee /ˌrefjʊˈdʒiː/ *n.* a person who flees for refuge or safety, esp. to a foreign country

middle management the middle echelon of administration

woozy /ˈwuːzi/ *adj.* stupidly confused; muddled

pipe dream any fantastic notion, hope, or story

gangster /ˈgæŋstə/ *n.* a member of a gang of criminals, esp. a racketeer

district attorney an officer who acts as attorney for the people or government within a specific district

irrevocable /ɪˈrevəkəbəl/ *adj.* unable to be revoked or annulled; unalterable —irrevocably *adv.*

obituary /əˈbɪtʃuəri/ *n.* a notice of the death of a person, often with a biographical sketch, as in a newspaper

imposter /imˈpɔstə/ *n.* also impostor, a person who practices deception under an assumed character, identity, or name

spent years of his life being successfully and utterly someone else: a Trappist monk, a doctor of psychology, a dean of philosophy at a small Pennsylvania college, a law student, a surgeon in the Royal Canadian Navy, a deputy warden at a prison in Texas. Demara took the protean itch and amateur's gusto, old American traits, to new frontiers of pathology and fraud.

Usually, it is only from the safety of retrospect and an established self that we entertain ourselves with visions of an alternative life. The daydreams are an amusement, a release from the monotony of what we are, from the life sentence of the mirror. The imagination's pageant of an alternative self is a kind of vacation one's fate. Kierkegaard did not really mean he should have been a police spy, or Nixon that he should have been a sportswriter. The whole mechanism of daydreams of the antiself usually depends upon the fantasy remaining fantasy. Hell is answered prayers. God help us if we had actually married that girl when we were 21.

In weak, incoherent minds, the yearning antiself rises up and breaks through a wall into actuality. That seems to have happened with John W. Hinkley Jr., the young man who shot Ronald Reagan* last year. Since no strong self disciplined his vagrant aches and needs, it was his antiself that pulled the trigger. It was his nonentity. The antiself is a monster sometimes, a cancer, a gnawing hypothesis.

All of our lives we are accompanied vaguely by the selves we might be. Man is the only creature that can imagine being someone else. The fantasy of being someone else is the basis of sympathy, of humanity. Daydreams of possibility enlarge the mind. They are also haunting. Around every active mind there always hovers an aura of hypothesis and the subjunctive: almost every conscious intellect is continuously wandering elsewhere in time and space.

The past 20 years have stimulated the antiself. They have encouraged the notion of continuous self-renewal—as if the self were destined to be an endless series of selves.

Trappist /'træpist/ *n.* Rom. Cath. Ch. a member of a branch of the Cistercian order, observing the austere reformed rule established at La Trappe in 1664

protean /prəʊ'tiːən/ *adj.* **a.** extremely variable and changeable **b.** (of an actor) versatile; able to play many kinds of roles

gusto /'gʌstəʊ/ *n.* **a.** hearty enjoyment, as in eating or drinking, or in action or speech **b.** individual taste or liking

retrospect /'retrəspekt/ *n.* contemplation of the past; a survey of past time, events, etc.

monotony /mə'nɒtəni/ *n.* wearisome uniformity or lack of variety, as in occupation or scenery

pageant /'pædʒənt/ *n.* a costumed procession

incoherent /ˌɪnkəʊ'hɪərənt/ *adj.* without logical or meaningful connection; disjointed; rambling

discipline /'dɪsɪplɪn/ *v.* **a.** to train by instruction; drill **b.** to bring to a state of order by training and control

vagrant /'veɪgrənt/ wandering or roaming from place to place

nonentity /nɒ'nentɪti/ *n.* **a.** a person or thing of no importance **b.** sth. that does no exist **c.** nonexistence

gnaw /nɒː/ *v.* **a.** to bite or chew on **b.** to waste or wear away **c.** to trouble or torment by constant annoyance

hover /'hɒvə/ *v.* **a.** to hang fluttering or suspended in the air **b.** to keep lingering about

subjunctive /səb'dʒʌŋktɪv/ *n.* the subjunctive mood or mode

Each one would be better than the last, or at least different, which was the point: a miracle of transformations, dreams popping into reality on fast-forward, life as a hectic multiple exposure.

hectic /ˈhektɪk/ *adj.* full of excitement and hurried movement

nimbus /ˈnɪmbəs/ *n.* a cloud, aura, atmosphere, etc., surrounding a person or thing, or a deity when on earth

evanescent /ˌevəˈnesənt/ *adj.* a. vanishing; fading away b. tending to become imperceptible

fervent /ˈfɜːvənt/ *adj.* showing great warmth or intensity of spirit, feeling, enthusiasm, etc.; ardent —fervently *adv.*

coalesce /ˌkəʊəˈles/ *v.* a. to grow together or into one body; b. to blend or come together

duet /djuːˈet/ *n.* a musical composition for two voices or instruments

For some reason, the more frivolous agitations of the collective antiself seem to have calmed down a little. Still, we walk around enveloped in it, like figures in the nimbus of their own ghosts on a television screen. Everything that we are not has a kind of evanescent being within us. We dream, and the dream is much of the definition of the true self. Last week Lena Horne said that she has always imagined herself being a teacher. Norman Vincent Peale says fervently that he wanted to be a salesman—and of course that is, in a sense, what he has always been. Opera singer Grace Bumbry wants to be a professional race-car driver. Bill Veeck, former owner of the Chicago White Sox, confides the alternate Veeck: a newspaperman. In a "nonfiction short story," Truman Capote wrote that he wanted to be a girl. Andy Warhol confesses without hesitation: "I've always wanted to be an airplane. Nothing more, nothing less. Even when I found out that they could crash, I still wanted to be an airplane."

The antiself has a shadowy, ideal life of its own. It is always blessed (the antiself is the Grecian Urn* of our personality) and yet it subtly matures as it runs a course parallel to our actual aging. The Hindu might think that the antiself is a premonition of the soul's next life. Perhaps. But in the last moment of this life, self and antiself may coalesce. It should be their parting duet to mutter together: "On the whole, I'd rather be in Philadelphia."

Cultural Notes

1. **Lance Morrow** (1939—) is a professor of journalism at Boston University. Author of 150 cover stories, including seven "Man of the Year" stories, Morrow has gained distinction as an essayist during his 32 years at *Time* magazine, for which he continues to write essays, book reviews and cover stories. He won the National Magazine Award for Essay and Criticism in 1981 and was a finalist for the same honor in 1991.
2. **Soren Kierkegaard** (1813—1855) was a profound and prolific writer in the

Danish "golden age" of intellectual and artistic activity. His work crosses the boundaries of philosophy, theology, psychology, literary criticism, devotional literature and fiction. As a precursor of modern existentialism, he cultivated paradox and irony throughout his life. His works include *Either/Or* and *Fear and Trembling.*

3. **Richard Nixon** (1913—1994) was the only American President to resign in disgrace. His crime was his involvement in the Watergate break-in at the offices of the Democratic National Committee during the 1972 campaign. Nixon denied any personal involvement, but the courts forced him to yield tape recordings which indicated that he had, in fact, tried to divert the investigation. Faced with what seemed almost certain impeachment, Nixon announced on August 8, 1974, that he would resign the next day to begin "that process of healing which is so desperately needed in America." In his last years, Nixon wrote numerous books on his experiences in public life and on foreign policy, and gained praise as an elder statesman.
4. **Norman Mailer** (1923—2007) was an American writer and innovator of the nonfictional novel. His novel *The Naked and the Dead* (1948), based on his personal experiences during World War II, made him world-famous, and was hailed by many as one of the best American novels to come out of the war years. In the mid 1950s he became famous as an anti-establishment essayist. In pieces such as *The White Negro: Superficial Reflections on the Hipster* (1956) and *Advertisement for Myself* (1959), Mailer examined violence, hysteria, crime, and confusion in American society.
5. **Eugene McCarthy** (1916—2005) entered politics as a Democrat, serving five terms in the US House of Representatives between 1949 and 1959. In 1966, he articulated his opposition to President Johnson's policy in Vietnam. The next year, he became a candidate for the Democratic Presidential nomination, supporting a negotiated peace in Vietnam. With the backing of large numbers of college students, McCarthy achieved great success in the early primaries, contributing to Johnson's decision to withdraw from the Presidential race in 1968. In 1971 McCarthy lost the Democratic nomination to Hubert Humphrey at the Chicago convention, which was the scene of what was later termed a "police riot" by Democratic mayor Richard Daley's law enforcement operations targeting the army of anti-war protesters. During the mêlées between protesters and police, McCarthy worried that Daley might have his children imprisoned, beaten, or murdered. The Chicago convention, in which CBS reporter Dan Rather was punched in the stomach on-camera by a plain-clothes detective, was one of the nadirs of American politics. Attempting

to reenter politics, McCarthy ran independently for President in 1976 and ran in a Senate primary in 1982, but was unsuccessful in both attempts.

6. **Ferdinand Waldo Demara Jr.** (1921—1982) was best known as "the Great Imposter." His career as an imposter spanned three decades and included a bizarre variety of pseudo-identities. Gifted with a sharp intellect and a photographic memory, Demara simply taught himself the techniques necessary for his deception by reading text books. Personal gain did not seem to be a motivation for him. He was an imposter for the sake of being one and described his own motivation as "rascality, pure rascality".
7. **Ovid** (43 BC—17 BC) was a Roman poet, whose narrative skill and unmatched linguistic and metrical virtuosity have made him the most popular of the Roman poets. In his middle period Ovid wrote *The Metamorphoses*, which is based on the transformations recorded in mythology and legend from the creation of the world to the time of Roman emperor Julius Caesar, whose change into a celestial star marks the last of the series.
8. **Ronald Wilson Reagan** (1911—2004) was born in Illinois. A screen test in 1937 won him a contract in Hollywood. During the next two decades he appeared in 53 films. He won the Republican Presidential nomination in 1980. Voters troubled by inflation and by the year-long confinement of Americans in Iran swept the Republican ticket into office. On January 20, 1981, Reagan took office. Two months later he was shot by an assassin, but quickly recovered and returned to duty. His grace and wit during the dangerous incident caused his popularity to soar.
9. **The Grecian Urn** in "Ode on a Grecian Urn" written by John Keats (1795—1821) is symbolic of something, which is both lively and lifeless, both mortal and immortal.

Comprehension Exercises

I. Please answer the following questions according to the text you have just read.

1. What might Kierkegaard have really meant to say when he wrote that he would have been much happier if he had become a police spy?
2. Why does Morrow say that it is Nixon who should have been the police spy? What might be Morrow's tone of voice in saying this?
3. What might be a proper definition of the term "antiself"?
4. What are the values of dreaming of an alternative self?
5. What is the function of the last sentence?

II. Are the following judgments correct according to the text? Write "T" if the judgment is correct, or "F" if the judgment is wrong.

1. This text might be written in 1990s.
2. Kierkegaard had a melancholy personality.
3. Kierkegaard had an unconscious desire for state power.
4. McCarthy had wanted to become the director of FBI.
5. McCarthy deliberately kept a low profile and successfully retreated from politics.
6. Ferdinand Waldo Demara Jr. had many professions throughout his life.
7. John W. Hinckley Jr. shot Ronald Reagon for political reasons.
8. It is normal for almost anyone to have his or her antiself.
9. It is harmful for one to change his career constantly.

III. Please paraphrase the following sentences:

1. On the other hand, Kierkegaard would probably have made an extraordinarily depressing sportswriter (*Fear and Trembling: The Angst of Bucky Dent*).
2. The soul at odd moments (the third trout, the fourth beer) will make woozy rushes at the pipe dream.
3. Demara took the protean itch and amateur's gusto, old American traits, to new frontiers of pathology and fraud.
4. The whole mechanism of daydreams of the antiself usually depends upon the fantasy remaining fantasy.
5. Hell is answered prayers. God help us if we had actually married that girl when we were 21.
6. For some reason, the more frivolous agitations of the collective antiself seem to have calmed down a little.

IV. Please translate the following sentences into Chinese:

1. The spirit stars itself in a brief hypothesis, an alternative, a private myth.
2. One rummages in closets for these revelations.
3. Kierkegaard's fancy about being a police spy is a dark, shiny little item: a melancholic's impulse toward sneaking omnipotence, the intellectual furtively collaborating with state power, committing sins of betrayal in police stations in the middle of the night.
4. Nixon's imaginary career—wholesome, all-American, unimpeachable—may suggest both a yearning for blamelessness (what could possibly be tainted in his writing about baseball?) and an oblique, pre-emptive identification with an old enemy: the press.

5. This wistful speculation often occurs in summer, when a vacation loosens the knot of one's vocational identity.
6. Each one would be better than the last, or at least different, which was the point: a miracle of transformations, dreams popping into reality on fast-forward, life as a hectic multiple exposure.
7. We walk around enveloped in it, like figures in the nimbus of their own ghosts on a television screen. Everything that we are not has a kind of evanescent being within us. We dream, and the dream is much of the definition of the true self.

V. How would you respond to each of the following statements?

1. It is only from the safety of retrospect and an established self that we entertain ourselves with visions of an alternative life.
2. Man is the only creature that can imagine being someone else. The fantasy of being someone else is the basis of sympathy, of humanity. Daydreams of possibility enlarge the mind. Almost every conscious intellect is continuously wandering elsewhere in time and space.
3. The antiself is a premonition of the soul's next life.

VI. Please provide a text, which might support your view on one of the statements in *Exercise V*.

Text B

Culture and Food Habits

*Joan Young Gregg**

All individuals must eat to survive—but what people eat, when they eat, and the manner in which they eat are all patterned by culture. No society views everything in its environment that is edible and might provide nourishment as food: certain edibles are ignored, others are tabooed. These food taboos may be so strong that just the thought of eating forbidden foods can cause an individual to feel ill. A Hindu vegetarian would feel this way about eating any kind of meat, an American about eating dogs, and a Moslem or orthodox Jew about eating pork. The taboo on eating human flesh is probably the most universal of all food taboos. Although some societies in

edible /ˈedɪbəl/ *adj.* able to be eaten safely
taboo /təˈbuː/ *v.* to take as too holy or evil to be touched, named, or used —taboo *n.* a strong social custom forbidding naming, touching or using sth.
vegetarian /ˌvedʒɪˈteəriən/ *n.* a person who does not eat meat or fish
orthodox /ˈɔːθədɒks/ *adj.* holding accepted religious or political opinions

the past practiced ritual cannibalism, members of most modern societies have resorted to cannibalism only under the most desperate of circumstances. The cases of cannibalism by the Donner Pass party* and recently by a South American soccer team* caused a great furor. Human flesh may be a source of protein, but it is not one that most humans are willing to use.

The ways in which human beings obtain their food is one of culture's most fascinating stories. Food getting has gone through several stages of development in the hundreds of thousands of years of humanity's existence on earth. For most of this time on earth, people have supported themselves with the pattern called hunting and gathering. This pattern relies on food that is naturally available in the environment. It includes the hunting of large and small game animals, fishing, and the collecting of various plant foods. It does not include producing food either by planting or by keeping domesticated animals for their milk or meat. Today, only about 30,000 of the world's people live solely by hunting and gathering.

Another ancient pattern of obtaining food is *pastoralism*, which is the raising of domesticated herd animals such as goats, sheep, camels, or cattle, all of which produce both milk and meat. Pastoralism is a specialized adaptation to a harsh or mountainous environment that is not productive enough to support a large human population through agriculture. The major areas of pastoralism are found in East Africa, where cattle are raised; North Africa, where camels are raised; Southwest Asia, where sheep and goats are raised; and the sub-Arctic, where caribou and reindeer are domesticated and herded. Pastoralism a lone cannot support a human population, so additional food grain must either be produced or purchased by trade with other groups.

The third major type of acquiring food is through *agriculture,* or the planting, raising, and harvesting of crops from the land. Agriculture, which

ritual /ˈritʃuəl/ *n.* one or more ceremonies or customary acts often repeated in the same form
cannibalism /ˈkænɪbəlɪzəm/ *n.* practice of eating the flesh of one's own kind
resort to to make use of; turn to (often sth. bad) for help
desperate /ˈdespərɪt/ *adj.* very difficult and dangerous(used of a situation)
furor /ˈfjuərɔː/ *n.* a sudden burst of angry or excited interest among a large group of people
game /geɪm/ *n.* wild animals, birds and fish which are hunted for food and as a sport
domesticate /dəˈmestɪkeɪt/ *v.* to make an animal able to live with people and serve them, esp. on a farm
pastoralism /ˈpɑːstərəlɪzəm/ *n.* the practice of herding as the primary economic activity of a society
caribou /ˈkærɪbuː/ *n.* American reindeer
herd /hɜːd/ *v.* to look after a company of animals feeding or going about together

is only about 10,000 years old, may range from simple, nonmechanized horticulture to farming with the help of animal-drawn plows, to the extensively mechanized agriculture of industrialized nations. Anthropologists generally agree that it was the gradual transition from hunting and gathering to agriculture that opened up new possibilities for cultural development.

horticulture /ˈhɔːtɪkʌltʃə/ *n.* the practice of growing fruit, flowers, and vegetables
anthropology /ˌænθrəˈpɒlədʒi/ *n.* the scientific study of the nature of man, including the development of his body, mind and society —anthropologist: someone who studies anthropology
nurture /ˈnɜːtʃə/ *v.* to care for and encourage the development of something or someone
inhabit /ɪnˈhæbɪt/ *v.* to live in a place
utilize /ˈjuːtɪlaɪz/ *v.* to use sth. in a practical way
millet /ˈmɪlɪt/ *n.* the small seeds of certain grain plants used as food
marginal /ˈmɑːdʒɪnəl/ *adj.* a. not very important or large b. on or in a margin
detrimental /ˌdetrɪˈmentl/ *adj.* having harmful or damaging effects
poverty /ˈpɒvəti/ *n.* the state of being poor
periodic /pɪəriˈɒdɪk/ *adj.* happening occasionally, usu. at regular times
famine /ˈfæmɪn/ *n.* very serious lack of food
bullock /ˈbʊlək/ *n.* a young bull which has had its sex organs removed so that it cannot breed
deprive /dɪˈpraɪv/ *v.* to take sth. away from someone

Cultural patterns of getting food are generated primarily by the natural, or physical, environment of the group. All human groups, like other animal communities, have developed special ways of making their environment nurture and support them. Where several groups share the same environment, they use it in different ways, so they can live harmoniously with each other. In a study of northern Pakistan, for example, Kohistanis, Pathans, and Gujars inhabit the same mountainous area. These three groups are able to coexist peacefully because each utilizes a different aspect of the land. The Pathans are farmers, using the valley regions for raising wheat, corn, and rice. The Kohistanis live in the colder mountainous regions, herding sheep, goats, cattle, and water buffalo and raising millet and corn. The Gujars are full-time herders and use marginal areas not used by the Kohistanis. The Gujars provide milk and meat products to the Pathan farmers and also work as agricultural laborers during the busy seasons. These patterns of specialized and harmonious relationships among different cultures in a local environment are typical of pastoral, or herding, people.

Some food-getting patterns or food habits are not so easy to understand as those described. The origins of many culturally patterned food habits still puzzle anthropologists. Some of these food habits appear on the surface to be irrational and detrimental to the existence of the group. For example, consider the Hindu taboo on eating beef despite the widespread poverty and periodic famine in that country. Yet anthropologist Marvin Harris views this Hindu taboo as an ecological adaptation—that is, as an adjustment to a specific environmental condition. Harris states that cows are important in India not because they can be eaten but because they give birth to bullocks, the essential farming animals that pull plows and carts. If a family were to eat its cows during a famine, it would deprive itself of the source of its bullocks and could not continue farming. Thus the religious taboo on eating beef strengthens the ability of the society to maintain itself in the long run.

It is also possible that there is a biological component to the avoidance of certain foods in specific cultures. The Chinese aversion to milk, for example, may be caused by the fact that lactase, an enzyme that helps digest the sugar lactose in milk, is missing in many Mongoloid* populations. As a result, the milk sugar, lactose, cannot be digested, and drinking milk frequently causes intestinal distress. Evidence to support biological reasons for food taboos is scarce, however, and at this point it seems safest to say that it is primarily culture that tells us which foods are edible and which are not.

in the long run in the course of long experience; in the end
aversion /əˈvɜːʃən/ *n.* a strong dislike for sth.
lactase /ˈlækteis/ *n.* (biochem)乳糖酶
enzyme /ˈenzaɪm/ *n.* 酶
digest /daɪˈdʒest/ *v.* to change food in the stomach into a form that the body can use
lactose /ˈlæktəus/ *n.* 酶
intestinal /ɪnˈtestɪnl/ *adj.* of the intestines, the tube carrying food from your stomach out of your body
distress /dɪˈstres/ *n.* great suffering, pain, or discomfort
scarce /skeəs/ *adj.* hard to find, and often not enough

Cultural Notes

1. **Joan Young Gregg** is teaching at New York Technical College. "Culture and Food Habits" is taken from her book *Communication and Culture—A Reading-Writing Text,* which offers ESL students a fascinating and successful way to strengthen their reading and writing abilities. A variety of absorbing, col lege-level readings give anthropological perspectives on multicultural issues such as family, gender roles, art, economics, time, and food.
2. **Donner Pass party** was a group of American migrants to California in 1846—47. Two families, the Donners and the Reeds, accounted for most of the 87 members of the party, which left Sangamon County, Illinois, in 1846, under the leadership of George Donner. After considerable difficulty crossing the Great Salt Lake in Utah, they were trapped by heavy snows in the Sierra Nevada in November. Forced to camp for the winter at a small lake, now named Donner Lake, they suffered enormous hardships, and members of the group resorted to cannibalism in order to survive. Forty-seven of them were eventually brought to California by rescue parties over what is now known as Donner Pass.
3. **South American soccer team** is another instance of humans driven by starvation to eat the flesh of other humans. It occurred in Chile in 1972, when 16 members of a Uruguayan soccer team survived for 70 days after their airliner crashed in the Andes Mountains.

4. **Mongoloid** is a member of the peoples traditionally classified as the Mongoloid race, marked by yellowish complexion, prominent cheekbones, epicanthic folds about the eyes, and straight black hair, and including the Mongols, Chinese, Koreans, Japanese, Annamcsc, Burmese, and, to some extent, the Eskimos and the American Indians. The word is no longer in technical use.

Comprehension Exercises

I. Please answer the following questions according to the text you have just read.

1. What is food taboo? Which food taboo is most universal in human society?
2. What psychosomatic illness is mentioned in the text?
3. What are the major patterns of getting food mentioned in the text?
4. Where is pastoralism mostly found?
5. What does the example of the Kohistanis, Pathans, and Gujars of the northern Pakistan demonstrate?
6. How does the anthropologist Marvin Harris explain the Hindu taboo on eating beef?
7. Why is it difficult for many societies of Mongoloid origin to digest milk? What effect has this had on their food patterns?
8. What conclusion does the text draw? Are you satisfied with the conclusion? Why?

II. Are the following judgments correct according to the text? Write "T" if the judgment is correct, or "F" if the judgment is wrong.

1. No people now live solely by hunting and gathering.
2. People in some areas still rely solely on pastoralism for a living.
3. The change from hunting/gathering to agriculture is not of great significance.
4. Cultural patterns of getting food are mainly caused by natural environment of the group.
5. Some culturally patterned food habits appear to be unreasonable and harmful to the survival of the group.
6. Many food taboos are for biological reasons.

III. Please paraphrase the following sentences:

1. Although some societies in the past practiced ritual cannibalism, members of most modern societies have resorted to cannibalism only under the most desperate of circumstances.

2. Pastoralism is a specialized adaptation to a harsh or mountainous environment that is not productive enough to support a large human population through agriculture.
3. For example, consider the Hindu taboo on eating beef despite the widespread poverty and periodic famine in that country.
4. If a family were to eat its cows during a famine, it would deprive itself of the source of its bullocks and could not continue farming.
5. These patterns of specialized and harmonious relationships among different cultures in a local environment are typical of pastoral, or herding, people.

IV. Please translate the following sentences into Chinese:

1. No society views everything in its environment that is edible and might provide nourishment as food: certain edibles are ignored, others are tabooed.
2. It does not include producing food either by planting or by keeping domesticated animals for their milk or meat.
3. Anthropologists generally agree that it was the gradual transition from hunting and gathering to agriculture that opened up new possibilities for cultural development.
4. It is also possible that there is a biological component to the avoidance of certain foods in specific cultures.
5. The Chinese aversion to milk, for example, may be caused by the fact that lactase, an enzyme that helps digest the sugar lactose in milk, is missing in many Mongoloid populations.

V. How would you respond to each of the following statements?

1. Food habits vary in different cultures.
2. Most animals do not practice cannibalism.
3. Vegetarianism is wholesome.
4. The Americans don't eat dogs for humanistic reasons.
5. The Chinese don't like drinking milk for biological reasons.
6. Food habits remain a mystery.

VI. Please provide a text, which might support your view on one of the statements in *Exercise V*.

Unit Eleven

Text A

Photographs of My Parents

*Maxine Hong Kingston**

Once in a long while, four times so far for me, my mother brings out the metal tube that holds her medical diploma. On the tube are gold circles crossed with seven red lines each—"joy" ideographs in abstract. There are also little flowers that look like gears for a gold machine. According to the scraps of labels with Chinese and American addresses, stamps, and postmarks, the family airmailed the can from Hong Kong in 1950. It got crushed in the middle, and whoever tried to peel the labels off stopped because the red and gold paint came off too, leaving silver scratches that rust. Somebody tried to pry the end off before discovering that the tube pulls apart. When I open it, the smell of China flies out, a thousand-year-old bat flying heavy-headed out of the Chinese caverns where bats are as white as dust, a smell that comes from long ago, far back in the brain. Crates from Canton, Hong Kong, Singapore, and Chinese Taiwan have that smell too, only stronger because they are more recently come from the Chinese.

Inside the can are three scrolls, one inside another. The largest says that in the twenty-third year of the National Republic*, the To Keung School of Midwifery, where she has had two years of instruction and Hospital Practice, awards its Diploma to my mother, who has shown through oral and written examination her Proficiency in Midwifery, Pediatrics, Gynecology,

ideograph /ˈɪdiəgrɑːf/ *n.* (also ideogram) **a.** a symbol that is used in a writing system, e.g. Chinese, to represent the idea of a thing, rather than the sounds of a word **b.** a sign or a symbol for sth.

gear /gɪə/ *n.* (usu. pl.) machinery in a vehicle that turns engine power (or power on a bicycle) into movement forwards or backwards

scrap /skræp/ *n.* a small piece of sth., esp. paper, fabric, etc.

cavern /ˈkævən/ *n.* a cave, esp. a large one

midwifery /ˈmɪdwaɪfəri/ *n.* the profession and work of a midwife, who is a person, esp. a woman, trained to help women give birth to babies

proficiency /prəˈfɪʃənsi/ *n.* ability to do sth. well because of training and practice

pediatrics /ˌpiːdiˈætrɪks/ *n.* the branch of medicine concerned with children and their diseases

gynecology /gainiˈkɔlədʒi/ *n.* the scientific study and treatment of the medical conditions and diseases of women, esp. those connected with sexual reproduction

"Medicine," "Surgery," Therapeutics, Ophthalmology, Bacteriology, Dermatology, Nursing and Bandage. This document has eight stamps on it: one, the school's English and gy, "Medicine," "Surgery," Therapeutics, Ophthalmology, Bacteriology, Dermatology, Nursing and Bandage. This document has eight stamps on it: one, the school's English and Chinese names embossed together in a circle; one, as the Chinese enumerate, a stork and a big baby in lavender ink; one, the school's Chinese seal; one, an orangish paper stamp pasted in the border design; one, the red seal of Dr. Wu Pak-liang, M.D., Lyon, Berlin, president and "Ex-assistant étranger à la clinique chirugicale et d'accouchement de l'université de Lyon"; one, the red seal of Dean Woo Yin-kam, M.D.; one, my mother's seal, her chop mark larger than the president's and the dean's; and one, the number 1279 on the back. Dean Woo's signature is followed by "(Hackett)". I read in a history book that Hackett Medical College for Women* at Canton was founded in the nineteenth century by European women doctors.

therapeutics /ˌθerəˈpjuːtɪks/ *n.* the branch of medicine concerned with the treatment of diseases

ophthalmology /ˌɒfθælˈmɒlədʒi/ *n.* the scientific study of the eye and its diseases

bacteriology /bækˌtɪəriˈɒlədʒi/ *n.* the scientific study of bacteria

dermatology /ˌdɜːməˈtɒlədʒi/ *n.* the scientific study of skin diseases

emboss /ɪmˈbɒs/ *v.* to put a raised design or piece of writing on paper, leather, etc.

enumerate /ɪˈnjuːməreɪt/ *v.* to name things on a list one by one

lavender /ˈlævɪndə/ *n.* **a.** a garden plant or bush with bunches of purple flowers with a sweet smell **b.** a pale purple colour

chop /tʃɒp/ *n.* official seal or stamp; trademark

wisp /wɪsp/ *n.* a small, thin piece of hair, grass, etc.

tendril /ˈtendrɪl/ *n.* a thin curling piece of sth. such as hair

posterity /pɒsˈterɪti/ *n.* all the people who will live in the future

snapshot /ˈsnæpʃɒt/ *n.* a short description or a small amount of information that gives you an idea of what sth. is like

bob /bɒb/ *n.* a style of a woman's hair in which it is cut the same length all the way around

The school seal has been pressed over a photograph of my mother at the age of thirty-seven. The diploma gives her age as twenty-seven. She looks younger than I do, her eyebrows are thicker, her lips fuller. Her naturally curly hair is parted on the left, one wavy wisp tendrilling off to the right. She wears a scholar's white gown, and she is not thinking about her appearance. She stares straight ahead as if she could see me and past me to her grandchildren and grandchildren's grandchildren. She has spacy eyes, as all people recently from Asia have. Her eyes do not focus on the camera. My mother is not smiling; Chinese do not smile for photographs. Their faces command relatives in foreign lands—"Send money"—and posterity forever—"Put food in front of this picture." My mother does not understand Chinese-American snapshots. "What are you laughing at?" she asks.

The second scroll is a long narrow photograph of the graduating class with the school officials seated in front. I picked out my mother immediately. Her face is exactly her own, though forty years younger. She is so familiar, I can only tell whether or not she is pretty or happy or smart by comparing her to the other women. For this formal group picture she straightened her hair with oil to make a chinlength bob like the others'. On the other women, strangers, I can recognize a curled lip, a sidelong glance, pinched shoulders. My mother is not soft; the girl with the small nose and dimpled underlip is soft. My mother is not humorous, not like the girl at the end who lifts her mocking chin to pose like Girl Graduate. My mother does not have smiling eyes; the old woman teacher (Dean Woo?) in front crinkles happily, and the one faculty member in the western suit smiles westernly. Most of the graduates are girls whose faces have not yet formed; my mother's face will not change anymore, except to age. She is intelligent, alert, pretty. I can't tell if she's happy.

The graduates seem to have been looking elsewhere when they pinned the rose, zinnia, or chrysanthemum on their precise black dresses. One thin girl wears hers in the middle of her chest. A few have a flower over a left or right nipple. My mother put hers, a chrysanthemum, below her left breast. Chinese dresses at that time were dartless, cut as if women did not have breasts; these younger doctors, unaccustomed to decorations, may have seen their chests as black expanses with no reference points for flowers. Perhaps they couldn't shorten that far gaze that lasts only a few years after a Chinese emigrates. In this picture too my mother's eyes are big with what they held—reaches of oceans beyond China, land beyond oceans. Most emigrants learn the barbarians' directness—how to gather themselves and stare rudely into talking faces as if trying to catch lies. In America my mother has eyes as strong as boulders, never once skittering off a face, but she has not learned to place decorations and phonograph needles, nor has she stopped seeing land on the other side of the oceans. Now her eyes include the relatives in China, as they once included my father smiling and smiling in his many western outfits, a different one for each photograph that he sent from America.

He and his friends took pictures of one another in bathing suits at Coney Island* beach, the salt wind from the Atlantic blowing their hair. He's the one in the middle with his arms about the necks of his buddies. They pose in the cockpit of a biplane, on a motorcycle, and on a lawn beside the "Keep Off the Grass" sign. They are always laughing. My father, white shirt sleeves rolled up, smiles in front of

pinch /pɪntʃ/ *v.* to hold sth. tightly between the thumb and finger or between two things that are pressed together
mocking /ˈmɔkɪŋ/ *adj.* (of behaviour, an expression etc.) showing that you think sb. /sth. is ridiculous
crinkle /ˈkrɪŋkəl/ *v.* to cause to become covered with fine lines by crushing or pressing
dartless /ˈdɑːtlis/ *adj.* (cloth) without a pointed fold that is sewn in a piece of clothing to make it fit better
skitter /ˈskɪtə/ *v.* to run or move very quickly and lightly
outfit /ˈaʊtfit/ *n.* a set of clothes that you wear together, esp. for a particular occasion or purpose
buddy /ˈbʌdi/ *n.* **a.** a friend **b.** a partner
cockpit /ˈkɒkpɪt/ *n.* an enclosed area in a plane, boat or racing car where the pilot or driver sits
biplane /ˈbaɪpleɪn/ *n.* a plane with double wings

a wall of clean laundry. In the spring he wears a new straw hat, cocked at a Fred Astaire* angle. He steps out, dancing down the stairs, one foot forward, one back, a hand in his pocket. He wrote to her about the Americancustom of stomping on straw hats come fall. "If you want to save your hat for next year," he said, "you have to put it away early, or else when you're riding the subway or walking along Fifth Avenue*, any stranger can snatch it off your head and put his foot through it. That's the way they celebrate the change of seasons here." In the winter he wears a gray felt hat with his gray overcoat. He is sitting on a rock in Central Park*. In one snapshot he is not smiling; someone took it when he was studying, blurred in the glare of the desk lamp.

stomp /stɒmp/ *v.* to walk, dance, or move with heavy steps

felt /felt/ *n.* a soft thick fabric made from wool or hair that has been pressed tightly together

blurred /blɜːd/ *adj.* **a.** not clear; without a clear outline or shape **b.** difficult to remember clearly

bang /bæŋ/ *n.* hair cut straight across the forehead

kidnap /ˈkɪdnæp/ *v.* to take sb. away illegally and keep them as a prisoner, esp. in order to get money or sth. else for returning them

There are no snapshots of my mother. In two small portraits, however, there is a black thumbprint on her forehead, as if someone had inked in bangs, as if someone had marked her.

"Mother, did bangs come into fashion after you had the picture taken?" One time she said yes. Another time when I asked, "Why do you have fingerprints on your forehead?" she said, "Your First Uncle did that." I disliked the unsureness in her voice.

The last scroll has columns of Chinese words. The only English is "Department of Health, Canton," imprinted on my mother's face, the same photograph as on the diploma. I keep looking to see whether she was afraid. Year after year my father did not come home or send for her. Their two children had been dead for ten years. If he did not return soon, there would be no more children. ("They were three and two years old, a boy and a girl. They could talk already.") My father did send money regularly, though, and she had nobody to spend it on but herself. She bought good clothes and shoes. Then she decided to use the money for becoming a doctor. She did not leave for Canton immediately after the children died. In China there was time to complete feelings. As my father had done, my mother left the village by ship. There was a sea bird painted on the ship to protect it against shipwreck and winds. She was in luck. The following ship was boarded by river pirates, who kidnapped every passenger, even old ladies. "Sixty dollars for an old lady" was what the bandits used to say. "I sailed alone," she says, "to the capital of the entire province." She took a brown leather suitcase and a seabag stuffed with two quilts.

Cultural Notes

1. **Maxine Hong Kingston** (1940—) is an American Professor Emeritus at the University of California, Berkeley, where she graduated with a BA in English in 1962. She is also a prolific academic and writer. Born as Maxine Ting Ting Hong to a Chinese laundry house owner in Stockton, California, she was the third of eight children, and the first among them born in the United States. Her works often reflect on her cultural heritage and blend fiction with non-fiction. Among her works are *The Woman Warrior* (1976), awarded the National Book Critics Circle Award for Nonfiction, and *China Men* (1980), which was awarded the 1981 National Book Award. She has written one novel, *Tripmaster Monkey*, a story depicting a character based on the mythical Chinese character Sun Wu Kong. Her most recent books are *To Be the Poet* (2002) and *The Fifth Book of Peace* (2003).
2. **The National Republic** refers to the National Republic of China (1912—1949), founded by Sun Yat-sen, the first president.
3. **Aiming** at training the Chinese women to heal their own people, both physically and spiritually, Dr. Mary Hannah Fulton (1854—1927) established the Kwangtung Medical School for Women in Guangzhou in 1899 under the auspices of the Board of Foreign Missions of the Presbyterian Church in the United States (North). With the generosity of Mr. E.A.K. Hackett, an American living in Indiana, the medical school was expanded to be the **Hackett Medical College for Women** in 1905. Together with the establishment of its affiliated institutions, the Hackett Medical College for Women was the first medical college for the training of Chinese women in the field of western medicine. The medical college played an important role in furthering women's causes from the late nineteenth century to the 1940s.
4. **Coney Island** is a peninsula, formerly an island, in southernmost Brooklyn, New York City, USA, with a beach on the Atlantic Ocean. The area was a major resort and site of amusement parks that reached its peak in the early 20th century. It declined in popularity after World War II and endured years of neglect.
5. **Fred Astaire** (1899—1987) was an Academy Award-winning American film and Broadway stage dancer, choreographer, singer and actor. He was named the fifth Greatest Male Star of All Time by the American Film Institute.
6. **Fifth Avenue** is a major thoroughfare in the center of the borough of Manhattan in New York City. Lined with expensive park-view real estate and

historical mansions, it is a symbol of wealthy New York. Between 34th Street and 59th Street, it is also one of the premier shopping streets in the world, on par with Oxford Street in London, the Champs-Élysées in Paris and Via Montenapoleone in Milan.

7. **Central Park** is a large public, urban park in the borough of Manhattan in New York City. With about twenty-five million visitors annually, Central Park is the most visited city park in the United States, and its appearance in many movies and television shows has made it famous. Central Park has been a National Historic Landmark since 1963.

Comprehension Exercises

I. Please answer the following questions according to the text you have just read.

1. What are the meanings the photographs of Kingston's parents might convey?
2. Why does Kingston say that the tube of her parents' photographs as well as crates from Canton, Hong Kong, Singapore, and Chinese Taiwan have the smell of China?
3. Why does Kingston describe her mother's photographs first and in greater detail than those of her father's?
4. Why is there a black thumbprint on the forehead of Kingston's mother in two small portraits of her?
5. What personalities of Kingston's parents can you infer from the article?
6. What is the function of telling the death of the couple's first two children in the last paragraph?

II. Are the following judgments correct according to the text? Write "T" if the judgment is correct, or "F" if the judgment is wrong.

1. This text might be written in 1970s.
2. Kingston's mother was not happy in the photographs.
3. Kingston's mother went to medical school because she has too much money.
4. Kingston's mother got her diploma in 1934.
5. It is rude to stare directly at whom you're talking to in the United States.
6. Chinese people usually require their relatives in foreign lands to send them money.
7. Kingston's father was born in the United States.
8. Kingston is the third child of her parents.
9. Kingston is proud of her parents.
10. People paint a sea bird on the ship to protect it against shipwreck and winds.

III. Please paraphrase the following sentences:

1. On the tube are gold circles crossed with seven red lines each— "joy" ideographs in abstract.
2. When I open it, the smell of China flies out, a thousand-year-old bat flying heavy-headed out of the Chinese caverns where bats are as white as dust, a smell that comes from long ago, far back in the brain.
3. Their faces command relatives in foreign lands—"Send money"—and posterity forever—"Put food in front of this picture."
4. Perhaps they couldn't shorten that far gaze that lasts only a few years after a Chinese emigrates.
5. Now her eyes include the relatives in China, as they once included my father smiling and smiling in his many western outfits, a different one for each photograph that he sent from America.
6. "If you want to save your hat for next year," he said, "you have to put it away early, or else when you're riding the subway or walking along Fifth Avenue, any stranger can snatch it off your head and put his foot through it. That's the way they celebrate the change of seasons here."
7. She did not leave for Canton immediately after the children died. In China there was time to complete feelings.

IV. Please translate the following sentences into Chinese:

1. It got crushed in the middle, and whoever tried to peel the labels off stopped because the red and gold paint came off too, leaving silver scratches that rust.
2. She stares straight ahead as if she could see me and past me to her grandchildren and grandchildren's grandchildren.
3. Most of the graduates are girls whose faces have not yet formed; my mother's face will not change anymore, except to age.
4. Most emigrants learn the barbarians' directness—how to gather themselves and stare rudely into talking faces as if trying to catch lies.
5. In America my mother has eyes as strong as boulders, never once skittering off a face, but she has not learned to place decorations and phonograph needles, nor has she stopped seeing land on the other side of the oceans.
6. He is sitting on a rock in Central Park. In one snapshot he is not smiling; someone took it when he was studying, blurred in the glare of the desk lamp.

V. How would you respond to each of the following statements?

1. Chinese do not smile for photographs.
2. It is usually easier for Chinese Americans to balance Chinese tradition and

American culture.

3. Chinese eyes are big with reaches of oceans beyond China, land beyond oceans.
4. Nostalgia is pleasant.

VI. Please provide a text, which might support your view on one of the statements in *Exercise V*.

Text B

Two Ways to Belong in America

*Bharati Mukherjee**

This is a tale of two sisters from Calcutta, Mira and Bharati, who have lived in the United Sates for some 35 years, but who find themselves on different sides in the current debate over the status of immigrants. I am an American citizen and she is not. I am moved that thousands of long-term residents are finally taking the oath of citizenship. She is not.

Mira arrived in Detroit in 1960 to study child psychology and pre-school education. I followed her a year later to study creative writing at the University of Iowa. When we left India, we were almost identical in appearance and attitude. We dressed alike, in saris ; we expressed identical views on politics, social issues, love, and marriage in the same Calcutta convent-school accent. We would endure our two years in America, secure our degrees, then return to India to marry the grooms of our father's choosing.

Instead, Mira married an Indian student in 1962 who was getting his business administration degree at Wayne State University. They soon acquired the labor certifications necessary for the green card of hassle free residence and employment.

Mira still lives in Detroit, works in the Southfield, Mich., school system, and has become nationally recognized for her contributions in the

debate /dɪ'beɪt/ *n.* an argument or discussion expressing different opinions

identical /aɪ'dentɪkəl/ *adj.* similar in every detail

sari /'sɑːrɪ/ *n.* a long piece of fabric that is wrapped around the body and worn as the main piece of clothing, esp. by East Indian women

hassle /'hæsəl/ *n.* **a.** a difficult argument **b.** a struggle of mind and body

fields of pre-school education and parent-teacher relationships. After 36 years as a legal immigrant in this country, she clings passionately to her Indian citizenship and hopes to go home to India when she retires.

In Iowa City in 1963, I married a fellow student, an American of Canadian parentage. Because of the accident of his North Dakota Birth, I bypassed labor-certification requirements and the race-related "quota" system that favored the applicant's country of origin over his or her merit. I was prepared for (and even welcomed) the emotional strain that came with marrying outside my ethnic community. In 33 years of marriage, we have lived in every part of North America. By choosing a husband who was not my father's selection, I was opting for fluidity, self-invention, blue jeans and T-shirts, and renouncing 3,000 years (at least) of case-observant, "pure culture"* marriage in the Mukherjee family. My books have often been read as unapologetic (and in some quarters overenthusiastic) texts for cultural and psychological "mongrelization." It's a word I celebrate.

Mira and I have stayed sisterly close by phone. In our regular Sunday morning conversations, we are unguardedly affectionate. I am her only blood relative on this continent. We expect to see each other through the looming crises of aging and ill health without being asked. Long before Vice President Gore's "Citizenship U.S.A." drive*, we'd had our polite arguments over the ethics of retaining an over-seas citizenship while expecting the permanent protection and economic benefits that come with living and working in America.

Like well-raised sisters, we never said what was really on our minds, but we probably pitied one another. She, for the lack of structure in my life, the erasure of Indianness, the absence of an unvarying daily core. I, for the narrowness of her perspective, her uninvolvement with the mythic depths or the superficial pop culture of this society. But, now, with the scapegoatings of "aliens" (documented or illegal)

cling /klɪŋ/ *v.* to hold on tightly to sb. or sth.
bypass /ˈbaɪpɑːs/ *v.* to avoid
quota /ˈkwəʊtə/ *n.* **a.** the limited number or amount of people or things that is officially allowed **b.** an amount of sth. that sb. expects or needs to achieve
merit /ˈmerɪt/ *n.* the quality of being good and deserving praise, reward or admiration
ethnic /ˈeθnɪk/ *adj.* of or related to a racial, national, or tribal group
opt /ɒpt/ *v.* to choose to take or not to take a particular course of action
fluidity /fluˈɪdɪti/ *n.* the quality of being likely to change or able to flow freely, as gases and liquids do
renounce /rɪˈnaʊns/ *v.* to give up; say formally that one does not own; say formally that one has no more connection with
case-observant: also observant, acting in accordance with law or custom (esp. religious)
unapologetic /ˈʌnəˌpɒləˈdʒetɪk/ *adj.* not expressing sorrow for some fault or wrong
mongrel /ˈmʌŋgrəl/ *n.* **a.** an animal, esp. a dog, which is of no particular breed **b.** a person of mixed race —mongrelization n
affectionate /əˈfekʃənit/ *adj.* showing caring feelings and love for sb.
ethics /ˈeθɪks/ *n.* a system of moral principles or rules of behaviour
erasure /iˈreiʒə/ *n.* the act of removing or destroying sth.
perspective /pəˈspektɪv/ *n.* a particular attitude towards sth.; a particular way of thinking about things
scapegoat /ˈskeɪpgəʊt/ *n.* someone blamed for sth. bad, though it is not their fault
alien /ˈeɪljən/ *n.* **a.** a person who is not a citizen of the country in which he lives or works **b.** a creature from another world
target /ˈtɑːgɪt/ *v.* to take sb. or sth. as a target

on the increase, and the targeting of long-term legal immigrants like Mira for new scrutiny and new self-consciousness, she and I find ourselves unable to maintain the same polite discretion. We were always unacknowledged adversaries, and we are now, more than ever, sisters.

"I feel used," Mira raged on the phone the other night. "I feel manipulated and discarded. This is such an unfair way to treat a person who was invited to stay and work here because of her talent. My employer went to the I.N.S.* and petitioned for the labor certification. For over 30 years, I've invested my creativity and professional skills into the improvement of *this* country's pre-school system. I've obeyed all the rules, I've paid my taxes, I love my work, I love my students, I love the friends I've made. How dare America now change its rules in midstream? If America wants to make new rules curtailing benefits of legal immigrants, they should apply only to immigrants who arrive after those rules are already in place."

scrutiny /ˈskruːtɪni/ *n.* a careful and thorough examination

discretion /dɪˈskreʃən/ *n.* **a.** the freedom or power to decide what should be done in a particular situation **b.** care in what to say or do in order to keep sth. secret or to avoid causing embarrassment or difficulty

adversary /ˈædvəsəri/ *n.* a person that sb. is opposed to, opponent or enemy

manipulate /məˈnɪpjʊleɪt/ *v.* **a.** to handle or control (esp. a machine), usu. skillfully **b.** to control and influence sb. skillfully, often in an unfair and dishonest manner —manipulative *adj.*

petition /pɪˈtɪʃən/ *v.* to make a formal request to authority

curtail /kɜːˈteɪl/ *v.* to cut short; reduce; limit

subtext /sʌbˈtekst/ *n.* a hidden meaning or reason for doing sth.

advocate /ˈædvəkeɪt/ *n.* a person who supports or speaks in favor of sb. or a pubic plan or action

expatriate /eksˈpætriət/ *n.* a person living in a country that is not his own

courteous /ˈkɜːtiəs/ *adj.* polite, esp. in a way that shows respect

gracious /ˈgreɪʃəs/ *adj.* kind, polite and generous, esp. to sb. of a lower social position

snap /snæp/ *v.* to say quickly, usu. in an annoyed or angry way

hysteria /hɪsˈtɪəriə/ *n.* a state of extreme excitement, fear or anger in which a person, or a group of people, loses control of their emotions and starts to cry, laugh, etc.

To my ears, it sounded like the description of a long-enduring, comfortable yet loveless marriage, without risk or recklessness. Have we the right to demand, and to expect, that we be loved? (That, to me, is the subtext of the arguments by immigration advocates.) My sister is an expatriate , professionally generous and creative, socially courteous and gracious, and that's as far as her Americanization can go. She is here to maintain an identity, not to transform it.

I asked her if she would follow the example of others who have decided to become citizens because of the anti-immigration bills in Congress. And here, she surprised me. "If America wants to play the manipulative game, I'll play it, too," she snapped. "I'll become a U.S. citizen for now, then change back to India when I'm ready to go home. I feel some kind of irrational attachment to India that I don't to America. Until all this hysteria against legal immigrants, I was totally happy. Having my green card meant I could visit any place in the world I wanted to and then come back to a job that's satisfying and that I do very well."

In one family, from two sisters alike as peas in a pod, there could not be a wider divergence of immigrant experience. America spoke to me—I married it—I embraced the demotion from expatriate aristocrat to immigrant nobody, surrendering those thousands of years of "pure culture," the saris, the delightfully accented English. She retained them all. Which of us is the freak?

Mira's voice, I realize, is the voice not just of the immigrant South Asian community but of an immigrant community of the millions who have stayed rooted in one job, one city, one house, one ancestral culture, one cuisine, for the entirety of their productive years. She speaks for greater numbers than I possibly can. Only the fluency of her English and the anger, rather than fear, born of confidence in her education, differentiate her from the seamstresses, the domestics, the technicians, the shop owners, the millions of hard-working but effectively silenced documented immigrants as well as their less fortunate "illegal" brothers and sisters.

pod /pɒd/ *n.* a long narrow seed vessel of various plants, esp. beans and peas
divergence /daɪˈvɜːdʒəns/ *n.* (of opinions, views, etc.) difference
demotion /dɪːˈməʊʃən/ *n.* the act of moving sb. to a lower position or rank, often as a punishment
aristocrat /ˈærɪstəkræt/ *n.* a person born in the highest social class with special titles
freak /friːk/ *n.* a person who is considered to be unusual because of the way they behave, look or think
ancestral *adj.* of an ancestor
cuisine /kwɪˈziːn/ *n.* a. a cooking style b. the food served in a restaurant (usu. an expensive one)
seamstress /ˈsiːmstrɪs/ *n.* a woman whose job is sewing
domestic /dəˈmestɪk/ *n.* a domestic servant, usu. female
referendum /ˌrefəˈrendəm/ *n.* an occasion when all the people of a country can vote on an important issue
betray /bɪˈtreɪ/ *v.* to be disloyal or unfaithful to —betrayal *n.*
elicit /ɪˈlɪsɪt/ *v.* to get, draw out, cause to come out

Nearly 20 years ago, when I was living in my husband's ancestral homeland of Canada, I was always well-employed but never allowed to feel part of the local Quebec or larger Canadian society. Then, through a Green Paper* that invited a national referendum on the unwanted side effects of "nontraditional" immigration, the Government officially turned against its immigrant communities, particularly those from South Asia.

I felt then the same sense of betrayal that Mira feels now. I will never forget the pain of that sudden turning, and the casual racist outbursts the Green Paper elicited. That sense of betrayal had its desired effect and drove me, and thousands like me, from the country.

Mira and I differ, however, in the ways in which we hope to interact with the country that we have chosen to live in. She is happier to live in America as expatriate

Indian than as an immigrant American. I need to feel like a part of the community I have adopted (as I tried to feel in Canada as well.) I need to put roots down, to vote and make the difference that I can. The price that the immigrant willingly pays, and that the exile avoids, is the trauma of self-transformation.

exile /ˈeksaɪl/ *n.* a person who chooses, or is forced to live away from his or her own country

trauma /ˈtrɔːmə/ *n.* **a.** a damage to the mind caused by the body having been wounded, or by a sudden shock or terrible experience **b.** a wound

Cultural Notes

1. **Bharati Mukherjee** (1940—) is an award-winning Indian-born American writer, and is currently a professor in the department of English at the University of California, Berkeley. Born in Calcutta, India, she received her M.F.A. from the Iowa Writers' Workshop in 1963 and her Ph.D. in 1969 from the department of Comparative Literature. Her novels *The Tiger's Daughter* (1972), *Wife* (1975) and *Jasmine* (1989) describe how people strive to understand the idea of an American identity in a world of hybridity and multiplicity. This is particularly evident in her more recent works *The Holder of the World* (1993), *Leave It to Me* (1997) and *Desirable Daughters* (2002) and *The Tree Bride* (2004). Her short story collection *The Middleman and Other Stories* (1988) won the National Book Critics Circle Award.
2. **Pure culture**, a microbiological term, describes "a nourishing medium that promotes the growth of one strong organism." This, of course, is a metaphor for one fully functioning organizational culture that is constantly clarified, nourished, and encouraged so that it can withstand the rigors of its environment.
3. **"Citizenship U.S.A." drive** was launched by **Vice President Gore** in April 1995 for speeding the elimination of the backlog of 600,000 immigrants who had requested naturalization, and promising new applicants naturalization within 90 days.
4. The United States Immigration and Naturalization Service **(I.N.S.)** was a part of the United States Department of Justice and handled legal and illegal immigration and naturalization. It ceased to exist on March 1, 2003, when most of its functions were transferred to three new agencies within the newly-created Department of Homeland Security.
5. **Green Paper**, in Britain and other similar Commonwealth jurisdictions, is a tentative government report of a proposal without any commitment to action;

the first step in changing the law. Green Papers may result in the production of a white paper. A Green Paper in Canada, like a White Paper, is an official document sponsored by the Crown. Many so-called White Papers in Canada have been, in effect, Green Papers, while at least one Green Paper, the one on immigration and population in 1975, was released for public debate after the government had already drafted legislation.

Comprehension Exercises

I. Please answer the following questions according to the text you have just read.

1. How were Mira and Bharati different in the debate over the status of immigrants?
2. What might be a proper definition of the term "mongrelization"?
3. How do you understand the term "pure culture"?
4. Why did Mira complain of feeling used and discarded in the United States?
5. Why does Bharati say that Mira's voice is the voice not just of the immigrant South Asian community but of an immigrant community of the millions?

II. Are the following judgments correct according to the text? Write "T" if the judgment is correct, or "F" if the judgment is wrong.

1. Mira and Bharati shared the same attitude when they arrived in the United States.
2. Bharati became an American citizen automatically after she married an American.
3. Mira resided in the United States legally for 36 years with a green card.
4. Mira and Bharati both married the grooms of their father's choosing.
5. Bharati likes to write books on "mongrelization".
6. Bharati was not satisfied with the immigration policy in Canada 20 years ago.

III. Please paraphrase the following sentences:

1. I am moved that thousands of long-term residents are finally taking the oath of citizenship.
2. Because of the accident of his North Dakota Birth, I bypassed labor-certification requirements and the race-related "quota" system that favored the applicant's country of origin over his or her merit.
3. She, for the lack of structure in my life, the erasure of Indianness, the absence of an unvarying daily core.
4. I, for the narrowness of her perspective, her uninvolvement with the mythic

depths or the superficial pop culture of this society.

5. We were always unacknowledged adversaries, and we are now, more than ever, sisters.
6. I feel some kind of irrational attachment to India that I don't to America.
7. America spoke to me—I married it—I embraced the demotion from expatriate aristocrat to immigrant nobody, surrendering those thousands of years of "pure culture," the saris, the delightfully accented English.

IV. Please translate the following sentences into Chinese:

1. We dressed alike, in saris; we expressed identical views on politics, social issues, love, and marriage in the same Calcutta convent-school accent.
2. By choosing a husband who was not my father's selection, I was opting for fluidity, self-invention, blue jeans and T-shirts, and renouncing 3,000 years (at least) of case-observant, "pure culture" marriage in the Mukherjee family.
3. Long before Vice President Gore's "Citizenship U.S.A." drive, we'd had our polite arguments over the ethics of retaining an over-seas citizenship while expecting the permanent protection and economic benefits that come with living and working in America.
4. But, now, with the scapegoatings of "aliens" (documented or illegal) on the increase, and the targeting of long-term legal immigrants like Mira for new scrutiny and new self-consciousness, she and I find ourselves unable to maintain the same polite discretion.
5. To my ears, it sounded like the description of a long-enduring, comfortable yet loveless marriage, without risk or recklessness.
6. My sister is an expatriate, professionally generous and creative, socially courteous and gracious, and that's as far as her Americanization can go.

V. How would you respond to each of the following statements?

1. There will be possibly an emotional strain that came with marrying outside one's ethnic community.
2. Immigrants are likely to have the feeling of being "aliens" even after they settled abroad for many years.
3. Living abroad, people usually face the choice of whether maintaining an identity of their native country or transforming it into the immigrant one.

VI. Please provide a text, which might support your view on one of the statements in *Exercise V.*

Unit Twelve

Text A

Three Types of Resistance to Oppression

*Martin Luther King, Jr.**

Oppressed people deal with their oppression in three characteristic ways. One way is acquiescence: the oppressed resign themselves to their doom. They tacitly adjust themselves to oppression, and thereby become conditioned to it. In every movement toward freedom some of the oppressed prefer to remain oppressed. Almost 2,800 years ago Moses* set out to lead the children of Israel* from the slavery of Egypt to the freedom of the Promised Land. He soon discovered that slaves do not always welcome their deliverers. They become accustomed to being slaves. They would rather bear those ills they have, as Shakespeare pointed out, than flee to others that they know not of*. They prefer the "fleshpots of Egypt" to the ordeals of emancipation.

There is such a thing as the freedom of exhaustion. Some people are so worn down by the yoke of oppression that they give up. A few years ago in the slum areas of Atlanta*, a Negro guitarist used to sing almost daily: "Been down so long that down don't bother me." This is the type of negative freedom and resignation that often engulfs the life of the oppressed.

But this is not the way out. To accept passively an unjust system is to cooperate with that system; thereby the oppressed become as evil as the oppressor. Non-cooperation with evil

acquiesce /ˌækwiˈes/ *v.* to agree, often unwillingly, without raising an argument; accept quietly —acquiescence /ˌækwiˈesns/ *n.*

resign oneself to to give oneself up; hand oneself over to

tacit /ˈtæsɪt/ *adj.* expressed or understood without being put into words; not spoken or written —tacitly *adv.*

become conditioned to to be trained to behave in a particular way or to become used to a particular situation

deliverer /dɪˈlɪvərə/ *n.* the one who rescues sb. from sth. bad

fleshpot /ˈfleʃpɒt/ *n.* a place supplying food, drink and sexual entertainment

ordeal /ɔːˈdiːl/ *n.* a difficult or unpleasant experience

emancipation /ɪˌmænsɪˈpeɪʃən/ *n.* liberation

yoke /jəʊk/ *n.* **a.** power; control **b.** the position of slavery or of being under the power of someone

slum /slʌm/ *n.* an area of a city that is very poor and where the houses are dirty and in bad condition

engulf /ɪnˈgʌlf/ *v.* **a.** to surround or to cover completely **b.** to affect very strongly

obligation /ˌɒblɪˈgeɪʃən/ *n.* a moral or legal duty

is as much a moral obligation as is cooperation with good. The oppressed must never allow the conscience of the oppressor to slumber. Religion reminds every man that he is his brother's keeper*. To accept injustice or segregation passively is to say to the oppressor that his actions are morally right. It is a way of allowing his conscience to fall asleep. At this moment the oppressed fails to be his brother's keeper. So acquiescence—while often the easier way—is not the moral way. It is the way of the coward. The Negro cannot win the respect of his oppressor by acquiescing; he merely increases the oppressor's arrogance and contempt. Acquiescence is interpreted as proof of the Negro's inferiority. The Negro cannot win the respect of the white people of the South or the peoples of the world if he is willing to sell the future of his children for his personal and immediate comfort and safety.

conscience /ˈkɒnʃəns/ *n.* an inner sense that know the difference between right and wrong, judges one's actions according to moral laws, and makes one feel guilty, good, evil, etc.

slumber /ˈslʌmbə/ *v.* to sleep

segregation /ˌsegrɪˈgeɪʃən/ *n.* the act or policy of separating people of different races, religions or sexes and treating them differently

coward /ˈkaʊəd/ *n.* a person unable to face danger, pain, or hardship; a person who shows fear in a shameful way

arrogance /ˈærəgəns/ *n.* pride and self-importance shown in a rude and disrespectful way

contempt /kənˈtempt/ *n.* a. the feeling that sb. or sth. is of a lower rank and undesirable b. lack of respect or admiration

corrode /kəˈrəud/ *v.* to (cause to) become worn or be destroyed slowly

temporary /ˈtempərəri/ *adj.* lasting or intended to last only for a short time; not permanent

permanent /ˈpɜːmənənt/ *adj.* lasting for a long time or for all time in the future; existing all the time

descending /dɪˈsendɪŋ/ *adj.* tending to come or go down from a higher to a lower level

spiral /ˈspaɪərəl/ *n.* a continuous upward or downward change

humiliate /hjuːˈmɪlieɪt/ *v.* to make sb. feel ashamed or stupid and lose the respect of other people

annihilate /əˈnaɪəleɪt/ *v.* to destroy or defeat sb. completely

convert /kənˈvɜːt/ *v.* to change or make sb. change their religion or beliefs

thrive /θraɪv/ *v.* to become, and continue to be, successful, strong, healthy, etc.

monologue /ˈmɒnəlɒg/ *n.* a long speech in a play by one actor, esp. when alone

brutality /bruːˈtælɪti/ *n.* violence and cruelty

A second way that oppressed people sometimes deal with oppression is to resort to physical violence and corroding hatred. Violence often brings about momentary results. Nations have frequently won their independence in battle. But in spite of temporary victories, violence never brings permanent peace. It solves no social problem; it merely creates new and more complicated ones.

Violence as a way of achieving racial justice is both impractical and immoral. It is impractical because it is a descending spiral ending in destruction for all. The old law of an eye for an eye* leaves everybody blind. It is immoral because it seeks to humiliate the opponent rather than win his understanding; it seeks to annihilate rather than to convert. Violence is immoral because it thrives on hatred rather than love. It destroys community and makes brotherhood impossible. It leaves society in monologue rather than dialogue. Violence ends by defeating itself. It creates bitterness in the survivors and brutality in the destroyers. A voice echoes through time saying to every potential Peter*, "Put up your sword*." History is cluttered with the wreckage of nations that failed to follow this command.

If the American Negro and other victims of oppression succumb to the temptation of using violence in the struggle for freedom, future generations will be the recipients of a desolate night of bitterness, and our chief legacy to them will be an endless reign of meaningless chaos. Violence is not the way.

The third way open to oppressed people in their quest for freedom is the way of nonviolent resistance. Like the synthesis in Hegelian philosophy*, the principle of nonviolent resistance seeks to reconcile the truths of two opposites—acquiescence and violence—while avoiding the extremes and immoralities of both. The nonviolent resister agrees with the person who acquiesces that one should not be physically aggressive toward his opponent; but he balances the equation by agreeing with the person of violence that evil must be resisted. He avoids the nonresistance of the former and the violent resistance of the latter. With nonviolent resistance, no individual or group need submit to any wrong, nor need anyone resort to violence in order to right a wrong.

It seems to me that this is the method that must guide the actions of the Negro in the present crisis in race relations. Through nonviolent resistance the Negro will be able to rise to the noble height of opposing the unjust system while loving the perpetrators of the system. The Negro must work passionately and unrelentingly for full stature as a citizen, but he must not use inferior methods to gain it. He must never come to terms with falsehood, malice, hate, or destruction.

Nonviolent resistance makes it possible for the Negro to remain in the South and struggle for his rights. The Negro's problem will not be solved by running away. He can-

potential /pəˈtenʃəl/ *adj.* existing in possibility; not active or developed at present, but able to become so

clutter /ˈklʌtə/ *v.* to make untidy or confused

wreckage /ˈrekɪdʒ/ *n.* the parts of a vehicle, building, etc. that remain after it has been badly damaged or destroyed

succumb /səˈkʌm/ *v.* to fail to resist an attack, an illness, a temptation, etc.

temptation /tempˈteɪʃən/ *n.* **a.** sth. very attractive **b.** the act of tempting or the state of being tempted

recipient /rɪˈsɪpiənt/ *n.* a person who receives sth.

desolate /ˈdesələt/ *adj.* **a.** (of a place) empty, making one feel sad or frightened **b.** very lonely and unhappy

legacy /ˈlegəsi/ *n.* **a.** money or personal possessions that pass to sb. on the death of the owner **b.** a lasting result

chaos /ˈkeiɒs/ *n.* a state of complete confusion and disorder

synthesis /ˈsɪnθɪsɪs/ *n.* the act of combining separate ideas, beliefs, etc.; a combination of separate ideas, beliefs, etc.

reconcile /ˈrekənsaɪl/ *v.* to make peace between, find agreement between

aggressive /əˈgresɪv/ *adj.* angry, and behaving in a threatening way; ready to attack

equation /ɪˈkweɪʒən/ *n.* **a.** a statement that two quantities are equal **b.** the act or fact of equating

right /raɪt/ *v.* to put sth. right or upright again

perpetrator /ˈpɜːpɪtreɪtə/ *n.* a person who commits a crime or does sth. which is wrong or evil

unrelenting /ˌʌnrɪˈlentɪŋ/ *adj.* continuous, without decreasing in power —unrelentingly *adv*

malice /ˈmælɪs/ *n.* a feeling of hatred for sb. that causes a desire to harm them

not listen to the glib suggestion of those who would urge him to migrate en masse to other sections of the country. By grasping his great opportunity in the South he can make a lasting contribution to the moral strength of the nation and set a sublime example of courage for generations yet unborn.

glib /glɪb/ *adj.* **a.** (of a person) able to speak well and easily, whether speaking the truth or not **b.** spoken too easily to be true

en masse /ɑn'mæs/ (from French) all together, and usu. in large numbers

sublime /sə'blaɪm/ *adj.* very noble or wonderful

enlist /ɪn'lɪst/ *v.* **a.** to (cause to) enter the armed forces **b.** to obtain (help, sympathy, etc.)

banner /'bænə/ *n.* **a.** a flag **b.** a long piece of cloth on which a sign is painted, usu. carried between two poles

By nonviolent resistance, the Negro can also enlist all men of good will in his struggle for equality. The problem is not a purely racial one, with Negroes set against whites. In the end, it is not a struggle between people at all, but a tension between justice and injustice. Nonviolent resistance is not aimed against oppressors but against oppression. Under its banner, consciences, not racial groups, are enlisted.

Cultural Notes

1. **Martin Luther King, Jr.** (1929—1968) was one of the pivotal leaders of the American civil rights movement. As a Baptist minister, he became a civil rights activist early in his career. He led the Montgomery Bus Boycott (1955—1956) and helped found the Southern Christian Leadership Conference (1957), serving as its first president. His efforts led to the 1963 March on Washington, where he delivered his "I Have a Dream" speech. Here he raised public consciousness of the civil rights movement and established himself as one of the greatest orators in U.S. history. In 1964, King became the youngest person to receive the Nobel Peace Prize for his efforts to end segregation and racial discrimination through civil disobedience and other non-violent means. King was assassinated on April 4, 1968, in Memphis, Tennessee, and was posthumously awarded the Presidential Medal of Freedom by President Jimmy Carter in 1977. Martin Luther King Day was established as a national holiday in the United States in 1986. In 2004, King was posthumously awarded a Congressional Gold Medal. "Three Types of Resistance to Oppression" is taken from his book *Stride Toward Freedom* published in 1958.
2. **Moses** was a 13th century BC Biblical Hebrew religious leader, lawgiver, prophet, and military leader, to whom the authorship of *the Torah* is traditionally attributed. According to the book of *Exodus*, Moses was born to a Hebrew mother who hid him when a Pharaoh ordered all newborn Hebrew boys to be killed, and ended up being adopted into the Egyptian royal family. After killing an Egyptian slave master, he fled and became a shepherd, and was

later commanded by God to deliver the Hebrews from slavery. After the Ten Plagues were unleashed on Egypt, he led the Hebrew slaves out of Egypt, through the Red Sea, and they wandered in the desert for 40 years. Despite living to 120, he did not enter the **Promised Land**, as he disobeyed God when God instructed him on how to bring forth water from a rock in the desert. A Hebrew kingdom was established in 1000 BC and later split into the kingdoms of Judah and **Israel.**

3. In Shakespeare's masterpiece *Hamlet*, the hero sighs: "the dread of something after death, the undiscovered country from whose bourn no traveler returns, puzzles the will and makes us rather bear those ills we have than fly to others that we **know not of.**"
4. **Atlanta** is the capital city of the US state of Georgia. During the Civil Rights Movement, Atlanta stood apart from southern cities that supported segregation, touting itself as "The City Too Busy to Hate." The city's progressive civil rights record and existing population of blacks made it increasingly popular as a relocation destination for black Americans. Blacks soon became the dominant social and political force in the city, though today some measure of demographic diversification has taken place.
5. Cain killed his younger brother Abel. When Lord asked him: "Where is Abel thy brother?" He answered: "I know not: Am I my **brother's keeper**?" (Genesis 4:9)
6. The phrase "**an eye for an eye**" is a quotation from *Exodus* 21:23-27 and *Leviticus* 24:20 in which a person who has taken the eye of another in a fight is instructed to give his own eye in compensation. However, in *Matthew* 5:38-39, Jesus says: "You have knowledge that it was said, **an eye for an eye**, and a tooth for a tooth. But I say to you, do not make use of force against an evil man." When people came to arrest him, he orders his disciple not to fight: "**Put up again thy sword** into his place: for all they that take the sword shall perish with the sword" (Matthew 26:52), and tells Simon **Peter: "Put up thy sword** into the sheath" (John 18:10-11).
7. **Hegelian philosophy**, also called Hegelianism, is a philosophy developed by Georg Wilhelm Friedrich Hegel which can be summed up by a favorite motto by Hegel, "the rational alone is real," which means that all reality is capable of being expressed in rational categories. His goal was to reduce reality to a more synthetic unity within the system of transcendental idealism.

Comprehension Exercises

I. Please answer the following questions according to the text you have just read.

1. What are the three characteristic ways King says that oppressed people usually use in dealing with their oppression?
2. What is King's purpose by mentioning the story of Moses 2,800 years ago?
3. What might be the meaning of "fleshpots of Egypt"?
4. Why is acquiescence not the way out according to King?
5. What does King want to say by mentioning Peter?
6. What is the definition of the "nonviolent resistance"?

II. Are the following judgments correct according to the text? Write "T" if the judgment is correct, or "F" if the judgment is wrong.

1. Slaves do not welcome freedom because they have to pay in order to gain it.
2. Acquiescence is a way of the coward.
3. Violence will never win because it destroys community and makes brotherhood impossible.
4. As a Negro, King understands both the Negro and the American whites.
5. The Negro can be given civil rights only when they work passionately and unrelentingly for full stature as a citizen.
6. It is unwise for the Negro to migrate en masse to other sections from the South.
7. The Negro's gain of civil rights means that justice comes back in America.

III. Please paraphrase the following sentences:

1. They would rather bear those ills they have, as Shakespeare pointed out, than flee to others that they know not of.
2. This is the type of negative freedom and resignation that often engulfs the life of the oppressed.
3. To accept injustice or segregation passively is to say to the oppressor that his actions are morally right.
4. The Negro cannot win the respect of his oppressor by acquiescing; he merely increases the oppressor's arrogance and contempt.
5. Violence as a way of achieving racial justice is both impractical and immoral.
6. Through nonviolent resistance the Negro will be able to rise to the noble height of opposing the unjust system while loving the perpetrators of the system.

7. By grasping his great opportunity in the South he can make a lasting contribution to the moral strength of the nation and set a sublime example of courage for generations yet unborn.
8. By nonviolent resistance, the Negro can also enlist all men of good will in his struggle for equality.

IV. Please translate the following sentences into Chinese:

1. In every movement toward freedom some of the oppressed prefer to remain oppressed.
2. To accept passively an unjust system is to cooperate with that system; thereby the oppressed become as evil as the oppressor.
3. Non-cooperation with evil is as much a moral obligation as is cooperation with good.
4. The Negro cannot win the respect of the white people of the South or the peoples of the world if he is willing to sell the future of his children for his personal and immediate comfort and safety.
5. It is immoral because it seeks to humiliate the opponent rather than win his understanding; it seeks to annihilate rather than to convert.
6. If the American Negro and other victims of oppression succumb to the temptation of using violence in the struggle for freedom, future generations will be the recipients of a desolate night of bitterness, and our chief legacy to them will be an endless reign of meaningless chaos.
7. With nonviolent resistance, no individual or group need submit to any wrong, nor need anyone resort to violence in order to right a wrong.
8. Nonviolent resistance is not aimed against oppressors but against oppression.

V. How would you respond to each of the following statements?

1. In spite of temporary victories, violence never brings permanent peace. It solves no social problem; it merely creates new and more complicated ones.
2. The old law of an eye for an eye leaves everybody blind.
3. Nonviolent resistance is not a struggle between people at all, but a tension between justice and injustice. Under this banner, in the end, conscience, not racial groups, are enlisted.

VI. Please provide a text, which might support your view on one of the statements in *Exercise V.*

Text B

Loneliness... An American Malady

*Carson McCullers**

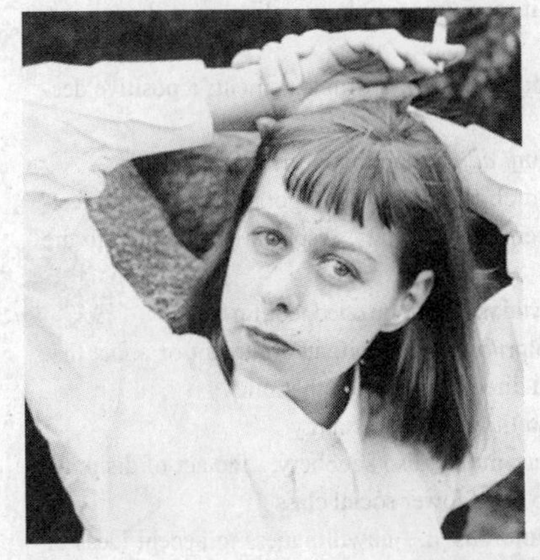

This city, New York—consider the people in it, the eight million of us. An English friend of mine, when asked why he lives in New York City, said that he liked it here because he could be so alone. While it was my friend's desire to be alone, the aloneness of many Americans who live in cities is an involuntary and fearful thing. It has been said that loneliness is the great American malady. What is the nature of this loneliness? It would seem essentially to be a quest for identity.

To the spectator, the amateur philosopher, no motive among the complex ricochets of our desires and rejections seems stronger or more enduring than the will of the individual to claim his identity and belong. From infancy to death, the human being is obsessed by these dual motives. During our first weeks of life, the question of identity shares urgency with the need for milk. The baby reaches for his toes, then explores the bars of his crib; again and again he compares the difference between his own body and the objects around him, and in the wavering, infant eyes there comes a pristine wonder.

Consciousness of self is the first abstract problem that the human being solves. Indeed, it is this self-consciousness that removes us from lower animals. This primitive grasp of identity develops with constantly shifting emphasis through all our years. Perhaps maturity is simply the history of those mutations that reveal to the individual the relation between himself and the world in which he finds himself.

After the first establishment of identity

involuntary /ɪn'vɒləntəri/ *adj.* happening without you wanting it to

malady /'mælədi/ *n.* **a.** sth. that is wrong with a system or organization **b.** an illness

quest /kwest/ *n.* a long search for sth.

identity /aɪ'dentɪti/ *n.* **a.** who somebody is or what sth. is **b.** the characteristics, feelings or beliefs that distinguish people from others

amateur /'æmətɜː/ *adj.* doing sth. for enjoyment or interest, not as a job

ricochet /'rɪkəʃeɪ/ *n.* the act of a moving object hitting a surface and come off it fast at a different angle

obsess /əb'ses/ *v.* **a.** to fill someone's mind continuously **b.** to worry continuously and unnecessarily

waver /'weɪvə/ *v.* to hesitate and be unable to make a decision or choice

pristine /'prɪstiːn / *adj.* **a.** fresh and clean, as if new **b.** not developed or changed in any way; left in its original condition

mutation /mjuː'teiʃən/ *n.* **a.** a process in which the genetic material of a person, a plant or an animal changes in structure when it is passed on to children, etc., causing different physical characteristics to develop; a change of this kind **b.** a change in the form or structure of sth.

there comes the imperative need to lose this new-found sense of separateness and to belong to something larger and more powerful than the weak, lonely self. The sense of moral isolation is intolerable to us.

In *The Member of the Wedding* the lonely 12-year-old girl, Frankie Addams, articulates this universal need: "The trouble with me is that for a long time I have just been an *I* person. All people belong to a *We* except me. Not to belong to a *We* makes you too lonesome."

Love is the bridge that leads from the *I* sense to the *We*, and there is a paradox about personal love. Love of another individual opens a new relation between the personality and the world. The lover responds in a new way to nature and may even write poetry. Love is affirmation; it motivates the yes responses and the sense of wider communication. Love casts out fear, and in the security of this togetherness we find contentment, courage. We no longer fear the age-old haunting questions: "Who am I?" "Why am I?" "Where am I?"—and having cast out fear, we can be honest and charitable.

imperative /ɪm'perətɪv/ *adj.* a. very important and needing immediate attention or action b. expressing authority

isolation /ˌaɪsə'leɪʃən/ *n.* a. the act of separating somebody or sth.; the state of being separate b. the state of being alone or lonely

articulate /ɑː'tɪkjʊlɪt/ *v.* to express or explain thoughts or feelings clearly

paradox /'pærədɒks/ *n.* a statement containing two opposite ideas that make it seem impossible or unlikely, although it is probably true

affirmation /əfɔː'meiʃən/ *n.* a firm statement; a positive declaration

haunting /'hɔːntɪŋ/ *adj.* remaining in the thoughts

charitable /'tʃærɪtəbəl/ *adj.* a. full of goodness and kind feelings towards others b. generous, esp. in giving help to the poor

bewildered /bɪ'wɪldərɪŋ/ *adj.* puzzled, confused

corollary /kə'rɒləri/ *n.* a situation, an argument or a fact that is the natural and direct result of another one

incertitude /in'səːtitjuːd/ *n.* uncertainty

snobbism /'snɒbɪzəm/ *n.* also snobbery, the act of disliking those one feels to be of lower social class

intolerance /ɪn'tɒlərəns/ *n.* unwillingness to accept ideas or ways of behaving that are different from one's own

xenophobia /ˌzenə'fəubiə/ *adj.* (disapproving) a strong feeling of dislike or fear of people from other countries —xenophobic *adj.*

For fear is a primary source of evil. And when the question "Who am I?" recurs and is unanswered, then fear and frustration project a negative attitude. The bewildered soul can answer only: "Since I do not understand 'Who I am,' I only know what I am *not*." The corollary of this emotional incertitude is snobbism, intolerance, and racial hate. The xenophobic individual can only reject and destroy, as the xenophobic nation inevitably makes war.

The loneliness of Americans does not have its source in xenophobia; as a nation we are an outgoing people, reaching always for immediate contacts, further experience. But we tend to seek out things as individuals, alone. The European, secure in his family ties and rigid class loyalties, knows little of the moral loneliness that is native to us Americans. While the European artists tend to form groups or aesthetic schools, the

American artist is the eternal maverick—not only from society in the way of all creative minds, but within the orbit of his own art.

Thoreau took to the woods to seek the ultimate meaning of his life. His creed was simplicity and his *modus vivendi* the deliberate stripping of external life to the Spartan necessities in order that his inward life could freely flourish. His objective, as he put it, was to back the world into a corner. And in that way did he discover "What a man thinks of himself, that it is which determines, or rather indicates, his fate."

maverick /ˈmævərɪk/ *n.* a person who does not behave or think like everyone else, but h independent, unusual opinions
ultimate /ˈʌltɪmɪt/ *adj.* a. basic b. most extreme; best, worst, greatest, most important, etc.
creed /kriːd/ *n.* a set of principles or religious beliefs
modus vivendi /ˈməudəs vivendai/ (from Latin, formal) an arrangement made between people, institutions or countries who have very different opinions or ideas, so that they can live or work together without quarrelling
deliberate /dɪˈlɪbərɪt/ *adj.* done on purpose rather than by accident
spartan /ˈspɑːtn/ *adj.* (of conditions) simple or harsh; lacking anything that makes life easier or more pleasant. From Sparta, a powerful city in ancient Greece, where the people were not interested in comfort or luxury
objective /əbˈdʒektɪv/ *n.* sth. that people are trying to achieve
frenetic /frɪˈnetɪk/ *adj.* involving a lot of energy and activity in a way that is not organized
pastoral /ˈpɑːstərəl/ *adj.* a. showing country life, esp. in a romantic way b. relating to the farming of animals
labyrinthine /ˌlæbəˈrɪnθaɪn/ *adj.* like a complicated series of paths, which it is difficult to find way through

On the other hand, Thomas Wolfe* turned to the city, and in his wanderings around New York he continued his frenetic and lifelong search for the lost brother, the magic door. He too backed the world into a corner, and as he passed among the city's millions, returning their stares, he experienced "That silent meeting [that] is the summary of all the meetings of men's lives."

Whether in the pastoral joys of country life or in the labyrinthine city, we Americans are always seeking. We wander, question. But the answer waits in each separate heart—the answer of our own identity and the way by which we can master loneliness and feel that at last we belong.

Cultural Notes

1. **Carson McCullers** (1917—1967) was considered to be among the most significant American writers of the twentieth century. She is best known for her novels *The Heart Is a Lonely Hunter* (1940), *Reflections in a Golden Eye* (1941), *The Member of the Wedding* (1946), and *The Ballad of the Sad Café* (1951).
2. **Thomas Wolfe** (1900—1938) was one of the great American novelists of the twentieth century. His opulent language and unique literary style as seen

in his autobiographical novels such as *Look Homeward, Angel* (1929), and *Of Time and the River* (1935) have elevated his life to legendary status.

Comprehension Exercises

I. Please answer the following questions according to the text you have just read.

1. What might McCullers have really meant by saying that loneliness is the great American malady?
2. What is the nature of the loneliness in New York City for McCullers?
3. How does an infant claim his identity according to McCullers?
4. What might be a proper definition of the term "moral isolation"?
5. Why does McCullers say that fear is a primary source of evil?
6. Why do American and European artists behave differently?
7. What is the function of quoting Thoreau and Wolfe?

II. Are the following judgments correct according to the text? Write "T" if the judgment is correct, or "F" if the judgment is wrong.

1. McCullers lives in New York City.
2. People go to New York for its loneliness.
3. Infant comes to know himself by exploring the bars of his crib.
4. Love makes people write poetry.
5. The loneliness of Americans comes from their intention of seeking out things as individuals.
6. Knowing "Who I am" helps people to be a better person.
7. Both Thoreau and Wolfe have found the meaning of loneliness.
8. McCullers has answered her opening question in the end.

III. Please paraphrase the following sentences:

1. The baby reaches for his toes, and then explores the bars of his crib; again and again he compares the difference between his own body and the objects around him, and in the wavering, infant eyes there comes a pristine wonder.
2. Consciousness of self is the first abstract problem that the human being solves.
3. In *The Member of the Wedding* the lonely 12-year-old girl, Frankie Addams, articulates this universal need: "The trouble with me is that for a long time I have just been an *I* person. All people belong to a *We* except me. Not to belong to a *We* makes you too lonesome."
4. Love is the bridge that leads from the *I* sense to the *We*, and there is a paradox about personal love.

5. The corollary of this emotional incertitude is snobbism, intolerance, and racial hate.
6. And in that way did he discover "What a man thinks of himself, that it is which determines, or rather indicates, his fate."
7. Whether in the pastoral joys of country life or in the labyrinthine city, we Americans are always seeking.

IV. Please translate the following sentences into Chinese:

1. While it was my friend's desire to be alone, the aloneness of many Americans who live in cities is an involuntary and fearful thing.
2. To the spectator, the amateur philosopher, no motive among the complex ricochets of our desires and rejections seems stronger or more enduring than the will of the individual to claim his identity and belong.
3. Perhaps maturity is simply the history of those mutations that reveal to the indivi dual the relation between himself and the world in which he finds himself.
4. After the first establishment of identity there comes the imperative need to lose this new-found sense of separateness and to belong to something larger and more powerful than the weak, lonely self.
5. Love of another individual opens a new relation between the personality and the world.
6. The xenophobic individual can only reject and destroy, as the xenophobic nation inevitably makes war.
7. While the European artists tend to form groups or aesthetic schools, the American artist is the eternal maverick—not only from society in the way of all creative minds, but within the orbit of his own art.
8. He too backed the world into a corner, and as he passed among the city's millions, returning their stares, he experienced "That silent meeting [that] is the summary of all the meetings of men's lives."

V. How would you respond to each of the following statements?

1. People keep on asking the age-old haunting questions: "Who am I?" "Why am I?" "Where am I?"
2. Having cast out fear, we can be honest and charitable.
3. There are different meanings in identity when we say "we" or "I".
4. Identity means how you define yourself in relation to others.

VI. Please provide a text, which might support your view on one of the statements in *Exercise V*.